I0823744

WILDERNESS OF MIRRORS

OLUFEMI TERRY

WILDERNESS OF MIRRORS

RESTLESS BOOKS
NEW YORK • AMHERST

This is a work of fiction. Names, characters, places, and incidents herein are either the products of the author's imagination or are used fictitiously. Any resemblance to actual events or persons, living or dead, is entirely coincidental.

First Restless Books paperback edition September 2025

Paperback ISBN: 9781632063984
Library of Congress Control Number: 2024953126

This book is supported in part by an award from the National Endowment for the Arts.

Cover illustration by Ngadi Smart
Cover design by Keenan
Text design and typesetting by Tetragon, London

Printed in the United States

1 3 5 7 9 10 8 6 4 2

RESTLESS BOOKS
NEW YORK • AMHERST

www.restlessbooks.org

WILDERNESS OF MIRRORS

Night has the color of old ink as he slips out of the city, first taking leave of his mother in the tall anteroom of her house in the suburbs. She is alone: his father is abroad attending a conference on money laundering at an alpine resort; on such days, the housekeeper is dismissed early.

Swift, murmuring embrace; the mother's face is averted. A farewell that goes as Emil has anticipated until the final moment. Holding the front door ajar between them, as if to bar his reentry or to confirm his exile, Vivian Silva offers a parting shot in her native argot: "Careful wat jy vind dar."

He gets in his car and, as if reluctant, which he partly is, pulls away from the curb. The trunk of the car contains a suitcase half filled with enough personal effects for a few weeks of travel. Three pairs of the crease-folded trousers he wears beneath his lab coat, and which are too formal for where he's going. Also in the case, which does not belong to him, is a canvas backpack stretched tight with monographs on clinical neurology and cognition.

The commuter traffic on the motorway is in full spate: late-model metallic blue or gray sedans rush north. It is fashionable now in the city to drive oneself rather than hire a driver, even for the outrageously wealthy. The city's remaining socialist newspaper—too often lately he finds himself reading it instead of his medical texts—has seized on the trend as proof of an epidemic of virtue signaling that harms workers.

From the elevated highway, he has a view over walds of bluegum and night-shadowed pepper trees: a fake forest concealing the slag hills out there where shackled men had delved and died for the gold that made the city rich.

When a moment came to reckon with the country's history, the city fathers made pragmatic choices, directing that fast-growing trees be seeded across undeveloped tracts of earth to heal the deep gouges made by quarrying machines. And they chose a new name: eGoli became eGeld. *Abode of wealth* replaced *the golden place*, a shift in emphasis that was both more and less subtle than it seems.

The ersatz bluegum forests efface eGeld's present as much as its past. Also out there, in the southwest and the east, are the barracas, the city's slums, which are invisible for commercial reasons. EGeld's municipal authority rations electricity based on economic output, so tenement precincts experience seven-hour blackouts each night, even in grayest winter. In the central business district and the northern suburbs, the nightlong glare of streetlights stains the atmosphere orange, erasing from sight astral constellations: the Chisel, the Furnace, the Fox.

More than once it seems that Emil has passed eGeld's outer limits, but the city is merely shape-shifting, its dwelling places becoming ever more provisional and tumbledown until, twenty miles from downtown, tent settlements stand on either side of the road; these thickets of canvas at last give way to swidden fields.

Careful what you find down there. He parses his mother's advice in two ways (her native tongue is well suited for subtly conveying obscenity). *Down there* reads straightforwardly—he is, after all, bound for the deep south of the country. But the words also gesture to the thing between his legs. They read as a dig about sexual immaturity, at his ignorance of all the uses for his prick. Nastiness is out of character for Vivian. He takes it as proof of a lingering rancor, toward which he is sympathetic. He has let himself be sucked into an errand of his father's, a fool's errand (which of them, father or son, is the bigger fool is not yet clear), in spite of Vivian's attempts at rescuing him.

Only a few months have passed (it feels quite a bit longer) since he told his parents he would take the coming year off. He did not mean to quit medical school—there was no chance of the one year away becoming three, and then final. But as burnout had begun to feel increasingly likely, now seemed the best moment to step away. There were eight years yet of intensive training ahead of him: three in general surgery and five more to specialize in neurosurgery.

Vivian had concealed her surprise—and pleasure—at his news. "You'll travel?" she'd said. "Or what will you do?"

"I'm not sure." The decision itself rather than what to do had preoccupied him. "I'd like, I think, to take a year just to live."

"'To live,'" Errol Silva said in echo, and not because he hadn't understood. Errol has been fortunate in life, very fortunate, and lucky chances had taught him not complacency but wariness, cunning. Skeptical, he waited for Vivian to press their son on his plans, but his wife sat very still, face glazed with thought, and said nothing.

Emil too refused to be drawn to elaborate, so Errol changed the subject. "How's the refresh coming?" A reference to the guest annex the Silvas had commissioned to be built behind the main house. The idea had been Errol's, his intention being to create a diversion for his wife until he turned sixty, when he expects to be named an ambassador. His old allies in government have promised no specific posting, but it will be somewhere in keeping with long service to the party. Errol has lobbied, discreetly, for Bogotá, San José (regrettably, Caracas must now be ruled out), or Rio de Janeiro (the consulate there would represent a small step down in rank, but no matter). Even Port of Spain would do, most any country with a Creole sensibility.

"The construction will go ahead before we landscape," said Vivian. She had seen through her husband but thrown herself anyway into overseeing the annex, even installing CAD software on her computer to review 3D blueprints. "The other way around would be too disruptive." The project has proved effective in staving off Vivian's reveries about diplomatic life in cities her husband thinks of as arid. Vienna. Luxembourg. Bern.

Errol had been content to let lie the matter of Emil's hiatus until the following family supper a fortnight later. He returned to it in his oblique, lawyerly way. "Either of you read anything about this Braeem Shaka? The one riling up folks down south with political rallies. Our folks. Apparently he's an anti-Semite, from what I'm hearing." *Our folks* was Errol's way of discreetly referencing Creoles.

Emil, so often only half attentive during these dinners, missed the abrupt shift in the conversation that followed. So, when his mother said "a year older," he did not know the question she was answering. After a beat, it became clear: Errol had asked him about his cousin Andres, and Vivian had answered on his behalf.

"The boy's not doing well, Celeste tells me." Errol addressed himself primarily to his wife. "Feuding with the brother, can't hold down steady work. Bothered me to hear that, I can tell you, Viv. So I asked Celeste, 'Should I call Andres up and talk to him?' I could fix a work trip down there, you know? Take that jungen out for beers and hard talk. Celeste just laughed. She said, 'Now, how would that work, Errol?'"

"You don't know him well enough for that." Vivian was brisk.

Errol had shaken his head. "You're right, you know. It's late in the day to start to play uncle." He gave Emil a meaningful look. "But you, it's not too late for you to connect with him. Both of your cousins and your Aunt Celeste."

Emil said, "How do you mean 'connect'?"

"Get to know them, build that family connection, you know. What do you think of the idea of going down there, spending time with Celeste, them? Andres and Torrance."

"Over the Christmas holidays, you mean?"

"I'm talking about living with them for six months, a year. These are your relatives, man. Your extended family."

Vivian cut in. "For what reason, Errol? It would be an imposition on Celeste, even for a few weeks."

"Funny you say that." Errol levered morsels of trout meat from his plate onto his fork. "Celeste is forever asking after Emil. 'How come he don't visit? He getting on at medical college?' This kind of thing. You know your aunt. She'd make a big fuss of you."

"I think Celeste needs moral support, Errol. You and I ought to go down for a week or so and visit with her. We *should* go down. We haven't seen them since Karel died."

Again, Errol shook his head. "It's not Celeste worrying me. I think she's rather taken to being a widow, if I'm honest. It's the boy. It's a lot to lose a father. Look, my thinking is, go down there, spend some time with him, with them, and when the moment is right, you deliver some tough love."

"And what if"—Emil chose his words with care—". . . what if Andres wants nothing to do with me?"

Errol seemed not to have considered this hitch. Looking at Vivian, he rubbed his middle finger along his cheek. "Well, if he's not interested, so be it. But it would still be an education for you, Emil. You know, reconnect with your roots."

"Christ, Errol," Vivian said. "You're wanting Emil to play babysitter *and* explore his roots, when all he wants is a break. Breathing space from the intense preparation to become a neurosurgeon. And are you really asking him to throw himself on the hospitality of his less well-off relatives, people he's not seen in five years? For a few months?"

"Christ yourself, Vivian." Errol shifted in his seat, and he turned now toward Emil. "What's breathing space? What does that mean? You're going to go lounge on a beach somewhere? See some sights? Rome, Venice, this kind of thing?"

"What's the implication here, Errol?" Vivian held tight to her sudden fury; her voice barely rose. "He's being shiftless because he wants a hiatus. That's your response?" The signs of her outrage were physiological. Vivid. She jabbed her arms in a birdlike motion, exposing the insides of her wrists; in her throat, the jugular vein stood out beneath the skin.

"It could work," Emil interjected, although he was careful to leave his meaning unclear. He felt embarrassed before his mother's ire. Shamed. He did not merit such a righteous defense. And he is conflict-averse enough that he'd already begun considering what going along with Errol's idea might entail. In the next breath, he said, "Maybe I can learn something from Andres too." Even though he knew this would inflame Vivian even more.

"What are you saying, Emil? What do you mean?" Vivian caught her breath. "This is crazy. If it's down to anyone to save Andres, that would be Celeste. And where in all of this is Torrance, where does he figure? Maybe he needs rescuing as well?"

"Let me think about it," Emil said. A fleeting pleasure, seeing his father quail beneath Vivian's anger.

"Yes. Sleep on it," the mother said. "I'm done with the topic, Errol. Done with concerning myself with Andres and Celeste as if they're children. And for god's sake, Errol, spare me any talk of roots in this house. Spare me. Keep that . . . kak for your comrades."

A family squall, and one blown out as abruptly as it flared. Were anyone peering in at the window, the Silvas would have presented a curious tableau. Vivian staring into her plate as if scrying. Errol slumped in his chair, wetting his lips with the tip of his tongue every few moments, chastened in the stony silence, awed too by his wife's capacity for outrage. There were stains in the bottoms of the wineglasses, the lees dark and gritted as coffee. At the lip of Emil's own plate was a row of translucent trout bones; Nanda, the housekeeper, had missed a few in her deboning.

One o'clock in the morning. The fuel needle at half and sleep an undertow tugging at him. He catches himself nodding a third time and pulls over onto the road's dirt shoulder and leans across to retrieve the thermos from where it has rolled beneath the glove compartment. The chill air of the hinterland steppe sends him ducking back inside the car for a sweater.

Out beyond the road shoulder is a blind darkness. Little by little, he makes out the forms of things: the livestock fence—three strands of fletching wire strung across plastic posts—and after the fence, unrelieved scrubland.

In the palm of his hand the lines are faint and silvery, catching he knows not what refracted light. His father had said once that men carry in them the seeds of their destiny. He snorts a grim half-laugh. The coffee is little better than tepid and tastes oily, but it revives him. As he downs a second cupful, his night vision, only just attuned to the gradations of darkness, fails, and he is again squinting just to make out the three-line fence.

With the dawn there is a view, toward the west, of foothills: a mountain range Emil is unable to identify, the ridge faces covered in a brown gorse resembling billiard-table baize.

A few kilometers beyond the village of Three Sisters are obsidian hillsides—vestiges of some drowned volcano—polished to a dim shimmer by wind and prairie sand. In a shallow depression, an antelope grazes among goats, its racer stripes faded in the distance.

In this place, neither winter nor summer bring adequate rain. The wadis—sand gullies left after streams have evaporated—are littered with man's plastic detritus. There are oases too which he cannot see: the desert trees crowding so closely over the rills and springs where water surfaces as to seem greedy.

A little before noon, he slows the car to a crawl and then a sharp stop; the tires kick up tall wavering wraiths of dust. Two boys scramble out from their tarpaulin shelter and give chase. They lug wooden crates with arms stiffly outstretched, protecting their wares from jostling. While he finishes pissing next to the car, they wait unmoving and discreet in the wailing silence.

They are jungen, these fruit sellers, but their faces are wizened from long days beneath the austral sun. Much of their liquid intake likely comes from the oranges and grapes they cannot sell; most of the water in these parts goes to irrigate the orchards. The faint bulge of their eyelids and the younger boy's upturned, staring nostrils are proof of the indigenous blood they carry. It is in Emil too, if less so.

Emil hawks to expel grit from his throat, and spits. He's unable to account for his high-handed manner toward the jungen, which cannot be explained away by fatigue. He is not Vivian, in important ways is very unlike her, but in his present brusqueness is an echo of her. The jungen are in fact his father's people, in more than one sense. Errol had been born not more than 150 kilometers from this place, had grown up in roughly similar conditions to these boys, by his own accounts.

Were he here now, Errol Silva would not go stiff and uptight but instead slip into the role of uncle (a persona Vivian finds irksome). Errol would demand of the youths whether they were still in school, what they planned to do after matriculating, perhaps even pressing as to whether they had considered two-year college.

Emil shakes his head at an offer of strawberries—too prone to bruise and weep in the heat—and gestures an interest in the mandarins, nodding as the taller boy counts out a handful.

For a great distance after he has left the fruit sellers, there is no one. Human traces, though, are everywhere: man releases his beasts, his castoffs, into the wildlands he has emptied of other creatures. A very few ancient place names are preserved: Mbazo, Umleni. After so long a solitude, the glare of a goat driver's red parasol—the striding figure is well behind his herd—is a kind of intrusion.

Near Worcester Town he passes a great dark-green steam train: an engine and five carriages running north even while seeming to remain motionless until vanishing from the terrain with startling speed. It is the luxury service, very popular with overseas tourists, which has stopped somewhere not far from Worcester to take on supplies for the final stretch to eGeld.

His eyes are fixed in a squint; he has wearied of the journey, of the confining car with its accumulating squalor of wrappings and rinds and spilled coffee. He steers now with one hand, now the other, to relieve overextended tendons in his wrists.

Still, he has crossed now into Cabo Province: the road signs tell him the coast is 120 kilometers distant. The late-afternoon traffic has begun to clot the suburban roads. If these are commuters, it seems to him they are going in the wrong direction. A mounting impatience to arrive, to sleep, causes him to become aggressive, even careless in his driving. Crabbing from lane to lane, he slips into spaces between cars, prompting furious honks from drivers. He is anxious too about what will meet him at Aunt Celeste's house.

Driving in this way, he does not immediately notice a mountain that is almost dead ahead. *The* mountain. Godsetafel, the Gods' Table: a red plateau with that now-familiar baize texture, looming over foothills. In the moment he recognizes it, a bank of gauzy cloud wafts across, concealing the mountaintop, and recalling for him a line of verse memorized in English class when he was maybe thirteen or fourteen: *Godsetafel, in her dream nimbus mantled.* He can recall now neither the poem nor the author's name. And he is not done remembering his old lessons. The aboriginals of the peninsula—the indigenous Boesvolk, or bush folk, pious of sea and earth and air, had revered the mountain as the meeting place of the deities and demiurges that ruled their universe. The old animism has mostly been abandoned, but the Gods' Table remains Stadmutter's numen.

He is near enough now to see houses in the highest quarter on the slopes below Godsetafel. He has the feeling of entering a fortress: Godsetafel and other peaks, less high, arrayed like ramparts. Within its encirclement of mountains and gelid sea, Muttie is iconoclastic: mystical and remote, pagan and yet modern.

The city's reactionary outlook is, in Errol's view, a result of its defensive geography. In Muttie, it is the AD—the Alliance for Democracy—rather than Errol's Movement Party that controls the government. In the most recent election for Stadmutter's governor, the Movement had stood a candidate—a Black woman, entrepreneur and ex-management consultant with a successful three-year stint in the national finance ministry behind her—who would have been irresistible in eGeld. After she lost the Stadmutter race badly, Errol remarked over family dinner that "Our folk down there are still fixated on shade and hair, sadly," and Emil had been surprised that Vivian nodded in agreement. Remembering the exchange, Emil wonders if Errol's fretting about Creole animus toward Black people might be linked in some obscure way to his preoccupations about roots.

A fork in the highway. Guided by the navigation app on his phone, Emil cuts left, sidestepping the city. His eye is drawn upward by the apparition of two tall blooms of smoke rising off the rounded brow of a peak alongside Godsetafel. Forest fire. A helicopter darts in close to the mountain face and discharges a sweep of snowy powder. Sand or some artificial flame retardant. He will learn later that this is the first forest fire of the summer season, the blaze a small one, as forest fires go. And then he is surrounded by the industrial parks of the city's port: the garment factories, warehouses. Industrial sprawl.

Celeste Wilson lives in the flatlands far outside the bowl of the city. Her street is a cul-de-sac of small two-story brick houses. The front yards are separated by buchu hedgerows. Emil supposes the area had been built for integration, but the Whites that had once lived here side by side with Creoles have since migrated to Australia or Brazil. He imagines the residents find ways to resist encroachment, to keep the division brown. The Whites that remain in the province are *tiblancs*—"small Whites" working as freeholder farmers, orchard keepers, tenders of bees—as opposed to Whites in eGeld, who are real people.

Number 9, Celeste's house, is the second-to-last one on Noel Road. Emil rings the front doorbell twice. Viewed from the front stoep of this maisonette south of the city proper, Godsetafel seems very far away, very high. Emil considers and discards the idea of peering in at one of the front windows. Self-conscious, he returns to his car to telephone his aunt, who answers on the first ring. "Emil, pet. Where are you? Just one sec, love." And she hangs up.

The front door opens and Andres, unmistakably him, steps out onto the stoep. "E, wat is aan?" he hollers as Emil gets out of the car. Andres comes to the curb and takes his cousin's hand in his own crushing grasp—no malice in it—clasping Emil's shoulder at the same time. Andres has the look of a rugby tighthead prop. "E," he says again, in unexpected wonder, and then coining a nickname Emil supposes is meant affectionately, he adds, "E-larnie." Gesturing back toward the house, he tells his cousin, "I didn't hear you buzz the door, you know. I was playing *Mortal*."

"It's fine. I got here just a few minutes ago."

Andres fetches Emil's case from the car trunk and, showing off, hoists it onto his shoulder. "Come on, E-larnie. You must want something to eat." Larnie means posh, pampered. Emil trails him into the house and up a flight of stairs. "You're in here, Torrance's old room," Andres tells him, shoving a door ajar with the ball of his foot.

Emil peers in. He has been steeling himself to sleep on a settee in Celeste's house, somewhere offering little in the way of privacy or comfort, and so he's unsure—pleased but also suspicious—about being offered a room to himself. "He moved out?" The room, while serviceable, has not been emptied completely of Torrance's things. Two button-down shirts hang in the open closet and there's a plastic crate of records peeking out from beneath the twin bed.

"Torrance? Ja, he moved in with his woman, Anne. About six months ago. Big flat out by that new mall in Saltrivier. They're renting it though."

"He's well?"

"Torrance? Ja, he's good. Torrance is hustling." Did Andres mean his brother was grifting? As Emil watches, Andres sets down Emil's case and nudges it against the baseboard with the toe of his slipper.

While Andres is in the kitchen seeing about some supper, Emil scrubs his hands to rid them of stickiness before making his way downstairs, not sneaking but not without stealth. The first door opens into the sitting room. In it is an immense flat-panel television depicting superhuman forms in mid-melee. Andres's game. Turning from the screen, Emil takes in the rest of the room. On one wall is a bricked-in fireplace, and over it a wooden mantelpiece decorated with a score or more of gleaming oval objects. Stepping nearer, Emil recognizes them as farmyard animals carved from small burnished knots of wood. These feetless geese, a cow, and some nubby dogs are probably unused bits from larger slats and hunks of timber.

Emil recalls that Karel, Celeste's husband, had earned his living as a furniture maker before his death; presumably Karel turned these fragments into totems. Leaning in for a closer look at the figurines while listening out for noises from the kitchen, Emil notices the unframed photos that are pasted to the wall above the figurines. Family photos, in more than one meaning, but looking over them on the wall is not unlike perusing photographs of strange people in a magazine. Emil has no visual memory whatever of Karel, and even Celeste's younger likeness is unevocative.

In one snapshot, Celeste stands with Karel on some headland, their arms entwined about one another. Emil's aunt and uncle are a little off-center in the image. With one hand, Celeste holds back her hair against the wind, smiling into the lens and coming across as a coquette. Karel has a self-effacing quality; it may be the look of unsmiling adoration he directs toward his wife. Easy to form an idea of their marriage from a single photograph. Karel, patient and stolid if somewhat glowering. Celeste as the vivacious, carefree one.

Visits between the families—Wilsons and Silvas—had been few; the truth of this accounts for his gauzy recall. He is aware that although the Silvas came to Muttie perhaps three or four times for visits (always staying in hotels), the Wilsons had never once traveled to eGeld. The reasons for this asymmetry are, in hindsight, even more unclear. The Silva house was more than adequate to host guests, annex or no. Perhaps Vivian had stood in the way of such a visit, although Errol could have been the obstacle just as well.

In some photos, the Wilson sons are present: Andres had been a slim boy, small and gap-toothed and beaming like his mother. The smirk had come later. Torrance is darker-complected, playful as most children are, but with some of the father's seriousness. It is easy to forget Andres is the elder brother. Even in these long-ago family snapshots, a sort of symmetry is evident. Torrance and the father, akin in temperament and coloring, on one side, whereas Andres and Celeste seem to mirror one another quite instinctively.

At the center of the mementos a letter is fixed to the wall. Standing on tiptoe, Emil can make out the words, although the light is poor. It is not meant to be read. This much he can tell: it is addressed to Karel, and Celeste and both sons have signed it. He presumes it was written after Karel's death, which would have been about eight years ago. He remembers Karel's funeral clearly, and wonders if the recollections of those few days have in some way effaced—replaced—his memories of earlier visits.

He would have been in the third or fourth form at the time. The funeral had been held in a parish church in Wanneburg, a town north of the city: Karel's birthplace, perhaps. A small service. Celeste wept throughout, gales of tears and whimpering that felt ostentatious to a teenager. Her inability to master her grief caused Errol to quarrel with Vivian, whom he accused of being unfeeling.

Before the Silvas returned north, Errol had taken his nephews aside for a few words. Emil was with him. The two Wilson boys bore up well under the strain of emotion and his cousins' composure had made an impression on Emil, who'd kept silent throughout the exchange.

Errol pointed out that Andres and Torrance were now the men in the Wilson house, and that their mother needed their strength and support. Support each other as well. Look out for your brother, Errol had said, or something very like it. In a difficult moment, it had been the right speech to make before bereaved teenagers, Emil thought. And yet the words struck him as hackneyed, a little sentimental, something that someone on TV might say. He had embraced his cousins in parting, an instinctual embrace, and then seen neither of them again until today. Has in fact barely given any thought to how they have fared.

In her graceful hand, Celeste had written, *May your soul rest in perfect peace*. In retrospect, his aunt must have been deeply shaken not merely by grief but also the puzzle of her husband's suicide, the sensation of being widowed young. The cause of death had been ingestion of carbon monoxide.

He steps back from the mantel wall a little self-conscious. If the sitting room has become a kind of shrine to Karel, it also clearly serves as Andres's den. On the carpet near the video game console are empty cans of beer and a leather wallet.

Andres calls from the kitchen, "Hey, larnie. Come nuh." To the Wilsons, the Silvas *must* appear to be snobs, Errol as much as his wife and son. Jetting in from eGeld and smiling in commiseration, buying dinner but never tarrying.

There is leftover goat meat and dumplings for his supper, with broiled brinjal, which is piquant. For dessert: an oddly virtuous half-pomelo. "It's good, neh?" Andres grins when Emil chokes slightly on pepperiness. Andres does not eat. He leans back in his chair sucking at a bottle of beer. "Ma's a dret good cook."

"It's excellent." Emil is embarrassed by his own formality. His belly sloshes with the water he has been gulping to temper the brinjal's oily spice.

Andres lingers after Emil has finished eating. "How long you down for, Cuz? Some sort of doctor training, is it?" In his sidelong looks is a wariness Emil cannot parse.

"Something like that." Emil squints at his cousin. The westering sun pours a blinding light into the kitchen, washing the surfaces of the table and counters red. He had been ever so slightly nodding into sleep, and mindful of coming across as aloof—as a Silva—he adds, "It's basically a fancy internship."

"What sort of medicine?"

"Neurosurgery."

"Brain, right? Makes sense. Didn't peg you as the family doctor type."

"Family doctor type?"

"You know, white coat, big leather bag with a stethoscope. Lollies for the sick kids. House visits to Oumas."

Andres's caricature is silly yet apt. In spite of himself, Emil is amused. As he's trying to work up a retort, there is the click of a key in the front door, and with a harried clacking of heels, Celeste rushes into the kitchen, teetering a little. "Look at you," she greets Emil, and circles an arm about his waist to draw him to her sideways on, the two of them hip against hip. His aunt's welcome is openhearted but with some of the same wariness Emil has sensed in Andres.

Celeste is handsome, ample, with none of the martyred air Emil had unconsciously anticipated. It may be Celeste is no longer that woman whose letter hangs on the wall. She appears too youthful for widowhood. The shared resemblance with Andres—mother and son both run to fat a little—that is evident in so many photos persists.

"You've eaten, pet? Andres give you supper?" From her handbag, Celeste takes a wrap of newspaper and sets it on the table. "I stopped in on the way home for fresh moreya. Dres used to go crazy for it, it's fried eel, but he doesn't much like it now, do you? Fix me a drink, would you?"

Andres fixes a tumbler with dark rum and a spoonful from the fridge of what looks to Emil like condensed milk. Celeste has pulled off her heels and she takes Andres's chair; he has gone back to the sitting room.

"Sorry I'm so late," she tells Emil. "Work has been a bit rough these last weeks. Stuff has been disappearing from people's desks. Paper, pens, that sort of thing. Weird, hey? Maybe someone's idea of a prank. And then yesterday, Tessa, my coworker, her mobile disappeared off her desk, and the supervisor decided enough is enough. 'It'd be a shame if we have to lay everyone off down here because of one bad apple,' he said." Celeste fetches a saucer from the drain basket and sets it on the table to catch cigarette ash. "I went to work this morning hoping Tessa had gotten the phone back, but nothing doing."

After a few moments, Emil says, "I'd like to contribute my share while I'm here, Aunt Celeste." Dredging out the words takes what remains of his strength. "I mean, groceries and utilities, this sort of thing. It would only be right."

"Wouldn't hear of it. And call me Celeste, please, Emil." She makes an abrupt switch of her own in the conversation. "You must go to the Pinelands festival while you're here. It's the second week of December. No, first week. Andres will remember. Anyway, it's a great time. If you're keen, you need to get your tickets quick. Dres!" Celeste hollers, rummaging in her handbag for her phone.

"I'm going up to bed I think, Auntie," Emil says. *Where is Andres?* He has been counting on his cousin's return to excuse himself, but Andres is not coming to relieve him.

"Yes, god, you must be finished from that drive. Go. Sleep." Celeste stands and embraces him properly. Her large breasts press his belly and he is aware of a scent, menthol cigarettes and something else a little musky, not at all light or flowery. Breaking off the hug, Celeste takes Emil's right hand in her strong fingers and holds it. "You go on up. Sweet dreams. And feel at home here, neh?"

Emil has showered and is falling asleep in Torrance's narrow, monkish bed, when a series of thumps rouses him. Scuffling, raised voices. He sits up, awake, yet retaining the sensation of dreaming. Feet clomp up the stairs and onto the landing. A rap at the door, as Emil has known is coming. From downstairs, more muffled shouts. Forestalling a second knock, Emil drags himself over to the unlocked door in his undershorts and pulls it open.

In the threshold stands a man Emil doesn't recognize.

"Hello, cousin."

Emil stiffens as the stranger, who is his doppelgänger, tries to clasp him in an embrace. Torrance is a version—a vision—of himself, akin in complexion, in stature, equally wiry, a resemblance Emil failed to notice in photographs. Neither Celeste nor Andres have mentioned it; perhaps he alone sees it, for Torrance also does not remark on it.

"I left a few things behind. Moved out in a hurry. I hope my stuff is not in your way." Torrance glances over his shoulder and back toward the staircase. Emil is suddenly a little more alert. *What time is it?* The reasons for the brothers' fracas are unclear, but it seems likeliest Andres had tried to bar Torrance's way upstairs. What was it Errol had said so long ago about Andres feuding with his brother?

"Come inside a minute," Emil says, beckoning. His thoughts are fast and slow.

Torrance shakes his head.

"Why? Let me . . . I'll come downstairs with you." Emil is casting about the room for his shoes, he cannot remember where he has last seen them. He will go with Torrance to his car if necessary; his presence ought to be enough to deter further scuffling.

There is some regret in Torrance's expression, a belated acknowledgment perhaps that it had not been worth it, whatever he had hoped for, coming upstairs. He presses something into Emil's hand, a stiff square of card. "I should get on. Need to get home. Anne waits up for me."

"What time is it?"

"We're hoping to have you round for supper, once you've settled." Torrance glances down at the card in Emil's hand as if to confirm its importance. He turns and is gone, making no noise as he passes down the stairs. Emil pushes away an impulse to go downstairs to confront Andres. Where *is* Celeste? For several moments after the front door shuts and even after the sound of a car engine has receded, he remains tense.

A long while since he has experienced such an agitation. When he is calm again—a startling calm—he reviews the last ten minutes. Celeste must have gone out after he'd retired to bed, before Torrance showed up. Andres, perhaps drunk, nursing a grudge against Torrance, had decided to prevent his brother from going upstairs, perhaps even force him from the house. An episode that already is shaping his impressions of the Wilsons, meaning Andres and Celeste. *Three's a crowd*. At the thought, he nearly laughs out loud.

He approaches the door and discovers it cannot be locked from within; curiously, the lock has been removed. And yet despite these many strangenesses, Emil falls smoothly back into sleep, stretched flat on his belly.

Andres receives 832 rands each month from the National Bureau of Workplace Health and Safety. Disability. The check and the accompanying form letter, displaced from its envelope, lie on the kitchen table, where they had not been the previous evening. Emil reads the administrative jargon without taking up the letter. He is waiting for the kettle to reach a boil. Spinal cord injury. Has Andres wished for him to find the letter? To win sympathy?

Is forbearance or pity possible when he is minded to view Andres as a bully, a narrative falling into place neatly: Torrance's growing isolation within the household after the death of the father. Odd man out. Celeste guilt-ridden and biddable enough to be turned against her younger son. What is it Vivian had asked over dinner that night? *Where is Torrance in all this, does he need rescuing too?* Torrance seems though to have rescued himself.

Last night, Emil had been a stranger to himself, capable of any decision, and this morning is the same. Here he is in the kitchen of an unfamiliar house, making himself at home, fixing coffee, on the cusp of putting from his mind the mystifying incident of his first night at the Wilsons'. He has slept without dreams and feels quite revived from his long drive.

When Andres comes downstairs in his singlet and long basketball shorts, a crust of drool at the corner of his lips, Emil finds himself saying, "Breakfast in the city, on me." Saying it with a cheeriness that does not feel particularly forced.

Andres curls his lip. "Why go into the city?" But he goes upstairs to dress.

Andres seems uncertain of the route; Emil navigates with his phone, Godsetafel as the destination. A different route than the one by which he arrived at his aunt's house. There is something old-fashioned about the small factories making running shoes or bathing suits or inexpensive cutlery that they pass. A contrast with eGeld's abstracted economy: the trading of rugby futures, swaps and wrapped stocks; he has never cared to understand any of it, but the glass towers near his home seem more impressive when he imagines them here in Muttie. In the high, gleaming rooms, incalculable transactions of immense value are taking place every second. As if in retort to his drawing comparisons, a sticker on a passing car announces: *Gefickt technocratie*. Fuck technocracy. On the windows and bumpers of other cars are similar stickers in two languages: *Resist tech. Kingdom of Muttie. Politically Incorrect.*

There is a disparaging old joke about Stadmutter's economy that his father and other senior Movement people never tire of relating: each month, it goes, Stadmutter's six old White masters dole two million rands into the hands of their retainers, and the bundle of notes and coins makes its way through the city, with each hand it touches peeling off a share, moving it along until everyone down to the city's lowest bergies and street drunks have received at least pennies. "They've consolidated," Emil once overheard Errol saying with a jeer. "It's only four White masters now."

Andres shifts in the passenger seat as if waking. "You want to go this way," he says, and Emil accepts the direction, thinking still about the joke, pulling at it to discern the truths it holds. Doubtless a parallel joke is told by people in Muttie about the insatiable greed of eGelders.

Andres is directing him through the Foreshore, a precinct adjacent to the port. The land already inclines steeply less than two kilometers from the water. Farther in, the city is a facsimile of old Amsterdam, although the buildings—a courthouse and other provincial offices for welfare and public health—are of ocher stone rather than brick.

The car tires groan over cobblestones. "See that?" Andres asks. They have entered a plaza with a small lawn that has a statue on a plinth at its center: a female form hewed with deliberate crudeness from some dark stone that is layered to resemble fabric. Striding toward higher ground, the woman points at the mountain, or some shelter from a storm perhaps. An avatar of the matriarch that has given the city its name.

But Andres does not care about monuments. His attention is drawn by the men about the statue's plinth and strewn on the plaza's benches, half asleep in their dusty clothes, huddled up against their fellows for warmth. They have passed the night here.

"These okes aren't homeless," Andres sniffs, and Emil glances at him, alert to a shift in mood. "Corvée. Corvée labor. That's where it's at down here. Construction bosses pull up one day a week and yell, I've got places for the five strongest workers. Show me how much you can work today and tomorrow, and I'll put you on my crew next week. Insurance, work permit, everything. Of course these Muntus jump up like the police is after 'em and rush the trucks, ready to work for niets. They might give these guys lunch, a kidney pie and a Coke and that's that. The next day, the bosses will drive to another place where there are fifty Africans waiting for that truck. Two days' work. As a crew boss, that's all you need for many of the really shit jobs. Demolition or carrying bricks. A psychological game for the bosses. They've got these okes living in this park waiting for trucks that rarely come. Police don't even roust them no more."

"Muntu?"

"Ja. It means one person, one oke, in this case an African. It's bantu, ain't it?"

Andres, Emil thinks, ought not to be underestimated. "Immigrants. Where do they come from?"

"Not really. I mean, they carry the same papers as you and me. They're from East somewhere. Libode, Komani, that side. Muntus." Andres gestures idly, shrugs. "Take this next left, will you?"

By the time they have taken seats inside Lola's, an American-style diner, Andres has forgotten his indignance. The restaurant is on Upper Langstraat, where nearly every shop or bar seems to offer a view up toward Godsetafel.

"What construction work were you doing?" Emil says.

"Roadwork mostly. Laying pipe." Andres emits a hiss of amusement, some inside joke perhaps that Emil misses.

"How's the money?"

"Used to be good. Not anymore. You saw why. Cheap Muntus. Even on government projects, which are supposed to exclude illegal labor, but it happens."

"What happens?"

"Bosses find a way to hire workers that come from outside the province." A flare of irritation. "Africans. There's ten other squares in the city like that one. I feel sorry for them okes, they're being exploited and yet they remain hopeful they'll get on a crew. Like they don't cotton to the scam. Of course they do. They do, but what else is there? I've worked crews with these guys. They put in work, take risks I never would. You hear stories. Someone gets caught in a cement mixer or falls off a scaffold. Know what these foremen do when someone dies or is injured? They tell the dead man's friends, 'Get rid of it, get rid of the body and keep it quiet. You don't want the police coming around asking questions any more than we do.'"

"How did *you* get injured?"

Andres nods, the question is overdue. "The jack. Vibration syndrome. Common enough injury. It starts with the wrists. You know what the flexor carpi is? You're a doctor. Got to the point where I could barely lift anything to my mouth. Arms ached so much I'd wake up in the middle of the night."

"You need a certificate to operate the jack?"

"Funny you ask. Nah. You don't. For cranes and diggers, you do. That's what I'm planning to get into once I'm finished with physio. Got about five months left. More job security working the crane, money better too. Only downside: a beer gut from sitting in the cage all day, but that beats the shakes."

Andres picks fussily over his breakfast. Is he ill at ease in a restaurant in which there are so many tourists? For Emil, the food is palatable if nothing extraordinary. Letting a few moments pass, he prods Andres. "So, none of those men in the square are immigrants?" He cannot bring himself to use the word *African,* much less *munt*. A callousness in that word from its nearness to *cunt*.

"Definitely not. Matter of fact, if a Congolese or whoever showed up in the square and tried to get in on a job, he'd get jumped pretty quick. Them Black guys pull box cutters on each other all the time."

Andres's interchangeable use of "Black" and "African" is disquieting. Unthinkingly, Emil has absorbed Errol's positions on race relations. *We are all Africans,* Errol likes to say of the country's citizens, and it is true many Whites have come around to this thinking, but it is not a popular view in the Creole community.

"I actually like the Congolese cats better," Andres admits. "Least they're real Africans. I like the sound of their language. All these parking guards out here are Congolese cats."

"I don't understand. Why can't bosses legally hire citizens of this country?"

"Law gives preference to our people for certain jobs. This is Muttie, man. Work bosses have to prove they can't find a local guy, and that won't happen. Lots of folks here out of a job theyself."

Emil has tired of the conversation. He calls for the bill and pays it with cash.

They are walking uphill, toward the mountain. In the time they've been inside Lola's, about an hour, the sun has moved high overhead; its heat has the force of physical weight on the crown of Emil's head. The pedestrians passing in the high street are Black men that are a little too nattily dressed for the hour, in felt homburgs, clinging gabardine trousers, dusted wing-tip shoes. In eGeld, going about in too-short trousers—crossing stream, they call it—is the waning fashion among a certain class of people.

"Watch your pockets," Andres tells him, slipping a hand into his own as they pass a knot of four men moving with the faintly mincing air of pimps. Emil's eye is sharpening. These are no vagabonds—the men are too preoccupied with cool for that—although they live precarious lives in spite of the carefully chosen clothes, lives not much less hardscrabble than the builders slumped dozing in the plaza. Stadmutter is what eGeld once was. *In Muttie, there are higher currencies than money*, Errol says, disdaining the South as a caste society. Emil understands this to mean that Whites and Creoles enjoy a cozy allegiance that shuts out progress and ideas about meritocracy.

Across Langstraat, the billboards are simple scaffoldings of paper and wood. Emil stares at them and tries to remember when last he'd seen billboards of this type. Andres, noticing his cousin, says a little defensively, "Digital ads were banned. Too many accidents." Andres's partisanship is a mirror reflection of Errol's own. Emil is too unsentimental for this sort of loyalty; eGeld is where his life is centered and he is comfortable there, but he anticipates—with neither eagerness nor reluctance—a time when he will go abroad for further training. More interesting for him is the fact that in eGeld, accidents owing to digital ads would not be a compelling enough rationale for their removal.

At the brow of the hill, just before another road runs perpendicular into Langstraat, is a public bathhouse. A couple of barefooted teenage girls loiter near the entrance. The first leans on one of its pillars; her companion, a plump girl perhaps a year or two older, with a birthmark like a livid bruise beneath one eye, has planted herself in the middle of the pavement and is entreating tourists.

The younger girl is arresting. Part of it is the lascivious way she presses against the stone column, keeping one arm embraced about it. Something causes her dark irises to dilate immensely, and she wears a threadbare, faded blue frock, its tattered tails gathered between her knobby knees: an inherited dress, something suited for a rustic feast in the rural Plattelands. Her breasts beneath it are overlarge for her age—perhaps fourteen—and for her gamine frame. It is, however, the rounded belly beneath the thin fabric that transfixes Emil. Malnutrition might be the cause: her bony hands and wrists—the hand not clasping the pillar is outstretched and partly cupped, and she bounces it in a manner suggestive of jiggling coins—appear enormous. But Emil is seized with certainty that the girl is with child. Unconsciously, he has slowed his stride to take a more careful look, aware that his fixation is not motivated solely by a curiosity to diagnose. Of course, it might also be fibromatosis, a condition that produces benign but visible abdominal tumors. Determining—non-invasively—the cause of the belly swelling would be simple, but he contemplates instead cutting into her, an operation to remove whatever is within.

He is trained not to reach prematurely for conclusions, but what seems likeliest is some *dopslaaf*, some bergie, covered this unripe child with his stinking body one night, forcibly or in exchange, in barter: a blanket, quaffs of some spirit. He reacts to the imagery of that rutting with revulsion but also a more-than-faint arousal, an echo of the same impulse to fantasize about operating—needlessly—on the child. Impossible to look on her swelling belly without being reminded of her lightly fuzzed cunt.

Careful what you find down there. From the far side of the intersection, he allows himself a last look at the ugly-beautiful child whose condition so discomfits him. Still draped about the pillar, the child extends her hand to a passing tourist couple as if for a caress. The woman, White, in her middle years, shies from the contact of those brown fingers.

"There's something I want you to see, Cuz," Andres says when they are in the car once more. He is alert now, even enervated, and he directs Emil south, along long arcs of road under the shadow of mountains reared by the same tectonic violence that created Godsetafel. The peaks become less high as the car advances down the peninsula, lands opening into a series of rolling valleys. Wine country: metal fences separate one terraced latifundium from the next. So early in the season, the trellises are bare of vine. A minor growing area that outputs wines primarily for tourists that stop by for lunch and tastings before going on to the beaches. Hidden among the plantings are hamlets where the pickers and stompers live, and there is a strip mall of four or five shops amid the cluster of farms. A 7-Eleven, a liquor store, a betting shop that is also a café.

"This is my patch," Andres announces when they have pulled to a stop in front of a pie shop.

"Your patch?"

Andres pulls out his phone and pecks in a number. "Waar is jy?" he asks, switching the phone to loudspeaker mode.

"I'm home. *Amome*. Why?" the dissatisfied male voice wants to know.

"I need you out here. I need to be seeing you out here, son. This is where you're supposed to be."

"Where? Where are *you*?"

"The fuck you think am at? I'm at Paco's."

"Int nobody in there."

"Don't matter, I should be seeing you in there. Folks int going to bother and come in there if they ain't seeing you."

"I'm coming, I'm coming. It's early in the day."

Andres turns off the speaker. Setting the phone to his ear, he says, "What you got? You good?" Then, "It don't look like much, do it?"

After a beat, Emil understands Andres is addressing him.

"You'd be wrong, Cuz. It look like slim pickings out here, but these farmworkers be fiends. Dop just don't cut it anymore."

"What are you selling?"

"Scag. Moonies. Effos sometimes."

"What's that, heroin?"

"Scag is fentanyl. Better than heroin. That's for evenings. In the mornings, these cats out here want a rock of meth so's they can work the whole day and take no breaks. My boet, Drool, says all these drugs are cooked up by doctors in eGeld wanting to make extra bucks. That you, Cuz? This why you came down, right? Scouting new markets for your side hustle."

Emil plays along. "No, but you're givin' me ideas, Cuz. Partners, you and me? Seventy-thirty split in my favor, as I'd be the one doing the hard work." It must not be so lucrative, he thinks, otherwise Andres would give up his real job.

Andres is putting all his cards out up front. Later that afternoon, a man walks into the house at 9 Noel without announcing himself and halts in the kitchen's threshold when he sees Emil at the table. Low light obscures his face, and Emil's first impression is that he is Black. After an inexplicable, theatrical pause, the man comes into the kitchen, moving with a flop-footed gait, and casts about in an exaggerated way, in obvious refusal to acknowledge Emil. Wavy hair gives away his South Asian origins. South Asian or Malay.

"Dres man, you here?" he calls out, staring straight into Emil's face. He holds himself easily, the long knobby forearms dangling at his sides. The ease of a man who feels able to protect himself. For Emil there is a rush of antagonism akin to the feelings he'd experienced in rugby matches.

Andres emerges from the sitting room. "Wh'appening, Drool?" The Malay grins at Emil, in some way vindicated, showing off gold-edged incisors and eyeteeth that appear to have been filed. This must be Andres's dealer, Emil guesses, although both must be middlemen.

"My cousin from eGeld," Andres says in introduction. Emil is startled when he adds, "Played rugby for his province."

"Ja?" The information is of no consequence to Drool, who is moving to mount the stairs. As if he is the visitor, not the host, Andres follows him: clearly, there is business to transact. Watching them go, Emil has an involuntary—a venomous—vision that buggery is about to transpire in Andres's bedroom: Drool, penis long and tapering, rearing stiffly over Andres, the dark Deccan skin vivid against his cousin's sallow hausvrow haunch.

If Emil has been deceived by the eventful first twenty-four hours in Stadmutter, he is swiftly disabused in the days that follow, which are slow and blue, feverish with directionless focus. The southern atmosphere with its hot austral air and clear light are disquieting: nature as an intrusive presence.

To acclimate, he begins an exploration of the Cabo peninsula, taking the car and, whenever possible, leaving it to walk as he gathers an impression of Muttie and its many suburbs. Out of season, the mown lawn of the provincial cricket ground at a place called Newlands lies under enchantment: green grass and freshly painted stands for a crowd of no more than five thousand. In the far south, the peninsula—which on maps resembles a beckoning finger—arcs into the Atlantic. The fishing villages along its entire length—Kommetjie,

Outstrand—would not look out of place in southern England or Normandy.

He is aware, with time, of his own reaction to something other than a tranquil gentility and persistent traces of caste. An ambivalence about modernity (he sees many stickers on car bumpers that read *Gegen technokratie* or *Nature was the first coder*) and a contrasting view about time, about life itself. Fatalism is the most apt word. Perhaps this is the ultimate lesson of that foolish joke about Muttie's six White masters. Life, what it brings, ought to be embraced rather than raged against.

After the initial burst of vitality, his excursions cease. Not that his curiosity is sated, but the city saps his energy.

Dissociation—retreating into himself—has long been part of his makeup. In his rugby days he'd experienced scoring tries at a remove, the one carrying the ball someone distinct from him. Perhaps this had made him a standout winger. The present disorientation though is new: afternoons in which he watches himself fall asleep in Torrance's single bed as if jet lag has felled him; nights of drifting through his medical textbooks and on into stirrings of rancor against Errol.

He has found idleness in the house at 9 Noel but little repose, certainly not the hiatus he envisaged months ago. But perhaps insufficient leisure had not been the problem he needed to solve. Quite the reverse: he does not take naturally to sloth; in fact, he is too inured to days that are structured by module lectures and clinical placements, evenings rereading study material over a beer.

Here, life is isolating, but the alternatives hold no more allure. He could join Andres in playing video games downstairs, but the sitting room's vibe—death shrine; bachelor den—is oppressive. And anyway his cousin has retreated from him, perhaps the instinctively hostile Drool has warned Andres off being too friendly. And Celeste? His aunt is mostly absent; Emil has intuited that her evenings away are spent with a lover.

One especially listless afternoon, Emil takes up Cormac's monograph on trauma in the prefrontal cortex, and a card falls from its pages. It is the one given him by Torrance the night of his arrival. He'd assumed then it was a calling card, but it is a sort of flyer, if a cryptic one. Wednesdays. Fridays. Eleven p.m. Bodhi. A party of some sort.

Bodhi is no lounge but a supper club, and it is not so far from where Emil and Andres had brunch that first morning in Muttie. The large interior is partitioned by two high, gray curtains that seem to amplify noise rather than dull it. The middle section is dominated by a banyan fig standing in a bed of earth, and tall enough that its topmost branches thrust out through an unglazed skylight into night.

An absurdly loud place in which to have a meal, as most people are doing; a great deal of the din seems to be coming from a party of ten or twelve near the back: their whoops and cheers reach all the way through to the short bar at the front, where Emil is waiting for a chair to become free. This happens after about fifteen minutes (it feels longer, owing to an acute self-consciousness about standing around), but before he's able to claim the vacant seat, a woman occupying the next one sets her handbag on it. She darts a warning glance at Emil that halts his approach. The bartender notices this interplay but does not intervene. Both gesture and look seem laden with racial meanings that Emil would not so readily reach for if this were eGeld. But then, in eGeld, he would also more likely insist on taking the chair. He turns away, moving with a deliberate slowness, and places himself where he will be out of the way of people coming and going.

A stocky brown man has come in off the road and, brushing past Emil, goes directly to the unused chair; taking up the woman's bag, he thrusts it brusquely into her hands. A brief glance passes between them and she returns to eating her dessert.

Swigging Bergkoenig beer from the bottle, Emil scans the front section of Bodhi through the gathering cigarette haze, and then as he turns once more in the direction of the bar, he finds that the stocky man is standing alongside him, so close in fact that he starts. "Yes," he tells Emil in response to some unasked question. A black notebook is in his splayed hand, and he jerks his head back in the direction of the bar. The woman with the handbag has left.

Strange, thinks Emil, even as he trails the man and goes to sit in the empty seat; from the bartender, he receives a noncommittal nod.

The stranger is writing lefthanded in his notebook. The next time the bartender looks up from the cocktail he is mixing, the stranger demands, "Some more hot water, thanks. For this man," he indicates Emil, "a gin and tonic."

"Thanks." Emil feels, if anything, more self-conscious now.

"Lukas Bolling." He extends a hand to Emil as the bartender moves to the other end of the bar. "Just Bolling, actually. You're at . . . Kloistendam, is it?" Bolling fishes something from the shoulder bag dangling by a strap off his knee and drops it into his glass. A dark and unidentifiable cube, it plummets to the bottom and disintegrates in clots that stain the boiled water muddy green. Bolling slides his hand free of the notebook and sets it page-down in his lap, managing drink, satchel, and notebook easily. "How are you liking it here?"

Something about that *here*, and Bolling's inscrutable, even insinuating intuitions, feels intrusive. "Adjusting still," Emil allows, struggling to retain balance.

"It's almost antitropical, this place," Bolling says, as if agreeing with Emil. "I don't think this water came to a proper boil." The liquid in the glass has gone a dingy brown. "It's cocoa tea," Bolling says, again answering the question Emil has not asked. "Every time I visit the city, I find I've forgotten how arid it is. Walking down Clifton Beach the other day, I looked up toward the mountains and thought, 'there's nothing up there much bigger than a lizard.'"

Emil, drinking the gin and tonic, tries to place Bolling within his own narrow universe, meaning medical school. He looks about thirty years old, so despite the burly frame, a rugby connection seems unlikely. Perhaps a lecturer in a department adjacent to his own—biology or chemistry. Bolling though does not seem like a university academic.

"We've not met, don't worry," Bolling says as if he wishes to let Emil down easily. Then he raises his voice above the music. "The environment here, as I was saying. It's very arid but no existential threat, you know. You're not constantly beating back bush as you have to do farther north, or stepping carefully to avoid snake bite. Modernity suits Muttie."

There are cobras out there, a very venomous subspecies, Emil is thinking, belatedly finding fault with Bolling's remark moments ago about the absence of wildlife on the mountaintop. He lets the thought about cobras remain in his head. He has the feeling of having arrived late to the conversation, also that facts are beside the point. While not entirely certain this stranger has not mistaken him for someone else, he persists in trying to place Bolling, about whom something is naggingly familiar. He is foreign, certainly, and going by the accent, English is not his native tongue, though he is fluent in it. What most gives Bolling away is not the accent so much as his airy way of speaking, the assurance with which he'd handled the woman at the bar earlier. Bolling wishes him to believe the two of them have some connection, without troubling to be explicit about it.

Emil is distracted as several diners holding cigarettes throng the tree: indoor smoke breaks are permitted in Stadmutter. In unison, they cant back their heads to blow smoke in the general direction of the skylight.

Scanning once more, Emil's eye passes over Torrance before he recognizes him. His cousin is talking to another man. "That's my cousin over there," Emil says, swiveling toward the bar once more. The impulse to claim Torrance feels immediately strange and childish. At least he resisted the urge to point, although it hardly matters: the chair next to his own is again vacant. Bolling has slipped off, and the bartender has already removed the drained glass of cocoa tea. He must be a grifter, Emil thinks, even if his con had not been discernible.

Torrance now stands behind the DJ table, performing a sort of ritual: twiddling knobs, removing the headphone earpiece on one side, and resting it on his cheek. The tempo of the music has altered; the rhythms also. Every so often Torrance looks up and across the room, reading it, but otherwise he remains slightly folded over the equipment table.

A woman sidles next to Torrance to take over from him, and Emil notices it is after midnight. He has moved on to his second gin and tonic, sleepiness being one effect of the unaccustomed drinking.

Torrance comes over to where Emil is sitting. "What did you think?" he asks, as if the two of them have already spoken.

"It's complex, the . . . mixing?"

"In the beginning, sure." Torrance accepts a glass of juice from the barman. "Once you get the hang of it, it's the most mesmeric experience. I lose myself for hours spinning."

"You have . . . gigs in several places?"

"Here and one other spot. For spare cash, really. In real life, I'm a sound engineer at Redmayne Playhouse. It's a theater and concert hall." Emil's face has betrayed his ignorance, and a faint defensiveness creeps into Torrance's tone. "Deejaying work is seasonal. This place, most of the bars really, are closed in June and July, no tourists then."

"Your girlfriend comes out to hear you?"

"She works very late, Anne. She'll only just be getting off work now. Ten-hour shift."

Teasing, Emil says, "I'm guessing your brother doesn't come out?"

"Andres hates this music," Torrance laughs. "'It's for goras and munts,'" he says, doing a sharp impersonation of Andres.

"Goras?"

"White folks. Places like this intimidate him. He came once when I was playing a spot in Kampsbaai and shocked me by staying for an hour. Afterward, the only thing he said was, 'drinks were expensive.' That's it! How was the vibe, I asked him. A bit fake, he told me. Larnies and hipsters." Torrance inclines his head. "Let's step out. Smoke in here is getting to me."

Emil settles his bill and follows Torrance from the supper club. He is ready to let the night end. Out of doors, the night does not feel so old: the last of the light is leaching from the sky. In his abrupt way—faintly reminiscent of Errol—Torrance tells Emil, "Stadmutter didn't change much for a long time. But all of a sudden, tourist money is making everything worse."

"How so?"

"Egos. Lots of complacency. Every Monday morning the news is citing some global survey naming Muttie a top-ten city."

"That doesn't seem a bad thing." Emil is still thinking of his father, the joke about the six old tycoons of Muttie.

"Depends. Things do need to change down here, but not so much, you get? Of course, we'll go too far and become eGeld, more or less, rather than something in between both places. Or the wrong things will change, like our maverick streak, you know, or . . . our animist feeling for nature. Or the right thing will change but in the wrong way." Torrance is speaking in earnest. "We'll get even more racialist than we are, rather than less."

"That's it." The voice cutting in is not loud, but both cousins start as if they have been caught conspiring. Bolling. "That's exactly it," he says. "And of course it will never come clear whether the end result is down to incompetence or . . . or bad planning, or malice." Bolling clasps Torrance's shoulder as if greeting an old friend, ignoring Torrance's evident confusion. "What I fear most is that animism will be abandoned, and folks will embrace the same evangelical craziness as in Central Africa. Prosperity gospel, that stuff."

"Torrance, this is Lukas. Bolling." Emil feels as awkward, as ambushed, as Torrance appears to. "This is my cousin."

Stiffly, Torrance inclines his head. Staring closely at Emil, he says, "I should head back in. May need to do a second set."

"Right now?" Bolling lets fall his hand from Torrance's shoulder. "If you've got half an hour, let's grab a quick drink?" He gestures. "Just down the hill here."

"Can't, I'm afraid." The rigidity in Torrance's tone is directed at Emil, and he backs up a step and spins on his heel. "See you."

"See you, Torrance," Emil says a little too loudly. He cannot fault Torrance's reaction to Bolling, to the intrusion. Emil is irritated too, because he had been about to swing the conversation around to Andres. And now he would like to make his excuses and extricate himself, but Torrance's abrupt departure has closed off this option. Out of an inexplicable decency, he feels bound to hang around with Bolling a bit longer.

It is thus easiest to simply go along when the man offers, "So, a nightcap somewhere down there?" Emil is curious too whether this might be part of the confidence game Bolling is working.

"It's paganism that rescues this place," Bolling tells Emil. They are walking now, and his tone, as earlier, is confiding but not really aiming at suasion. "Keeps it from becoming insufferable. Worshiping nature—the mountain spirit, sea naiads, that stuff. Europeans now want to return to their pre-Christian cosmologies, but they're gone. Irretrievable. It's only ideology left. Ideology, reason, and faith all mucked up together into a big mess."

Three men, Whites, are moving upslope toward them. Obviously drunk, faintly listing, they are sufficiently far gone that merely putting one foot in front of the other seems to demand a trancelike concentration. Bolling watches them come, but not warily. Two of the men have grown their light-colored hair out in shoulder-length dreadlocks, and they walk unshod, heedless of stones and broken glass on the pavement.

"No shoes," Bolling says, just as the men are going past; he seems not to care he might be overheard. "Staking their connection to this land through bare feet. As if ties of blood and soil are so easily bypassed," he muses, almost fondly.

Emil is diverted from parsing Bolling's elusive, jarring remark by the sight just ahead of the top of Langstraat; there is the bathhouse where he had seen the girl who might be pregnant. He puts her from his mind, not entirely certain Bolling cannot pluck his thoughts.

Several people lie sleeping in half-light beneath the pillared eaves of the bathhouse covered by rough industrial blankets of the type used to swaddle furniture for transport; they resemble corpses laid out for a mass burial. The girl is not there. These are the forms of adults.

At the Donahan Hotel on Breestraat, the bar has already closed, and Bolling turns to Emil. "I don't fancy going anywhere else. Back to mine? I'm parked around the corner."

"Where do you live?" An opening to be off is presenting itself, but in Emil's present state he is too torpid to seize it. Given how tired he feels, the prospect of the uphill trek to retrieve his car is unappealing.

"Come on." Bolling has sensed Emil's inertia. "A friend of mine, Braeem Shaka, should be at mine."

The name has a distant familiarity. At the same time, something in the casual way Bolling throws it out raises Emil's suspicion.

"Braeem," he repeats. "I think you two'd get along."

It is both apt and unsurprising that Bolling gets around Muttie in a Jaguar of twenty-five years' vintage. And he drives with a careless assurance—signaling every turn well in advance while scarcely bothering to check the rear mirrors—which suggests he knows the city well, even if something he said in the bar leads Emil to suspect he does not live here.

The house, high over Stadmutter's south shore, is on a knife-edge ridge overlooking two popular tourist beaches on the Atlantic side. The quarter is less fashionable than the precincts directly beneath Godsetafel but likely more expensive. Behind the house, the hillside, barren scree, drops straight down toward the bowl of the city.

Bolling tosses his satchel onto the couch. "Braeem," he calls twice. The interior of the house has a Nordic style: unpainted blonde pinewood and insulated windows of bare steel and double-layered glass. Some design feature deadens the reverberation of voices, creating a stillness that feels airy. Almost to himself, Bolling says, "He might have gone to bed. He sleeps a lot these days." Emil is rethinking his view of Bolling as a hustler. If this is grifting, it is at a high level. Of course, Bolling might not be the owner of either the car or the house.

Something jogs Emil's memory. "Braeem Shaka? Isn't he the one demanding reparations for Creoles?" He recalls something about anti-Semitic views as well.

Bolling appears genuinely thrown by the question. "Yes."

Emil settles himself across the living room from his host. "What's your connection? To Braeem, I mean."

"Hold on, let's have something to drink first." Bolling slides his palms against one another as if affirming a decision. When he returns to the room, he is carrying two glasses of clear liquid. Emil accepts one and sets it on the table. "It's bush tea," Bolling says. "Herbs. Nonalcoholic, of course." Emil again takes up the glass with its lukewarm slosh more viscous than water. Bolling has already emptied his glass in one draft. "What's my interest in Braeem? He's finding his way in local politics, and I have some ideas that could be helpful. I'm advising on his political platform."

The bush tea is earthy and tastes of leaves, oily but not unpleasant. Emil sips. "You knew him . . . before?"

Bolling misunderstands. "Before the business in the States? Actually, no." Seeing the confusion he has caused, he adds, "Braeem was deported from the US, and it was after that when I met him. He was job-hunting, not very well, unsurprisingly. Come in the kitchen a minute." Bolling stands, signaling a slight impatience with the conversation. "I need my fix."

His fix is more cocoa tea. Perhaps he is a teetotaler. With the tea brewing in a saucepan, tended idly by Bolling, there is a pointed silence during which Emil tries to work out the man's origins. An alien stress on the words *he's finding his way* is partial confirmation of his earlier hunch. The atmosphere in the kitchen feels dense, its air even more benumbed than in the salon, yet without any hint of staleness or odor. Emil misses the noises of ordinary kitchens—even high-end fridges emit sighs. And what time is it? Two a.m.? Later?

Some aspect of Bolling's persona—not entirely distinct from the assertiveness Emil had admired at Bodhi—makes his silence unremarkable. Nor is he perturbed or offended that Bolling makes precisely enough cocoa tea for himself, which is surely no accident. Tasting it, Bolling says, "Better you don't mix bush tea and cocoa tea. Not just yet." A new timbre has come into his voice, a vibrancy that had not been there minutes before. Bolling too seems aware of it, or rather, seems to catch Emil's reaction. He nods. "That's the iboga. The bush tea. It's altering your perception. Let's go sit."

"A psychoactive?" Emil's voice too is changing shape.

"Yes, ibogaine. But not highly so. A four out of ten in terms of potency, I'd say; not more than five."

They are sitting and once more facing each other across the pine chest that serves Bolling for a coffee table. "Why did you give it to me?" Emil asks in a tone the mildness of which is startling. He cannot gauge how he feels about being dosed without consent. Aggrieved, afraid? But then he is unable to make out Bolling's response: the words come from his mouth hesitatingly. Whatever reason seems to not much matter; he hears himself asking an unrelated question. "Do you speak argot?"

"I can make it out." Bolling's voice is nearly normal. "German is my mother tongue, but I'm Creole too. Antillean, from Hispaniola. I'm not sure you can appreciate how seductive a place called Muttie is for Germans."

Four out of ten. Emil's physiology is experiencing alteration, the surface of his skin shedding heat, pleasantly, even if the iboga is not yet distorting his thinking. Nothing prevents him from entering a bathroom and retching; nothing save intrigue or maybe the scientific impulse—one he rarely experiences—to experiment on himself.

There is no sudden swoon into hallucination, the transition is rather a closing off, a retreat from the outer world and then proprioception. Every five minutes, he takes hold of his left wrist to get a reading of his pulse: the rate is normal, if anything a little torpid. Bolling is confessing a late-developing distaste for France or is it Germany, a resentment he first experienced during the year he spent in Haiti. *Motherland.* His voice sounds more resonant than ever, mollifying, wise.

Emil is finding it ever more difficult to discern the German himself. To feel certain he is physically present. In some moments it seems Bolling has vacated the room but left parts of himself behind. Cheshire cat. Or glitchy pixels that waver and change colors, as when a video stream has not quite buffered. He can no longer detect a pulse in his wrist but there is as yet no nausea (he anticipates the ibogaine trip to be a welter of lucid and semilucid hallucinating punctuated by fits of vomiting, incontinence).

He relives the night of his arrival in Muttie: a reimagining in which there is no fracas between the brothers in the house at 9 Noel and he has remained awake, sitting on the bed in an upstairs room waiting for Torrance. The knock comes and Torrance stands in the threshold. The advice he offers is not entirely unexpected. *You can't trust Braeem. Shaka. Don't trust him at all. Be careful of Bolling too. He's not who he says he is.* Torrance moves off and Celeste takes his place on the landing and there is a White stranger there too, a man with dreadlocks. Dream-Emil notices he is wearing shoes that are soaked in blood.

Here is Andres now: sitting on a sand dune playing his video game. There's a man behind him looking at photographs on a wall. The sitting room of Celeste's house has become a stretch of beach. The man leans in close, inspecting photos of himself and his family, a gesture Emil himself has made. With a sudden whoop, the man runs past (through?) Andres and into the ocean, disappearing from view beneath the waves.

Andres, Andres, Emil calls, testing the boundaries of delusion. *Why are you playing your video game at the beach?* Andres shifts uneasily on the sand, conscious of the queerness of it. He is playing his game against someone; the same man that had run into the ocean—Karel—has come to sit on the other side of the console, a towel across his damp shoulders. Karel plays the game without a controller, perhaps telepathically, but still he is losing to his son. Dream-Emil expects to look up and see Torrance and Celeste approaching down the beach.

The bush tea has endowed incomplete omniscience, (partial) access to the thoughts and motives, the identities of those in the dream via a sort of osmotic, one-way flow. The sequences that unfold in parallel: are they his own unconscious thoughts wrenching him into first one world then another? Has he thus reconfigured the Wilsons against the grain of real life? Andres with Karel, Torrance and Celeste.

Another sliding shift is underway; as his sight is redirected elsewhere, Emil retains an awareness of Andres and his father—screen within a screen—on that peninsular beach as the tide draws in. Hospital consultation room. The man in a lab coat flicking a pen against the palm of his hand is unknown. A woman and child are also present, but the woman withdraws shortly (to the next room), leaving her son behind. The man in the white coat sits on the floor to observe but otherwise leaves the boy to himself.

The child has not reacted to the mother's disappearance, nor is he drawn to the toys scattered about the floor. The doctor—it comes to Emil that his name is Septmann—takes from his pocket a string puzzle and holds it out to the boy, who accepts; for several moments, the child busies himself with unraveling it.

Septmann watches the child for signs of autism: fixity of concentration, detachment. He has noted the child's indifference and lack of concern about his mother's departure. Still, the doctor is noncommittal, on her return, about what he has observed. This is to avoid creating premature alarm. The boy is still too young to be assessed thoroughly. With certainty, Septmann will say only that the child is highly curious and shows no preference for either hand.

Drool, Andres's business associate, is also in the hospital. Drool has come in as an outpatient to see Emil. *Male problems. Summat that needs a man doctor to look at for me.* The Malay is tugging down his undershorts even before the door to the consultation room is closed. Emil is preoccupied with the identity of the dispassionate child clinically observed by Septmann. Drool's affliction is an arresting one. A leechlike parasite has swallowed his penis, covering it entirely. The incidence of urethral hirudiniasis—the presence of a leech inside the urethra—is infrequent but documented; what Emil sees is unknown. The patient, Drool, is exceedingly cheery despite confessing to experiencing quite a bit of pain. The parasite in this case resembles a leech certainly, but this is atypical leech feeding behavior. Nor do leeches have large mouthparts. *Are you able to pass water? Is there bleeding?* None at all.

Hallucinations mount in complexity and form. It is as if Bolling's salon functions as a screen onto which unseen projectors on all sides cast images for Emil's viewing. In the welter of apparition and light, Emil is both audience and actor, bound to the room as if by some psychic tether. Almost throughout the dream, he has a paranoiac's perception of another presence that skulks at the edge of the visions, spinning them out according to some ineffable pattern. Signs point to Bolling, who displayed prior knowledge about Emil from their first meeting. But how can Bolling have knowledge of Drool's existence? Of what seem to be deeply buried details from Emil's own childhood?

Emil looks on as the country's history begins unspooling: a potted, lurching history: a highlight reel of indigenous slaughter and the gathering of human ears for bounty. Slaves confined underground. And then a great leap forward to the onset of national peace talks: here are Blacks and Whites facing off across a wooden table that is much too broad for the narrow room. Perhaps the European diplomats had thought it wise to keep the two sides from being able to physically get at one another.

Two or three of the men have faces that seem familiar. They might be friends, comrades of Errol Silva: ex-bush guerrillas as well as lawyers, clerks with immaculate Afros and shabby suits made for other men. Black men proud of their roughness, of years stretching behind them spent in the so-called frontline states waging war for which they were lightly armed and mostly untrained; or lives of subsistence in cold-water flats in Gelsenkirchen, Nottingham, Malmö—service in exile to the revolution.

The Whites, contrastingly, carry themselves like civil servants or accountants, even the colonels among them, yet their jackets fit just as poorly. It might be subterfuge, a bit of marketing aimed at international public opinion. Both sets of men—no women sit around the table, no faces that are recognizably Creole—belong altogether to the 1970s.

The peace negotiations seem a kind of morality theater playing for a global audience. A humanist allegory. The Blacks and Whites alike understood they were expected to perform rituals of magnanimity and atonement, and neither side had any doubt over which role was theirs and what was at stake. Nothing less than rejoining the community of nations.

The Whites had the more demanding role: formulas of contrition were well and good, but around the world there was a strong feeling that some deeper display of self-abasement was needed by the racialists. Some public rite that carried echoes of the humiliation they had meted out. A complicated business, weighing wrongdoing. And there had been sympathy in some quarters for the view that Antipodean Whites were also victims of history.

"I have something for you." Bolling's salon has reconstituted itself, is once more merely a well-furnished room. The tall windows admit glimmers of early-morning sky just turning blue. Here is Bolling himself, too real to be a delusion. Emil however is prone on the floor next to the large wooden chest, and so looking up at the German. Has he slept? The iboga dream elides the passing of time as REM dreams do. A little embarrassed, Emil sits up, scanning for evidence of incontinence. His clothes are dry and unsoiled, the floor too. His mouth is acrid. *About four out of ten in terms of potency*. Bolling's amusement is faint though unmistakable. Just as suddenly, he leaves the room, and Emil scrambles to follow on feet grown stiff from inertia. The hallucinations have entirely dissipated but the beat of his pulse remains ponderous.

The top floor of the house is a long attic room with windows set above the eyeline. It is vacant, perhaps too large to be properly furnished or used, but it opens onto a second room through an entryway without a door. As Bolling passes this threshold at the far end, Emil, hurrying a little, glimpses movement within the second room.

In this room, which is furnished, a woman is seated in an armchair. Although awake, it seems to Emil from the way she moves that she has been drugged.

"She's quite sick," Bolling tells Emil, as if no further explanation for her presence here is needed. "Terminal and near death, in fact."

"Cancer?" Emil finds his voice steadier than expected.

"Yes. In the cervix. She's a Seventh-day Adventist, so even though doctors caught it early, she refused treatment, both chemo and surgery, on religious grounds. The pain would be unbearable if I didn't have her so heavily sedated. The cancer has eaten right through her. She might as well be kept under a permanent general anesthetic."

Emil does not understand what Bolling means by this remark. "You want me to do something for her?" The woman, who is not more than sixty years old, watches the two of them with bird-bright eyes.

"I can have a room ready at a private clinic in two hours with a nurse to assist."

"Assist with what? She's terminal, you said."

"I'm offering her to you, her body, her brain, to operate on as you like. Look at her. I've had so much psilocybin and fentanyl pumped into her system, she may as well be in heaven already. You won't get an opportunity like this for another five years."

Emil can find no response that fits the grotesque offer. In the next moment he's turning away, and he manages a single step through the open doorway before retching, once, twice, staggering with the need to void his system. As if the nausea brought on by ingesting iboga can no longer be held back.

Lukas Bolling, which is perhaps not his real name, is Antillean German, both and neither. For years, he has lived in hotels, traveling under other names; he even enjoyed moderate success as an installation artist in Berlin. This had been the partial cause of a collapse from nervous exhaustion. He had been working obsessively on an installation he'd already named despite having no more than a loose concept of the form it would take—*Absolving Otto Weininger*—and perhaps it was this running ahead of himself that triggered the breakdown that followed.

Telling no one, he decamped to Gonaïves in north Haiti, renting an old plantation house to recuperate and read the writers he'd never gotten around to reading. It was in Gonaïves—where his mother Marie-José had been born—that the contours of his German identity came into view. And he'd been surprised at how comfortable he was with this unwonted indulgence in clichés—the rundown manse on a derelict plantation; self-discovery through exile.

He'd arrived with an image of Haiti and the United States as twinned. After overthrowing their European masters, each country balanced on a knife's edge: choose revolution or counterrevolution. America's oldest instincts were reactionary, whereas Haiti's insurgent spirit had been snuffed out by wary outsiders before it could be transmitted.

Marie-José was already dead when Lukas arrived in the town of Saint-Marc; she had died in Miami a few years earlier, and his father Georg shared the news without explaining how he had come by it. Lukas had never known his mother: Georg cut Marie-José off after she refused to leave Haiti for a new life in Germany. Unyielding Georg—he left a suitcase of cash in a house at Petionville for the mother of his child and, without a look back, returned to his own country with the infant boy, who bore the name Matthieu, along with three suitcases containing the wealth he had amassed in Haiti. Within a week of arriving in Bremerhaven, Georg had taken the two-year-old to a small country church and rechristened him Lukas.

In Gonaïves, Bolling became acquaintanced with Matthieu, his counterfactual self. Matthieu, he decided, would coast on his sallow chabin complexion. And while going mostly with women, he would occasionally, discreetly, enjoy men. Lukas though resisted laying hands on any of the young men in the town, even if several caught his eye. Parts of himself he allowed to die: the fantasy of being—of emerging as—a contemporary Fanon. Some irony that, in that revolutionary hinterland, he left off reading about Jacobins Black and White and turned his attentions toward the occult.

He arranged for the books of Miguel Serrano to be shipped to him from Miami; the sums involved were considerable, but he could afford it. Voudon rituals held no interest (it was with a certain satisfaction that he observed no one mentioned Baron Samedi in his hearing during three months in Gonaïves).

Gonaïves was useful, in the end, not for offering space to recuperate but for spurring a recalibration. After six months, he no longer aspired to be feted at Art Basel, rather taking pleasure in a new appreciation for formlessness, mostly his own, but also for societies that seemed to him protean, as Haiti did.

Gonaivans had a gentility he had scarcely found anywhere else. One day, at the supermarket where he frequently shopped for water and stunted local vegetables, a woman in the line behind him produced eighty gourdes from somewhere on her person and passed it to him. The cashier's till contained no change: five-gourde coins were so scarce in the city (hawkers of fruit and plastic water cartons hoarded them, Bolling suspected) that he was frequently offered cheap Mexican candies or tiny bottles of Dominican cane spirits in lieu of change worth less than two hundred gourdes.

He'd dismissed this spontaneous generosity but it occurred again and again, and so often that to defend against it he began paying for the groceries of those behind him in the line, his prospective benefactors. A strategy that sometimes averted the problem but equally often prolonged his shopping trips. Being German, he was deeply affected by the generosity of those materially less well-off, but he fretted that too many Germans would be so affronted by poverty in Gonaïves as to miss the dignity of its people.

Another day, ambling through town, not shopping precisely, he became aware of a commotion up ahead. Yells and scuffling. As he was deciding whether to go on and see what it was about, a local man of about sixty years old, natty in his homburg and suit jacket but clearly underfed, took Bolling's elbow. "Gason," he greeted him with a Haitian endearment—his tone confiding rather than diffident—before going on in English, "better you pass this way." And he steered Bolling down an alley that seemed to open up miraculously, holding him all the while. And when the man let go his grip, he did it so subtly that moments passed before Bolling realized the stranger had left him. Later, he learned that a common thief was being lynched with a rubber tire. The older man had simply done him, a foreign visitor, the courtesy of seeing to it that he did not witness the violence of a mob.

He dallied in Gonaïves for longer than was fruitful primarily because the prospect of returning to his earlier life had grown so unappealing. Berlin was on the way to becoming London. What exactly had he given up? He had never been conventionally social, even if he'd taken undeniable pleasure in immersing himself in crowded, fuggy urban spaces (which was most of Berlin in winter), in having access to aspiring artists and subversives. If industrialized cities are the primary arena for the eternal series of contests that is modern life, he had no use for them. He already had money and he had lost all appetite for fame. Perhaps he was merely channeling his mother; rejecting Berlin meant rejecting Germany.

What spurred his departure from Haiti at last was a growing fixation with ibogaine. After much wavering, he decided to travel to Lagos and live for a time with a Yoruba Babalawo he had contacted online, and who had offered what he billed as a safe haven to ingest the psychedelic. After the slow gentility of Gonaïves, Lekki—a newer part of Lagos—and the unflagging ambition of the Lagosians he met, felt young. Younger than

Haiti, which had dissipated its energies in survival, although Nigeria's kingdoms had a more ancient lineage. *Nigeria is rising*, he was told by the driver of the Uber car that brought him from the airport to his hotel. He heard it many more times.

The meeting with the Babalawo, Kenneth Ajegunle, did not go well. The man was trying to hustle him, Bolling felt, and as he grew lukewarm on the idea of doing ibogaine under Ajegunle's care, the hustle became more insistent. Ajegunle had guessed at Bolling's wealth and pressed him to invest in a range of ventures, including a megachurch in Lekki.

In fact, all the great energy of Lagos seemed directed toward raising God and amassing wealth. Fervor for capitalism was so great, Bolling questioned his own indifference, and on an impulse attended an investment conference (there were two or three each week; fertilizer and cement seemed to be real growth areas) on Victoria Island. He had on him a handful of calling cards with his name and the title of Vice President, Mergelsberg GmbH, a construction firm based in Hamburg. This was enough. It was startlingly easy to pass as a serious investor visiting Lagos to assess whether to take a stake in a local company. Perhaps the whiff of ease about him worked in his favor, for he certainly lacked fluency in the jargon.

Were he more patient, more outgoing, he felt certain he would encounter amenable people in Lagos, more easily perhaps than in Hamburg or Haiti, but an antsiness was driving him that had everything to do with the long stint in Gonaïves, and after two weeks in Lagos he boarded a flight to eGeld and from there went on to Stadmutter, attracted by a clinic with positive online reviews and offering the sort of ibogaine experience he was looking for.

Some of Bolling's biography Emil has gleaned from the iboga dream. For if Bolling had peered profoundly into him as he hallucinated, the reverse also seems true: Emil has acquired quite a lot of data on the German.

Overcome by the aftershocks of his lucid dreaming, he searches out a bedroom on the middle floor of Bolling's house and crashes into sleep. Much later, half roused by an insistent touch on his hip but dazed, he does not really resist as Bolling sucks him off. The intensity of ejaculation sends him into a renewed blackout. In the instant of swooning, he understands that the sexual exchange marks the surrender of any real power he might have exerted over the German. *Be careful . . .*

He wakes in his undershorts. It is plain day outside, well past noon. He lies where he is, trying to sort out what is real from delusion. Bolling's offer of the dying woman keeps drawing him back, the amorality of it, extravagance wrapped about stone-hearted pragmatism. The behavior of a man answerable to no one. *Are there gaps between the iboga dream and waking?*

Dressed but barefoot, he goes for a look around the second level of the house. He is in no hurry just yet to see Bolling. In an unused study, he is transfixed by a wall etching in bronze or brass, with a patina of verdigris: six elongated, angular humanoids side by side. A work of great patience into which the artist has poured a concentrated attention into every gouge and hew. He perceives the figures as extraterrestrials, envoys of some Afrofuturist colony. Could he get it out of Bolling's house unnoticed? Perhaps tucked into his waistband with his shirt tugged over it. The fierceness of his longing to take this thing, to have it, is irrational enough that it feels of a piece with the last fifteen or so hours. And Bolling's boldness has given him leave to be vengeful, yes, but also aggressive. Pulling his phone free of his pocket, he goes to photograph the work before changing his mind and leaving the room.

He finds Bolling in a cramped office downstairs off the kitchen, a converted scullery. The German is hunched over a high draftsman's desk. "I left my car in Kloofstraat," Emil announces, following a sharp rap on the ajar door. What's there to say about the previous night? "I'm going to catch a taxi over there."

Bolling is impatient to get on with his writing, this is evident, but he gets up and walks into the kitchen and fetches Emil a glass of water. A needless courtesy; Emil has not asked for anything. With Bolling gone, he unthinkingly snatches one of the black notebooks stacked on the writing desk. They are identical, and he hesitates over which one to take, then regrets choosing to pull free the fourth one from the top. The pile threatens to topple as he shoves the notebook down the front of his trousers.

"It's only water, right?" he asks, accepting the glass from Bolling and taking a long drink.

Bolling ignores the jibe. Gesturing toward the pile of notebooks, he says, "You like my Schwarze Hefte?"

What if he has cameras? Emil's eye goes to the ceiling corners; and then, his glass of water emptied, he sees himself out and finds he is hoping Bolling will discover his theft.

In the days after drinking iboga, Emil is afflicted by a partial blindness. The wavering gray haze shot through with blinking colors might be unconsummated visions. Those sunstruck mornings—it is not even high summer—are when the aftershocks of the iboga are sharpest. Drawn-out convalescent days in which he remains confined in Torrance's old room.

The hallucinations recede, and increasingly he misremembers what persists. And there is the problem of confirming the truth in what he has seen. One image that does not fade: the child psychiatrist Septmann seated on the floor studying a brown child.

When eyesight allows, Emil reaches beneath the bed and fetches out the stolen notebook. Many of the pages are filled with notes and aphorisms. Bolling has an immaculate penmanship; in Emil's present mood—indolence lacing the iboga hangover—he returns often to one observation that reads quite pointedly:

> *Once man learned to lie his way out of danger from nature, could he ever learn truth again?*

The notebook contains few dates, no explanatory notes. Nor is it obvious to Emil what has induced Bolling to write in English on some pages and elsewhere in German. Translating on his phone is arduous.

Kultur ist ein Exoskelett. Darunter gibt es nichts Einheitliches, nichts Wesentliches, das man Seele oder Willen nennen könnte. Schopenhauers Beschreibung des Willens als körperlos, als ätherisch, ist zutreffend. Kultur ist der Panzer, der den Menschen vor der Auflösung bewahrt.

Culture is an exoskeleton. Beneath it is nothing unitary, nothing essential, to call soul or will. Schopenhauer's description of will as disembodied, as ethereal, is right. Culture is the carapace that holds humans together against dissolution.

The writings, abstracted, at times idiosyncratic, have demolished Emil's earliest impressions of Bolling. The German is no grifter. He has inherited great wealth and influence.

Human capitalist systems mimic nature's brutal simplicity, albeit veiled in pieties. Having fled natural selection, we crafted a poor simulacrum that is rigged in our favour; and yet still we seem to be losing.

The true romantics of our world are hunter-gatherers.

Only those who never left nature need no myths about returning to it.

Emil spends festering hours reading from the notebook or hunting for details about Julius Evola (quite neutrally described in Bolling's writings as a turgid sort of monarchist rather than a pure fascist), alternating with internal monologues in which he rails against Errol, though he does not spare himself. By presenting as aimless to his father, he'd stepped into a trap he ought easily to have avoided.

Vivian telephones. "How is Andres?" she asks, the frostiness of recent weeks only lightly thawed. Emil cannot fault her for wanting still to punish him. In response to her coolness—and his own feelings of foolishness—he is evasive. "I've been busy learning my way around," he tells her in a bright voice. "Andres has a lot going on." What else can he say if he will not lie? His cousin has gotten good at absenting himself from the house. Many days, the only sign that Andres remains present is when Emil's already restless sleep is roiled by the sound of his footfalls on the stairs in the small hours of morning. Peddling a vial or two to grape stompers, perhaps.

No reference is made to Torrance, who in Emil's view is the more deserving target of the Silvas' assistance. Torrance, the striver, the forgotten man. Emil's efforts to contact him since that night at Bodhi have been unsuccessful.

Be careful what you find down there. Vivian had warned not against Andres, nor the Wilsons more generally, but about Stadmutter. The city is the trap. It has not taken long to jettison (relinquish?) the mission to save Andres, but this is little comfort. *Who will save me?* The thought is no more than half mocking.

Bolling? What the German is extending is not an offer of friendship, for which Emil has little use anyway, but rather sex—on Bolling's terms—and a kind of tutelage Emil will not find in any textbook. He feels certain: Bolling will wait for him to initiate the next contact, thinking he has set his hooks deeply enough.

Andres's aloofness toward Emil has not escaped Celeste. "You're taking your cousin round, I hope?" she says whenever the three of them find themselves together in the kitchen. A running joke directed at Andres but which mocks all of them. After all, Celeste herself is absent. That is only part of it. As Emil sees it, the teasing is Celeste's way of owning up to what her elder son is: someone who sees little need to carry his weight within the household. Celeste is stuck with Andres, and he with her, and with Torrance departed, Celeste is free to indulge Andres without shame.

In Emil's view, Torrance has made a happy escape from 9 Noel and yet, seeking human interaction, he finds pretexts to wander downstairs. And when Celeste makes her familiar joke, Emil smiles to show he's game for a little teasing.

Celeste is readying for an evening out, a date, she calls it. Rinus, a man in her office, has asked her out to a jazz club. Emptying her tumbler—the familiar condensed milk floating over Caracas rum—she rises from the table and, humming open-mouthed some mid-tempo Latin tune, dances with arms raised the few steps to the countertop to fetch her nail lacquer. "God, I need another cigarette. How do I look?" It is the second time of asking.

"Just be yourself, Tannie. You look very nice," he says. *Tannie?* Plumping Celeste's vanity is the precise diversion he needs from Bolling's black notebook but he is also curious, pruriently so, about where his aunt has been spending the nights she is away from 9 Noel. Celeste sits and blows on her freshly painted nails with pouted lips. Deliberate provocation? "You're the woman," Emil adds. "Let him, Rinus, worry about making a good impression."

"I don't know if he ever married. Does it make a difference, do you think?"

It is the commuting hour. The roads are clogged. Rinus, running late, telephones. Emil fetches the phone out of Celeste's handbag to spare her nail polish and holds it up to her ear. Will Celeste come to the curb to be picked up, Rinus wants to know. His voice blares down the line, the distraction of driving making him sound brusque. It is not his usual way, Celeste tells Emil after she's rung off. He knows what it is to be a gentleman. The band is to begin its first set in less than thirty minutes.

Outside, Celeste loops her arm through Emil's and draws him near as they walk the short path to the curb. "So glad you came to be with us, pet. I miss Karel more than I can bear sometimes. I'm still a young woman, you know." A defiance directed not at Emil but at fate. "I feel young, you know. I must say 'young widow' sounds more glam than it really is. My needs haven't gone away. Oh, what I am telling you that for?"

"I understand, Celeste."

"It's Andres who has really struggled with this," she confesses. "He misses Karel more than his brother does. The two of them were into their rugby and their fishing. Torrance was always closer to me." A startling, unexpected detail. Celeste's candor touches him, but the next moment sentimentality seems to lift, and her attention is pulled back to the evening ahead, the dancing. On the narrow path, she sways to the rhythm in her head, bumping Emil's hip. "Beautiful night."

A car is coming down Noel Lane at moderate speed, straddling both sides of the road. Drunk driver, is Emil's first thought, but then he guesses this must be Rinus, looking at the numbers on the houses so intently he has missed seeing that there are two figures ahead at the curb.

"Yoo-hoo," Celeste says, waving. "That's Rinus." She unlinks her arm from Emil's, shifting her stance so her back arches. Still waving to catch the driver's attention, she crosses one leg in front of the other. "I don't have lipstick on my teeth, do I?" Celeste makes a grimace. "You'll open the car door for me?"

The car veers across the road toward them until, at the last instant, the driver hauls on the steering wheel to spin it about in a squeal of tires, positioning the passenger door directly in front of Celeste.

Emil, embarrassed by this stunt, peers over the half-raised window glass into the car and glimpses pale eyes in a worn, cussed face. Cat eyes, Creoles call these irises that are muddy green or amber. "Get in, girl," Rinus says with pretend impatience, and he leans across the gearshift to shove the passenger door ajar. His dyed jet hair has been combed flat with brilliantine. "We can still make this thing."

Celeste kisses her nephew's cheek. "Don't wait up, love," she teases Emil, who is guiding her into the car. There is an awkward moment as Celeste tries and fails to avoid disclosing too much skin over her knee as she settles into the passenger seat. A modesty aimed at Rinus? If so, the mystery of where Celeste has been spending her nights deepens. Emil shuts the door behind his aunt and steps back as the car pulls away.

Ten minutes later, Emil is behind the wheel of his own car heading in the general direction of the city bowl, with no fixed destination in mind. Turning on the radio, he learns from a news bulletin of a mountain blaze menacing the city. The frequent fires around and above Stadmutter are a result not only of the arid terrain but also local topography. The encircling mountains create a funnel through which strong winds pull fires into the city bowl. And there is a news item that prompts Emil to think of Bolling. Braeem Shaka is threatening to march two thousand people up to the gates of Parliament Hall . . .

A red helicopter crosses above Emil in the darkening air, signal light flitting; an echo of the day of his arrival in the south. He descends a highway ramp and passes beneath the mountain that is afire. He cannot see the blaze—the road runs too close to the peak's stone roots—but the taint of scorched grass is in the wind.

From the upper stories of the houses in Langstraat, the main thoroughfare, uptilted faces peer out, tracking the dart and flicker of helicopters. From Langstraat there are occasional glimpses of the fire itself far up on the mountain's sheerest face, a lone petal of flame—so small—that is covered over again almost at once by the night and creeping smoke.

Too swiftly, Emil has bypassed central Muttie, arriving once more at the periphery. A carrefour, the left fork leading toward the Godsetafel cable car. Floodlights set in the rock face illuminate the looming mountain. A glance in that direction blinds him for an instant, but he does not slow. In his wing mirror is a panoramic view of the city and the peninsula, the mountains running nearly the entire length of the isthmus, with man-made light clustering most thickly near their feet.

The road shears rightward to pass along the brow of a cliff and through stands of montane pines. On Emil's right, far out, is a void that is the Atlantic, waters that lie dark save in one spot, where a moored ship casts a poor glow. He descends from the high ridges and pulls the car over on one of the streets that tips toward the shore. As he's getting out, there's a movement in the deep shadows along the sidewalk. There, stooping protea bushes absorb the ambient light, and he is unsure whether he has seen anything. Someone has risen from a seated position and, holding up a cigarette lighter, flicks it alight. A woman. By illumining her face, she means to reassure him. Between her feet is an upended soft-drink crate lugged from god knows where, a perch to sit on.

She is a parking guard. He digs out seven rands from the car console and she accepts the coins from his hand without a nod. There are few other cars. This will be a lean night; her patch of sidewalk is far off the ocean road. Down there, on the strip, parking guards can earn more than a hundred rands on a Friday night. Down there, it will be only men—Andres has told him that parking guards maim one another with razors to protect heavily trafficked stretches of road.

A wind whips at him as soon as he steps onto the beachfront. Kampsbaai. The ocean road running south through here connects to Llandudno and then Hout Baai. *Llandudno.* An alien name to Emil's ear. A stream of cars crawls along the main strip. Across the road is a coved beach popular for swimming and surfing. The bars and restaurants Emil walks past are named to evoke foreign rivieras. Here, an open-fronted place, is Antibes. Its neighbor Janeiro has been painted in blues, greens, and yellows. Down a few doors is a whitewashed concrete house that bears the name Amalfi in tricolor paint.

He chooses Ayia Napa, although it is a name that means nothing to him. A clamor washes over him, human noise rather than music, an atmosphere fuggy with blue cigarette smoke. He's already decided what he will drink but he pores over the menu anyway before signaling the barman to order.

The evening feels young, although about him are faces that are slack with spirits. He's missed the sunset, an occasion in Muttie for drinking sundowners, a ritual entertainment of the summer. Night has come in very fast but there are, in the upper sky, one or two persistent smears of rose-colored cirrus cloud. With a swallow of gin and tonic inside him, he scans the room. High up on one wall, a television plays the news with the sound cut. The photo on-screen is an old one of the nation's father; the chyron beneath has four words: *Ubaba in stable condition.* Emil rattles the glass to hasten the melting of ice and dilute the alcohol.

Small likelihood, Emil muses, that anyone in the bar has spared a thought for the nation's father, the first president of the country post-unification. Over the car radio, he had heard that the old man is showing signs of recovery after being rushed to hospital with a sudden pneumonia.

"Excuse me." Emil does not hear the words so much as feels them, the sibilants particularly, in the brush of lips near his earlobe. In the pack of bodies there's no room to give way, scarcely space for Emil to turn about and face his interlocutor. Craning his neck, he meets the eye of a man who looks too young to be in any bar. It is the current fashion for men to tease the hair at the forehead into a thicket with gel, whereas the adolescent facing him has combed his dark red hair with water so it lies flat across his scalp. He is unfamiliar but he has recognized Emil.

"Silva, isn't it?" Emil allows the stranger to pump his hand in greeting. His mouth opens and shuts but Emil hears no more than snatches of what he is saying: ". . . behind you at KES." Emil nods to confirm, yes, he is an old boy of King Edward's School. It is four years since he matriculated. *Let's get away from this,* the stranger seems to signal, inclining his head and indicating the claustrophobic space. Shy as a child, he catches Emil's wrist to lead him away.

Outside, beneath the patio awning, the air smells pleasingly of asphalt. Sand whips off the beach, flicking across Emil's cheeks and nose. The red-haired boy half turns for a look back, keeping hold of Emil's wrist. "I remember that try you made at Garsfontein. Ran fifty-five yards, I think it was. I must have been in second form then. We talked about that one for ages." He is laying claim to Emil, to something greater than a shared experience.

He halts before a vacant seat and lets go of Emil. There is an awkward moment in which it appears they have arrived in a place where talk is possible, but with no more to say. The youth is bending down to speak to a woman seated in the next chair who stares into her phone. He looks toward Emil and indicates that he should sit. Leaning in although he is easily audible now, he says, "Be right back with drinks. Oh, I'm Wareing, by the way. Adam." And then he is gone.

Odd behavior, fetching Emil out of the bar's interior and then going off again without troubling to ask whether he'd like a drink. He is mulling whether to go back inside or to a second bar, and so several moments pass before he realizes the woman Wareing had spoken to is holding out her hand. Emil accepts.

Her name is Tamsin. "You're some sort of rugby god at KES, Adam says."

He is amused. "I matric-ed from KES four years ago." Adam himself must be soon to matric; Emil puts him at about seventeen years old. Tamsin is several years older, older too than Emil, who is trying not to stare at her hair with its unnatural color: something out of a packet, a cheap dye or one she has applied carelessly—deliberately so, probably—into hair and scalp.

The drab hair and wan skin are quite deliberate, he thinks: they are to draw a contrast. *In Muttie, pale hair and sun-darkened skin are a numinous gift*. The sentiment is from Bolling's notebook. What is the true color of your hair, he wants to ask, but holds back.

The beach is emptying. Youths mount the sidewalk and begin moving in squads down the strip, peering in at the windows of Ayia Napa and the other bars. Tamsin's phone flickers once, twice, and she comes to her feet at the precise moment that Emil, deciding it is the moment to leave, also stands. Adam's reappearance without drinks creates another uncomfortable moment.

Tamsin says something to Adam and his head jerks back in displeasure, and then the siblings are talking over one another and Emil waits a little foolishly to say goodbye, having no interest in interrupting the quarrel. Tamsin steps away from Adam and comes to Emil, standing so close they are nose to nose.

"I have a quick errand to run just up the hill. Will you come with me?" Her breath smells of nothing at all. "It'll be ten minutes." And she catches his hand in a surer grip than her brother's, but with a similar purpose: laying a claim. Awed by her assertiveness, Emil allows himself (once more) to be led, out the main door and into the night.

Adam follows them outside and squares up to his sister, his throat the livid red of a weal. "It's a bad idea, Tams." There is an unsteadiness about him that is more than pique. Has he quietly downed several drinks at the bar?

"It's fine, Adam. Your . . . your friend will go with me."

"You don't know him. You can't even tell me his name, can you?"

Tamsin lets go Emil's hand and walks away from her brother a second time. Adam stares after her as she moves off down the strip and then surprises Emil by ducking back into Ayia Napa. Free to leave, Emil hesitates before going after Tamsin, whose movement is hindered by long skirts. He catches up to her as she is turning into the first intersection. Not quite daring to take her hand as she had his.

"It was so White in there," Tamsin says. For a moment he does not follow. Had it been so obvious he would chase after her? The road inclines sharply up into darkness; a ghostly movement three hundred yards upslope, a will-o'-the-wisp, resolves into the forms of two parking guards wearing reflective vests. They stand in the middle of the road to better scout for approaching cars.

At the next corner, Tamsin raises her hand as if to hail a taxi. A car slides away from the opposite curb, a foreign model with a lowered chassis, the undercarriage so low it seems to crab over the tarmac. The driver flicks on his headlights. The parking guards stationed in the road are gurning in the glare of high beams. The rear door of the car swings ajar, letting Tamsin rabbit-hop onto the seat, with Emil a step behind.

"Tamsin Freudsniffer," the driver says in greeting, and he hunches forward to get a look at Emil in his driving mirror.

The car's heating system has been running. "Ekow, are you cold?" Tamsin lets out a small giggle, which strikes Emil as uncharacteristic.

The driver guides the car with easy skill, keeping to the side roads. "There's a stiff breeze up Chapman's, nights, Tams, you know that." *You know that* is faintly suggestive. Ekow shifts to take another look at Emil. The whites of his eyes gleam. By looks he is African, Emil guesses, but his clipped way of speaking is British. Ekow turns up the volume on the audio system as if to better hear a yawp of horns and then cuts it down again. "This another one of your brothers then, Tams?" His dark mouth shapes to say something more but he thinks better of it.

Instead, Ekow passes a package back to Tamsin, something he has retrieved from between his feet. Tamsin accepts the bundle and teases the folds apart to fetch out the contents. With a curt wave, she signs to Ekow that he should put out the car's ceiling light. With the same hand, she passes him the bills wadded tight between index finger and thumb, a discretion that deceives no one. "We're good, I think, fam," Tamsin says. She is teasing Ekow. And then, recalling the question from a few moments ago, "This one? He's my foster brother. The sporty one." She pats Emil's knee in a way he dislikes.

Ekow says, "I'll let you and your bruv out by the Pick n Pay, yeah?" The car has doubled back more than once, but Emil is certain they are above Kampsbaai moving southward, in the general direction of Llandudno.

"You in a rush?" Tamsin wants to know.

Ekow holds up his phone. "Yeah. I've to be in Constantia in eighteen minutes."

Before they get out, Tamsin bows her neck to sniff, dabbing at the edge of first one nostril, then the other. She raises a balled fist to Emil's cheek—it seems a menacing action, and he stifles the reflex to shy away; Ekow is watching. The vial of powder is tucked against Tamsin's palm, secured and concealed by her thumb. Emil shuts his eyes and sniffs. His understanding of cocaine and its effects is entirely academic.

Ekow eases the car to a standstill before a large well-guarded house. "The Pick n Pay's just down the road from here." He points with two fingers. "You'll be alright, I think." Then he turns up the volume on the stereo, an unmistakable signal.

The two of them stand exposed on the unlit pavement of a residential street. The next house is some way down the road, and Ekow's silver car has already rounded a bend and moved out of view with its deceptive sidling velocity.

Out of Ekow's presence, Tamsin is different, diffident, and she looks at Emil in expectation. The direction that suggests itself is downslope: follow the curve of the road to reach the shore. Tamsin lets out a sinusy grunt, perhaps a reaction to the tickle of powder in her throat, a sound so improbable Emil has to bite back amusement.

"This way." He is pleased at sounding, feeling calm. Spooking Tamsin will only increase his own jumpiness. It is not yet eleven o'clock, is his guess. Tamsin rabbits her nose, another reflex against the cocaine, and falls in beside him. There are houses below, but these stand in darkness. Already he can hear the jostle of open water, and within a few minutes they arrive at a T-junction that gives onto the ocean road leading back toward the tourist strip. Here though there is no beach abutting the road. Beyond a narrow grass verge is sheer cliffside that falls into deep roiling water.

Either Ekow's bearings are awry or he has played a malicious joke putting them out here. Crashing waves spit up sea spray, smearing their vision: the lights of the Kampsbaai bars and nightclubs are a Fata Morgana of bleared neon green, blue, red. The road is winding; he estimates that returning to Ayia Napa will require at least fifteen minutes of walking, and along a stretch of road empty of habitation.

Emil has hold of Tamsin's forearm. Still, he is careful not to lengthen his stride and give an impression of hurrying her along. The pebbles of the murram track make for unsteady progress. And the track narrows where the cliff wall leans out over their heads, in one or two places nearly hangs over the road, towering and providing small comfort against the sensation of being exposed. No car has yet passed in either direction.

Tamsin wipes the spritz of sea mist from her forehead and eyelashes. "What does Freudsniffer mean?" Emil asks. The water droplets are bitingly cold against cheek and top lip, reminding Emil of how far south they are in the world. Between Muttie and Antarctica is a void of sea and grinding ice.

"A private joke." Tamsin sounds winded. "Freud was very fond of cocaine."

Freud? "And what was Ekow saying about Chapman's peak?"

"Oh, it's one of his kicks, racing that car up and down Chapman's nights with the headlights off. It's his fetish. He takes the engine apart every few months and reassembles it. You know, my father grew up here before Kampsbaai was a real resort. It was scrub all the way up to the mountains and maybe five houses, barely a village." Is Tamsin trying, in changing the subject, to reassure *him*? "My grandma used to go over the ridge for groceries in her little Beetle."

Sudden laughter on the air. The mumble of human voices. Emil is confused at first by the direction of it, and glances back over his shoulder before identifying its source up ahead. Male voices, high-spirited and talking over one another, not in English but in Creole argot. Jungen. And fast approaching, by the sound of it, but still out of view. He assumes he and Tamsin are also not yet visible.

"Hy dink hy schelm," one boy tells his mates in a cracking voice. *The guy thought he was clever.* The first two jungen move into view from around an arc of the road just ahead; they are in close conversation, their heads leaned together, nearly touching. Another three are a few steps behind and one of these is the loud-voiced boy. How young they seem; and it is strange too that their carrying voices convey some haste, the impatience of the young, although they are not walking particularly fast. *Where are they going?* At this hour, it is unlikely taxi vans ply the ocean road south of Kampsbaai; nothing will go past here except private cars.

Emil catches Tamsin's slippery-dry hand in his own and moves ahead of her on the path. He has experienced dread since the first sound of approaching voices, and not for himself. The next moments throng with sensation, leaving him no time to speak. An image flashes in his eye, real as life, but he knows it for a fever dream, aftershock perhaps of the iboga. Two prostrated forms, the larger, juddering one almost entirely obscuring a supine form beneath, a sprawl of pale wrists and long-toed feet bared and arching. Tamsin. The violator might be Emil or one of these jungen but it scarcely matters; he and they share a physical likeness that collapses distinction.

Just in the instant the two jungen in front reach Emil and Tamsin, there is the putter and snarl very close by of a revving motor. The first boy sees Emil—Tamsin is slightly behind him—only at the last moment. He starts and pulls up short, his eyes going very round. In that place hemmed in by road and cliff, he is close enough for Emil to smell five-rand menthol cigarettes on him, maybe the same brand Celeste smokes. He grunts as the hitch in his forward momentum fetches the next boy stumbling into his back.

"Hai," calls a commanding voice, and a motorcycle rider swerves his machine up over the curb and onto the murram track, driving straight at Emil as if to run him over. Taken unawares on two sides, real fear flares in the faces of the jungen.

The motorcyclist is bareheaded. Emil knows him. Bolling. "Here you are," he says, killing the engine. He straddles the immense motorbike easily. Emil lets go of Tamsin's hand. As if there's nothing extraordinary about meeting on an isolated stretch of road beyond the city.

"Why you run that kindtrike at us?" one boy jeers. His mates break out in nervous grins at the analogy—a child's three-wheeler—but when Bolling looks at each of them, they don't know what to do. The explosive arrival, the humped immensity of the motorcycle continues to unsettle them.

"Get on," Bolling says, leaning the motorcycle to one side to ease Tamsin's mounting. Her upper thigh is bared as she swings a leg across the pillion, but the anticipated catcalls do not materialize. The jungen shuffle their feet, seeming eager to be off but curious also to see how this encounter will turn out. Once Tamsin is astride, Bolling walks the motorcycle backward into the road and kicks the engine to life. Cutting the handlebars, he hauls the machine about in a tight arc. Emil gets up behind Tamsin on an old-fashioned wedge seat.

A brief ride. Within minutes, Bolling noses the machine up to the curb at Ayia Napa. The strip has quieted, a lull perhaps before the late-night crowd comes in. Two women sit nearby on a doorstep, forearms on knees; one of them, weeping, seems unable to stop. Her friend looks witheringly at the three of them and Bolling's motorcycle.

"It was just kids back there," Bolling tells Emil, gesturing over his shoulder. Emil has slid off the wedge seat. Tamsin seems in no rush to dismount and merely lifts her hand from Bolling's shoulder. "Nothing serious." But what had Bolling seen? Feeling—wonder mingling with resentment—swells in Emil and he is unable to respond. With a glance of reproach toward Tamsin, he goes off down the strip. No one calls him back.

The motorcycle ride has dried the sea mist to a stiff salt mask on his cheeks and forehead. He walks as if he has a purpose other than getting his head clear. Six young girls stand in the road up ahead, a less frequented section of the corniche with its 7-Eleven and betting shop. Black girls. Each one has a pattern daubed on her forehead and throat in luminous paint. Stars or dots in a diamond formation, snaking lines. Twelve hands settle on hips in very grown-up fashion. A dance is commencing, a sight that distracts him from his anger by driving grievance toward new targets. These are children; the hour is late. And the costumes, brief string skirts and halter necks fastened tight over breasts that are mere nubs, sharpen their vulnerability. One or two of them are as young as eight years old.

But the children are not unchaperoned. The ensemble leader sits well back from the dancers, his shoulders braced against the darkened window of a shop. He begins striking the drum encircled by his thighs (like an opponent wrestled into submission). The drummer wears a kirtle of some haired fabric dyed to mimic the pelts of civets or brown hyenas. He raises a varying rhythm on the cowhide with the heels of his palm. Despite the precision of his beating, the man's face has an unfocused look.

Emil has no yardstick to measure the children's skill. For whom do they dance? Not pedestrians, who are very few in number here and are anyway preoccupied with their phones. Behind him though is a restaurant patio, six tables on a raised platform overlooking the bay with a cordon of wrought-iron fencing. Every table is occupied. Nearest where Emil stands on the sidewalk, a couple's table is laden with platters of shellfish and half-eaten slabs of what must be buffalo or eland steak. Game meat for the tourists.

But it is the diners themselves, florid, listless with drink, that absorb Emil. He is glaring, in fact, and wonders that they remain unaware of his eyes on them. They are American or British, certainly affluent, and yet he doubts they eat so richly at home as in Muttie. Exchanging dollars or sterling for rand favors the tourists immensely, and Emil suspects this is the reason the couple have ordered a meal too large to eat at one sitting, likely the dearest wine too. When the bill is presented, the satisfaction at how little it has all cost likely exceeds the savor of the lobster or springbok loin; it is this that will feature most vividly in the memory. The true source though of Emil's loathing is the couple's insensibility to the dancing children.

To the mumbling of the drum, the girls have formed two lines facing one another. The ones nearest him bend forward until they are on hands and feet, mimicking beasts. One by one, they roll to the tarmac and lie still. The dance might be retelling the cattle killing, the legend about a warlike people in the country's southeast that very nearly achieved self-annihilation through a mass slaughter of their own herds.

After Emil has stalked off down the promenade, Bolling helps Tamsin from the motorcycle, and by a tacit sort of understanding they find a place on the vacated beach to sit. In answer to Bolling's questions, Tamsin admits she is working toward a doctorate in the history of psychoanalysis, going as far as to share the working title of her thesis: "Sigmund Freud and the End of Iconoclasm." Something about Bolling, his manner certainly, but also what he'd told Emil in front of Ayia Napa, dissuades Tamsin from being evasive. She herself missed the aspect of the encounter with the jungen that has so disturbed Emil, whereas Bolling had sensed it even as he was arriving on his motorcycle.

Bolling knows not to underrate Tamsin. Under differing circumstances, the two of them might have discussed Freud and Jung until dawn, Bolling's own position being that both men had gotten peripheral parts right but a great deal wrong. But instead, he clams up. He has seldom found use in his life for women, and there had never been more than two or three friends. In fifteen minutes of conversation (long enough to let Emil cool off), Bolling shares nothing of his earlier stint as a conceptual artist. Yes, he is German, he admits; Tamsin has a good ear. He is in the country to help his father out with one of his businesses, a construction firm.

And then Tamsin comes to her feet and brushes sand from her skirts. "I should go and find him," she says, as if of a child that has wandered away. Yes, Bolling answers. It isn't clear to either of them why Tamsin should go after Emil. Bolling stands and watches her walk off before he returns to his motorcycle.

The whiff of exploitation that hangs over the children has pinned Emil in place. He watches to see if anyone will give a donation. The children dance with greater and greater fever. The drummer whips them up. The dancers—the drummer also—have nothing to sell but their culture.

At last, Emil drops some rand notes into the battered paper cup on the pavement—so easily kicked over by heedless feet—and as he is straightening to leave, to return to his car, a voice says into his ear, "Can I get a ride home?" He faces Tamsin with a flush of embarrassment warming his face, but she is looking over his shoulder at the children, still dancing. Not at him.

Emil sets aside the newspaper he's been skimming. "What do you think of Braeem Shaka?"

Andres looks up from scanning his phone. Shaka is pushing ahead with plans to march two thousand people through Stadmutter. A blackmail rally, the newspapers are calling it.

"I agree with some of the things he says. He's not the one to be saying it though."

"What do you mean? Who should say it?"

"He's a Black American. I know that for a fact, Cuz. Drool overheard him in a nightclub one time speaking in his normal accent. He doesn't speak our language. Having said that, I'm on board with reparations; dankie viele for the check. I'm not on board with seceding from the rest of the country—folks down here ain't ready for that."

"Meaning?"

"I'm a realist, Cuz. You have two kinds of people in Muttie: good-time Charlies work to live, to enjoy life, whiskey, and zoll and abalone, all that. That's me and that's Ma. Good-time Charlies. The other lot, the backras, are different, worse. Backra Johnnies, we call them—people who came to Christ after everyone else and only got to sit on the last pew in church, the back row. No wafers for them, that was for the White folks in the front bench. No wine, neither. Backras like to suffer, they're meek and mild, work hard but don't expect any reward. In fact, reward makes them suspicious. Confuses 'em. You're thinking that doesn't sound as bad as a good-time Charlie, right? Self-sacrifice. Humbleness. At least they're not drunk every Friday night, but you can't build an economy on backras. They work hard, but there's no ambition."

Emil is amused. Andres, camped in front of the sitting room television or else selling vials of meth out of his car, a good-time Charlie? He asks, "Is Torrance a Charlie?"

"Torrance? Torrance is neither. That's his problem. My brother doesn't fit in down here, that's why he'll end up moving to eGeld. Sooner or later. Folks down here don't trust Torrance's kind. That ambition, taking night classes, working two jobs. Shit like that messes with folks' heads. Messes with my head. Backras need the Charlies, and the Charlies need the backras. There's no room for anyone who puts both sides to shame. Torrance knows it. In a year, two tops, he'll be gone. Good thing he's got his larnie Uncle Errol to help him get on."

Andres is warming to his theme. "Thing is, I don't think the backras will get on board with Shaka's reparations idea. They're all about suffering in this earthly life, yada yada. They're not going to give that up for a check."

Can this be the explanation? That Torrance is a breaker of the social order, that he has brought ostracism down on his own head, even in his childhood home? Emil has one more question but it is one he cannot ask: whether dead Karel had been a backra or a good-time Charlie.

Days of unseasonal rain. Flooding flushes the city's vagrants from the culverts and underpasses, forcing them to search out higher ground. Brawls break out between brown and White men over stashes of bottle caps. Shopping trollies overloaded with belongings clog the traffic on Buitenkant Street and one or two other intersections close to the feet of the mountain.

For Emil, the German's writings are easier going than his medical textbooks at present. Bolling has written:

> *Technocracy is an attempt to democratise the will to power, a concept the utopians have repurposed from their old enemies, the romantics.*

He treats the aphorisms as a child responds to a clever puzzle. He is induced to turn them this way and that in an attempt to solve them. And there is this:

> *Hard to understand this country's Lebensraum history when its interior territories remain so sparsely populated even today.*

The little Emil has come to know about romanticism makes him skeptical, particularly the part about opposing sensation to science, to the Enlightenment.

Errol telephones at last, although Emil tells himself he has not been waiting for the call; it is merely his due. Errol though has not rung to learn how Emil is faring in the south, still less to apologize. He wants to discuss Braeem Shaka's blackmail rally.

"What are you hearing down there?" Errol's tone is one of suppressed excitement.

Nothing more than is in the papers, Emil admits.

"If your governor down there doesn't step lively, he'll force our hand." By *our*, Errol means the government; frequently, he forgets he's on the outside. "Let Shaka unleash his riot and there will be a state of emergency. No one comes out of it looking good if we have to send in police reinforcements. Least of all Governor Kob. He will feel that at the polls, I tell you." Emil listens, saying nothing. After Errol rings off, he wonders if his father has been trying to use him to pass a message.

Later that same day, Bolling shares a curious intelligence via text message: Braeem Shaka has agreed to sit down for secret discussions with Kob's people. Emil's guess is that the governor is hoping to defuse the threat of reparations before it gathers steam. He considers passing along the information to Errol but decides his father will find out anyway, if he is not already aware.

What is he to make of this sentence, with its paradox that he grasps but cannot fully penetrate: *Since progress foreclosed any possibility of actual freedom—a feral barbarian existence beyond reach of the state—fascism has exerted an enduring pull.*

Unable to comprehend the reasoning, he can neither refute nor corroborate it, nor still dismiss it as feverish speculation, perhaps because he is invited by these writings to consider ideas he ordinarily would not, and in ways that lead away from the universe of scientific knowledge and practice. Bolling's writings seem to imply that some questions lie beyond science's power to answer (subliminally Emil knows this, although his view is that the answers are merely yet to be discovered). The tone of the asides in the black notebook suggests that there are truer paths than science.

Ibogaine is presumably one of these, or the occult more broadly, which seems to be another of Bolling's things, one connected in some way to romanticism. And what about instances when the German has demonstrated prior knowledge that is not easily accounted for: a pinpoint awareness of where along the Kampsbaai road to find Emil, and more staggeringly, Emil's state of mind in the moments of the encounter with the jungen.

Late morning one Saturday, a text message from Tamsin. One word: *swim?* To which he replies: *Where? I'll come fetch you,* she responds. *Address?* Forty minutes later, another one-word missive. *Outside.*

Emil leaves the house holding nothing but wallet and phone. A more humid day on the peninsula than any in the weeks before, an atmosphere that feels swollen with heat.

"Quiet neighborhood," Tamsin observes, turning the key in the ignition. Emil's memory of her—her appearance, her voice—is awry, but he cannot pinpoint what he misremembers.

Tamsin brings them to Soutrivier. A weekend market with great throngs of families and tourists moving about beneath pavilions trying samples of smoked fish, hams, hummus, fortified cider, freshly made pizzas. The vendors, local Whites and Creoles, bray out what they are selling.

Behind Emil, just a few steps inside the entrance, someone says, in a simpering voice, the accent foreign, *Your country is so beautiful*. Innocent remark, with no special emphasis on the word "your," yet open still to misinterpretation. Might it be praise of this sort that keeps a vestige of small Whites from emigrating to Perth, to Christchurch? The takings from operating a weekly market stall probably amount to several hundred rand at most.

Tamsin senses an edge in the mood. "People are nervous. This Braeem Shaka thing." She has downed one bottle of cider and her wrist presses a second bottle against her ribs, freeing her hands so she can taste the morsels on offer. A fiddler band is playing old songs beneath a second canopy, where there are tables and bales of straw for sitting.

Hunting out a seat for himself and Tamsin, Emil bumps into Adam. "Hard not to pick you out in this monochrome," Adam tells him. In the heat, his forehead is shiny and the button-down gingham shirt he's wearing seems an odd choice. Behind Adam is a Black girl of the same age. He looks toward her rather than at Emil as he presents her. "Emil, this is Dipha. Also from eGeld. We all have our own Whiteys nowadays, eh?" He gives Emil a square look.

"What the fuck, Adam?" Dipha is indignant.

"I don't say it. I'm quoting that journalist. Paraphrasing, rather. What's his name? The one who said everyone has their own Black."

Tamsin comes laden with two large paper bags. She offers Dipha a nod that strikes Emil as a little cool. "Surprised to see you here at the White people market, Adam," she tells her brother.

"Well, food's good." Adam will not be drawn.

Tamsin thrusts one of her bags into Emil's hands, jerking her head. "I've got everything."

"She's too old for you, Silva," Adam says in parting.

Emil catches Dipha rolling her eyes. "What is it with your family and race?"

Tamsin brings them not to Muizies, a surfers' beach, as Emil has anticipated, but into the upland interior of the peninsula via a narrow road filled with switchbacks. "We're swimming at Silvermine tarn," she tells him firmly, as if he has protested her decision. There had been a working mine here even before the eGeld gold rush, but artisanal scale, Tamsin says; not rich enough to transform the region. And now no more than the name remains for a place that is popular with locals when the ocean beaches are choked with tourists.

Emil stands taking it in, discreetly allowing Tamsin to change into her bathing suit on the car's back seat. The far shore seems busier, perhaps because a proper beach rings the waters on that side. In the shallows, the tarn—a little less than a kilometer across lengthwise—is rust-colored. Invisible underground springs charge its waters. Excited children play fetch with a retriever, its blonde head shining; the volleys of shouts carry across from the opposite side as if bouncing off the impenetrable surface.

"The water here terrified me as a kid." Tamsin has come to stand at Emil's elbow. She is long-waisted but not so tomboyish in build as he had previously thought, even in the austere black two-piece, and surely no older than twenty-six. If Tamsin notices his appraisal, she does not comment; she wades straight in until the water is at her waist. By the time he has undressed to undershorts and set his phone and wallet alongside her bag, she has gone out quite a distance. Following, he is surprised that apart from an occasional stone meeting his toe, the bottom is loamy underfoot, firm but with a faint suck. And it is not the tarn floor staining the water rust-colored but some characteristic of the water itself, some dissolved rock.

Pedaling his legs, he luxuriates in the interleaved drifts of cold and warm water, which are soapy against bare skin. The inscrutable surface is a disquieting thrill: visibility is little more than a hand's width. Silvermine has no fish, Tamsin said, the concentration of minerals is too high, the water highly alkaline; not even dragonflies flit overhead. In the childish shrieks that reach Emil from the opposite shore is an echo of his own instinctual fear about what the depths might conceal.

Tamsin has switched from a lazy crawl to lolling on her back, her buoyancy easier than his own. He feels compelled to exert himself, to match her. His limbs recall something of the patterns of swimming freestyle.

She is watching his approach, and when he is within reach she catches his shoulders with both hands and rears out of the water, using her weight to press him beneath its surface. He has seen previous glimmers of Tamsin's silliness and accepts the unfamiliar game, offering no resistance, letting his body be borne down limp and blind into terminal darkness. Her grip on him persists until, with a double kick that he feels as beats of water on his forehead, she flees, pulling for the surface. The water has an unusual pull, not irresistible certainly, but like a weak tide.

If the lake hides some pitiless creature in its void, it would be a smooth-fanged fish, scaleless and glass-skinned, narrow-bodied to withstand pressure, and inured to the ammonia scald of high alkalinity; unseeing in deep darkness. Emil is offering himself as temptation, almost hoping to feel the catch of soft, strong fishy lips over his foot. His eyes are tight shut (as if it makes a difference) and thirty seconds, forty, a minute go by. The pincer-tight pressure at his eardrums has dissipated to an ache. Ninety seconds.

He breaks the surface, and the scald of the sun on his head is like a benison. Scattering droplets from lash and brow with a finger, he allows his eyes to open. The dog has not ceased its barking. What of Tamsin? She has returned to wallowing on her back. The attempt to frighten her has failed and, laughing, he snorts water and gags—a real if momentary fear of drowning—until he flips onto his back to recover breath.

A little later he sits on a scalded rock with his arm folded around his knees. The skin of his flank retains a soapy sort of sheen and he traces his finger back and forth. "It's the water." It is Tamsin's turn to observe him, and she does so over one shoulder; the two of them are seated side by side on the curved rock. She has covered her head with a brimmed raffia hat, somewhat battered, that she pulled from her bag.

"Will you specialize?" she says, changing the subject. "Medical college, I mean."

"Neurosurgery." He looks at his hands.

"What's that, ten more years?"

"Something like that."

"Where are you doing your summer res?"

"I'm not, just yet. I deferred for a year."

"How do you view psychiatric practice?"

"Is that what you're studying?"

"History of psych. PhD."

"Ah." Emil is thinking of Ekow, Tamsin's dealer. "Freudsniffer?"

"Yes, Sigmund Freud. Mostly him."

"I don't know very much about psychiatry. A few studies, deep brain stimulation as a therapy for mental disorders. It's not my area."

"Nor mine. Almost was. I don't have a temperament to see patients, but I was going to go ahead and do it anyway—credit to my father, who talked me out of it. He convinced me to get close to Freud and Charcot by studying history."

A brown man in stained trousers approaches down the trail, leading a young boy by the hand, and when he passes near their rock his eyes fall on Tamsin and Emil. Something causes him to frown and then to slow his pace. Emil watches him but the man seems to want Tamsin to look at him, to mark his disapproval; her face though is turned from the stranger.

"Why?" Emil asks, smiling at the man, taunting him a little. "Do you have the wrong temperament for patients?"

"Too little patience. More prurience than empathy, maybe. Anyway, I'm more interested in Freud's life, which would be inconceivable today. Freud was the final iconoclast. The very last one, just as Einstein was the final genius, maybe. When I was at uni, someone told me, 'Our nation's father is an iconoclast.' I didn't respond but I was pricked by this, and I thought about it for a long time. Maybe a month before I decided he wasn't. He's saintly. Inhumanly saintly, but that's not iconoclasm."

"What is it about . . . Freud. For you?"

"His paradoxes worked. They make sense because there was an obvious sense of futility at the heart of them. Freud wanted to make a science of mapping the human mind, but he was also dubious about human reason. It's the right balance of skepticism and . . . and idealism. I remember learning as a teenager that early physicists theorized that sight was nothing more than the light from our eyes hitting some object, an apple falling, say. That's wrong of course as a matter of physics, but it's a perfect metaphor for human cognition, epistemology. Our eyes impose on an essentially chaotic world taxonomies of meaning. Freud knew it was foolish to use the scientific method to understand human thought, conscious and unconscious, but he still made it his life's work."

Epistemology. He has at best surface understanding of this term. Reaching for solid ground, he says, "Answers to these questions come from studying the brain itself."

"Not the answers I'm interested in. Synapses firing, that's dull stuff, no offense."

"Dull is neither here nor there in medicine." He accepts the zoll cigarette that Tamsin has lighted and, doing so, is diverted from what he had been saying. "What's . . . provable? What can be replicated?"

"Sure. But neurologists are no closer than psychiatrists to mapping the brain to the mind. Synapses, neurons, acetylcholine. Those are bits of flesh, chemicals. It's qualia I'm interested in. Can you get that from an MRI?" She is shaking her head. "Tell me, what diagnosis would you make for a patient whose prefrontal cortex scanned normal but who had begun to display erratic antisocial behaviors. Mood swings, violent outbursts, that sort of thing?"

"Do more tests. That's what I'd do. Look at non-neurological factors. It could be a pathology that lies elsewhere than in the brain."

"Is this a brain fixation you've got, Emil?"

"I've wanted to be a surgeon for a long time." He laughs, shrugs. "When I was eight, I had a rugby coach who used to tell me, 'You've got surgeon hands.' Delicate, I think he meant. Delicate but strong. Perhaps that had some influence. And I grew up thinking that answers are always out there."

"Through science, you mean?"

"Yes. We might not find them, but they're out there."

He takes a final drag on the zoll, which has warmed his skin still more; he feels overheated in the high sun-sharp atmosphere of Silvermine. He swings down from the rock with the thought of reentering the water; instead he crosses the short distance to a second rock lying in the shade of a stand of pines and, abruptly drowsy, drapes himself face down on it.

What wakes him is the sensation of prickling skin on his arms and thighs. A wind has come up that carries a faint chill. Sitting, he swipes drool from the side of his mouth. Tamsin's shoulder bag and sandals are on the nearby rock, but she herself is gone. He has been asleep for nearly an hour. Sitting on the first rock in late afternoon sunshine (he is thankful for the glare in spite of the headache building at his temples), he locates Tamsin in the tarn, quite far out. She treads water, her head a dark indistinct dot on the surface. She is aware he has woken. He suspects her eyes are on him right this moment and he pretends he has not found her, scanning the horizon in an exaggerated way. The far shore of the lake has fallen into shade. The family with the swimming dog has departed, although he hears still the noise of playful barks; another dog perhaps. The beach opposite is in fact nearly deserted. A lone figure, androgynous at this distance in white clothes, stands motionless at the water's edge.

Zoll and dehydration have fouled his mouth. Stepping from stone to stone, retreating from the water, Emil finds a rocky copse and pisses a brief yellow stream; in his hand, his penis is a sullen inert thing.

On the drive back, Tamsin, beating her thigh to an old song playing, abruptly cuts off the radio. "How's Lukas?"

"Lukas? Bolling. I don't know."

"You're friends, I thought."

"Friends?" Emil muses. "I don't know. He sucks good cock." He cannot say whether it is a fatuous joke or a confession.

Tamsin takes it in the spirit of the former. "So that's how he found us in Kampsbaai?" She goes on patting her thigh in the same rhythm without music. Of course she had noticed that too. What would she make of Bolling's notebook?

There is little urgency for the excursion to end, it seems. Tamsin stops to buy fizzy water at a service station and when she returns to the car, she is holding a piece of paper. "This is today." Getting in, she thrusts it at Emil. "Braeem Shaka. Shall we go and see what the fuss is about?"

Emil scans it. The flyer is quite crude, although this might be the point. An evening rally, taking place at a beach he doesn't know. There is no overtly political sentiment in the flyer's message, which is in English. No propaganda. Simply a beach gathering for lovers of music and straight talk.

The anodyne language piques Emil, and they turn once more toward the south and follow the dual carriageway as far as it goes, and then a single-lane road toward the nail bed of the fingerlike peninsula with cliffs falling toward wild seas in nearly every direction. The trees are grown in more densely here than farther north, a terrain mostly vacant not only of humans but of wild things.

The gravel road runs a kilometer or so and then comes to an end. Cars line it along either side. The metal sign reading Todfrowenstrand—the awkward concatenation squeezed onto a single line—stands salt-bleached and twisted by the strong winds. Dead Woman's Beach.

"We could get in there," Emil tells Tamsin in a tone he thinks inoffensive. Tamsin has passed up a parking berth.

"You park it then." Tamsin lurches from the driver's seat, leaving the engine running. She stands next to the road, hugging herself, as Emil clambers across into the vacated seat and maneuvers the car into the space. More cars are arriving behind them. A breeze carries the sound of music up to the road: reggae, with the rich imprecision of live instrumentation.

In the descent over broken ground, Tamsin moves haltingly, a sulkiness in the hiked set of her shoulders. And when she stumbles in her flip-flops, Emil reaches out a hand to steady her before pulling back in the last instant. Through stunted trees, they pass onto mudflats, the earth damp and smooth. A tidal floodplain of some estuary now depleted or shifted in its course. The seasonal southern winds have strewn the loam into gyres and drifts. At the edge of hearing is the ebb tide hiss and swell of the ocean.

There is a rough amphitheater perhaps five or six hundred yards beyond the tree line. Jerry-rigged scaffolding for the lights and the man-high oblong shape of the loudspeakers, which are the source of the music. Tamsin and Emil are still making their unsteady way toward that stage when the singing and drums stop suddenly and sounds previously drowned out become apparent: the droning of the diesel generator powering the floodlights and audio equipment, and the low ambience of voices.

"Starving," Tamsin tells him once they have settled themselves on damp and unyielding ground not far from the stage, having no blankets. Food smells are all about. And they have left their own picnic—what is left of it after Silvermine—in the car's trunk. She demurs, a little stiffly, when Emil offers to trek back for the food. His own appetite is slight. He has noticed with surprise how many families are in that crowd, which is made up mainly of Creoles. The presence of White folks is perhaps not so surprising, given Shaka's politics, but there are greater numbers of Blacks than he's expected.

The stage is nothing more than wood pallets stacked three high with a tarpaulin draped over them that does not conceal them entirely. And when a tall thin figure steps onto the stage, Emil assumes it is someone who will introduce Shaka.

"On this beach," the man says into the microphone, his voice strong but overstrained as if he has been addressing crowds all day. The lack of preamble comes across awkwardly. "On. This. Beach." He jabs his finger toward the earth with every word. "A woman did die, yes." Emil understands now that this is Braeem himself speaking, that no one is going to introduce him—and his reaction is to doubt the size and influence of his movement. And there is shock too that Shaka is speaking in English.

The first thing to notice about the man is how whippy he is physically, how tall: he is well over six feet. He has the reddish undertone of skin Creoles call kaffir red, but nothing in his features is particularly striking. Shaka has an oval, regular face, neither handsome nor ugly. His clothes are a little odd for a firebrand, a word that seems inapt now, even grandiose. Shaka's attired for an evening out at a supper club: wine-colored polo shirt, well-cut trousers that are off-white. Is this Bolling's influence? The effect is disarming, at odds with the newspaper stories about a man hungry for race war, a demagogue. Emil suspects even his father might be disarmed.

"I had long assumed the dead woman was one of our people," Shaka goes on. "A brown woman. Creole. We all did. Thing is, she was a Dutchwoman, and she didn't actually die on the beach, on those dunes a little ways over there. She died offshore, died on a little rowboat in 1883. Anja Koenma was her name, and she was far gone in childbirth, a difficult delivery, and the captain of the ship she was on thought she and her baby might be saved if he got her to shore. But Anja Koenma died and the child died too. A sad story. But when I learned the reason for the beach's name, sad wasn't the first thing I felt. I experienced a strange feeling that I could only put a name to after thinking about it for weeks. I felt cheated, as if something had been stolen from me. Why? Because I'd felt certain the name of this beach honored one of our ancestors. One of our foremothers. Because our presence on this peninsula goes back much farther than a hundred and thirty years. We come from an ancient lineage of humankind that is deeply rooted here. Didn't this particular spit of sand have a name before Anja Koenma died here?"

What Shaka has, his affect, is a sort of anticharisma; no one will confuse him for a standard politician with this talky desultory style. He says, "If I'm honest, I felt relief also that the place name had nothing to do with another massacre of the ancestors. There were so many, it's sort of miraculous any of us are here if you think about it. But that's not a winning combination really, feeling cheated and relieved. Neither of those is a pleasing emotion. So often a sense of relief is followed immediately by a feeling we've settled for something okay but not great. I have the same sort of gut reaction when I think about what Kob is doing for us." With heavy irony, Shaka adds, "Our Kob September."

At this mention of the governor's name, a slight quickening of interest passes through the crowd. Emil is remembering the exchange he had with his father about Governor Kob, about the need to respond to Braeem Shaka. Also, the intelligence from Bolling about secret talks, and he understands in an instant that the talks, whether or not they have begun, offer Shaka additional leverage. Even now Shaka might be securing a soft landing for himself.

"Kob's problem, and this is where unnu come in, actually where all of us out here on this beach count, is that he's got it twisted. He acts as if, for the working people of Athlone and Ottery and Blousrivier, there is no alternative to him. He can do the bare minimum for us, and we won't kick up a fuss. And yes, it's true we don't want a Movement government down here. We don't, do we? But we could return a coalition during the next elections. A split government. That'd keep both the AD and the Movement honest, and put Kob on notice that actually he has no other constituency but us brown folk. If we turf him out down here, he's not going to be able to go up to eGeld and contest elections. They won't want him in eThekwini either. Bloemfontein. But I'm not saying we should wait until the next election two years from now to send Kob a message. To let him know what we want."

Emil glances at Tamsin. Her eyes are narrowed to a squint. It is not obvious what she thinks of Shaka's speech. For himself, he has been expecting taunts, whereas Shaka seems to be playing a subtle game. But perhaps the man is only warming to his themes.

"I think Kob is starting to realize we're not just talking." Shaka circles a down-pointing finger to take in everyone on the beach. "He can't get away with labeling us extrademocratic, our rallies, and so now he's signaling that he's willing to sit down and talk. He says he wants to hear what we have to say. Personally, I think the governor hopes we will sit down to work out some backroom deal with him. That way, he can keep everyone onside. The businessmen down here, the political folks up in eGeld, the government folks. Makgaletha and the rest of the Movement guys. Thema and Tebisa and Phineas Semenya. We know these guys, I know Tebisa personally. They're greedy, they want Cabo to open up fully, open up to private money, and they want it quick. They don't like our labor quotas, our unemployment benefits, our rules about local participation. They're pressing Kob to liberalize. Let's create more jobs, cut red tape, diversify the economy. Race-to-the-bottom stuff."

Near Emil, a young woman nods, but the emotion is not all with Shaka. There are moments of palpable impatience. The crowd seems to agree with Shaka's assessment of Kob and the Movement, but in the moments when he strays, the shifts in mood signal some persisting ambivalence. Emil suspects there are doubts over the identity of the messenger, of Shaka's fitness to lead the faction he is trying to build. What is it Andres had said of Shaka? He's a Black American. He's not one of us. Sentiments of this sort are likely to find some purchase among Creoles. Not for the first time, Shaka strikes Emil as an unlikely firebrand. His accent is nothing like that of Andres or Celeste. Even Torrance, who has worked to smooth his accent, cannot entirely conceal that he is a native speaker of Creole argot. Whereas Shaka's speech is reminiscent of eGeld, where it is difficult, over the telephone, to tell Black from White or Creole. Shaka has the accents of money. Not simply having it or chasing it but being shaped by it.

Shaka is speaking now about the idiosyncrasies of Cabo and its Creoles. "The Movement government, they don't get us. Our roots are in matriarchal hunter-gatherer communities, not patriarchal cattle-keeping ones." Here it is, Emil thinks. A racial distinction that is not so veiled as to elude listeners. Also, he thinks, perhaps this is the link to Bolling. A romanticization of hunter-gatherers.

"Our ancestors, men and women, took lovers. Women and children insulted the meat. You know what I mean, don't you. Inequality is built into the traditional Bantu way of life though, isn't it? Some men having lots of wives, others only one. Kraals and soldiers to guard the king's herds. Anyway, keepers of cows and goats are not really bound up with the natural world as hunter-gatherers are. The world of sea and mountain and stream, wild animals to kill or be killed by. For me, Bantu pastoralism leads quite naturally toward the sort of modern life we see in eGeld. Prosperity gospel. Free-market systems. Unending competition. Stock markets and digital currencies. So much abstraction is not suited to the earthly people we are."

Emil is recalling a sentence or two from Bolling's notebook. *If blood and soil can be literally invoked anywhere in our world, it is Cabo province. One hundred thousand years of blood and soil.* And he senses the audience's gathering receptiveness to Shaka's message. Tamsin has noticed too. She is looking about her with a slight unease.

Shaka has demonstrated that he can stir his listeners. What is less obvious is whether he can build a movement extending beyond racial essentialism, or whether he even aspires to. He seems to be feeling his way toward a course of action, along with the few hundred people that have joined him on the beach. A sense that he will need time, forbearance too, to fully evolve as a leader.

Most affecting for Emil is the mingled mood in the air on the mudflat beach. He is little moved by Shaka's rhetoric, but its influence on the strangers around him is triggering a resurgence, in slightly altered form, of old doubts. That he has not lived, has experienced no great feeling in his life, romantic or political. Even his ambition to become a neurosurgeon seems open to question now. It rests entirely on intellectual affinity and lacks any emotional dimension. Perhaps he does have a brain fixation. How can he aspire to perform life-retrieving operations on fellow creatures for whom he lacks moral feeling? He who has struggled to establish rapport with others, his own parents included. The iboga dream had revived doubts, but Muttie itself—the atavistic permissiveness that is part of the city's atmosphere—has widened the fissures inside him. Attuned to the stirring that Shaka has evoked in a crowd of hundreds, he finds in himself confusion and self-pity. Shaka is no prophet, but Emil is not ready to dismiss him as a charlatan. *Not yet.*

For much of the drive north, Tamsin is silent. The sign for the Ottery exit ramp seems to rouse her from her thoughts. "What did you think of it?"

A beat or two passes before Emil hears himself say, "My father is in the Movement. I realized I've internalized his views about racial solidarity. More than I knew."

If Tamsin notices his evasion, she does not give any sign. "Whatever happens, however things fall out with Shaka's plans, secession or what-what, there won't be a place in this country for people like me."

"People like you?" In the silence of the car, it seems both he and she have been contemplating their own futures rather than that of the country.

"Yes. I don't mean Whites. For my mother, eGeld will always be home, but Muttie has been my place. It's more hospitable for academics. Journalists. I thought that when I completed my PhD, this was where I'd end up. A wave of mostly White academics left five years ago, long before anyone ever heard the name Braeem Shaka. The ones that left then weren't like earlier exiles, at least that's what they told themselves. They didn't hate the country, they didn't hate minority status. They went to American and British universities seeking opportunities to advance their postcolonial studies. I stayed. After my BS, I had offers from PhD programs in Britain and the US. I had begun to fancy Santa Clara but I stayed, partly because it felt like the wrong moment to emigrate. And there was a professor here I really wanted to work with. In Muttie it's always been easy to pretend the racial politics had nothing to do with me."

"You think Shaka is going to change that?" She is perhaps older than he has guessed. His mind is being pulled, as so often now, to words Bolling has written:

> *The Creole perceives himself as neither victim nor protagonist in the country's Passion Play. And even post-Partition, he has struggled to develop an image of himself, and in particular one outside the existing binaries: protagonist—antagonist?—and victim. While these roles have shown themselves*

fluid, capable of switching between Whites and Blacks, they remain, for the Creole, out of reach.

Or something very like it. How, though, does causation flow? Is Bolling influencing Shaka according to his philosophical musings or are the German's writings a response to Shaka's ideology and culture? Out loud, Emil says, "Agency and racination go together in this country, or in the Creole's case, re-racination." The aside, from another section of the notebook, had made an instinctive sort of sense, but he is no longer so certain as Tamsin shoots him a quizzical look. The last minutes of the drive pass in silence. And then, as Emil is getting out of the car in front of 9 Noel, Tamsin thanks him.

"For what?" He hesitates. What is he to Tamsin? A guardian, a more stimulating and amenable younger brother than Adam? The age gap between them—four or five years—is reason enough to wonder. More to the point, what is she to him?

"For the company today. Hey, listen," she says, looking toward Celeste's house meaningfully. "If you ever have a hankering to get away from the banlieues, my mother has a place in Scarbs . . . Scarbrough. You're welcome to use it. She goes there to write, but she's just finished a book so you'd have it to yourself."

"Thank you," he answers. But whether he is grateful for her offer of the getaway, or her own company, is not clear to either of them.

His muscles are stiff with the earlier exertion at Silvermine, and he enters the house looking forward to reading a few pages in the notebook and falling asleep. His mood is fouled the moment he steps into the foyer. Celeste is at home, and from the sounds of it she is not alone in the kitchen. Unfathomably, she has switched on nearly all the downstairs lights.

The detritus of takeout Indian food lies on the kitchen table: foil packaging and half-torn disks of paratha bread in wax paper. Celeste and Rinus are talking softly and drinking beer from the bottle; Emil's aunt is telling her boyfriend something about America. *Ah-may-rikka*, she renders it. Seeing movement in the kitchen threshold, she interrupts herself. "Emil. That you, pet?" And when he comes in, "You remember Rinus?"

Rinus stands to a stoop, as if Emil merits less than his full height. He scarcely resembles the man glimpsed through the car window weeks ago; his hair is free of brilliantine, and in the too-bright light his eyes are an ordinary brown. Emil takes Rinus's hand. Fixing an age to him is difficult: the sallow complexion and gaunt frame add years. Rinus wants it understood that his grip is strong enough to crack bones. The fingernails are closely clipped save the right pinkie nail, which he has allowed to grow overlong and then filed to a point, as Andres has. A weapon of last resort, perhaps. Has Rinus been in prison? "Sit with us a moment, jung," Rinus tells him. "You might learn a thing or two."

Celeste too seems keen for Emil's company. "Dish you up some biryani?"

Emil drags over a chair, curious in spite of himself to find out what Rinus hopes to teach him. "Thanks, Auntie. A little bit. I'll sit a few minutes before I head upstairs."

"Emil is my brother Errol's boy. He's visiting from eGeld."

"How old are you, jung? You're small but you look fit. I don't guess you've got shop floor experience?" A response seems beside the point, so Emil keeps silent. "A man needs a job of work, you know. Idle hands and all that. I should know." Rinus takes up his fork and empties his plate of rice and beef with an unexpected delicacy. When Emil calls him sir, he answers, "No need to address me so formal, jungie. Call me Uncle."

There are a few reasons why it should be Andres rather than himself sitting over a table of fast-congealing food and beer talking job prospects with Rinus. His cousin has a knack for well-timed absences. More frustrating is Celeste's silence in the face of Rinus's foolish questions and remarks. *Did you matric yet? Celeste, I must bring this boy to a bordel or what?* Emil could of course get up from the table at any moment, but in his perverse mood he waits, vainly, for her to interrupt and tell Rinus what she knows well: her nephew is in medical college and about to begin specialization for neurosurgery.

"I'm studying veterinary medicine." An untruth to test his aunt, and to avoid lashing out in a way that will shock her. Celeste misses the lie or opts to overlook it.

"Vet? How far along are you, eh? What, you want to spend your life with one hand up rindarschen? Oh, it's canines, is it? Is that good money?"

"I need to sleep," he announces. Fifteen minutes are the limit of his patience with his aunt. Standing, stars crowd his vision, and swaying, he is unsure whether it is an act. There is a feeling in him, small, unexpected, of gratitude for his parents. Mounting the stairs, he bites back a howl of laughter at overhearing Rinus tell Celeste, "What's going on with that one? Doesn't seem in top form."

He wakes, damp-chested, weak with some sudden ague. Getting up off Torrance's narrow bed, he stumbles. He is shivering and pulling the window closed has no effect.

And then sometime after dawn, a thumping rouses him. Andres and Torrance once more, he knows. The bedroom door is flung open, and he wonders what the brothers might be fighting about now. But Andres is alone. "Larnie," he says with mock fierceness, "where you been?" On his feet are running shoes of a poisonous green hue. He cannot get a proper visual fix on his cousin. Andres wavers in and out of sight; in one moment he is right up alongside the bed, and the next in the threshold.

"Come here," Emil orders his cousin. Thirst is unbearable. Andres appears to be considering whether to approach the bed. Emil shuts his eyes and forces himself up onto one elbow. Water. He has hoped to never need anything of Andres, certainly nothing so urgent as the present craving for water. Fever. It must be.

"What's up, E?"

"Give me something to drink." It must be Silvermine's water that has sickened him.

The water Andres fetches is cold enough that his gums ache. "You hungover, E?" Andres taunts. "Need a katzenjammer?"

"You meet Rinus?" A little of Emil's strength has returned. "No?" Emil finds himself laughing maniacally at Rinus's aside. *Not in top form*. The mirth is a sharpness behind his ribs. Sleep is pulling at him, but he needs to piss. "Where is my mobile, Andres?"

Andres stares and does not answer.

He falls into sleep and opens his eyes as Andres is lifting him on the bed to drink, one arm about his waist. He holds the glass so Emil will not choke. His cousin has warm sweetish breath, like green apples, and he peers into Emil's face with an unreadable expression. "Do you need the toilet, Cuz?"

At times Emil cannot make out what Andres is telling him, and there are other voices. The fever has stolen his eyesight, or perhaps it is the iboga again.

"Go on to work, Ma." Andres's voice rises suddenly from a clamor of speech. "I'll keep my eye on him."

"But what is it? What's wrong with him?"

Andres switches to argot, and Emil cannot follow. He is preoccupied with making a diagnosis of what has felled him. Bacterium that is resistant to Silvermine's alkaline black water. It must be the zoll.

"He's too thin," Celeste complains.

The fever has turned. He no longer sweats, has left off shuddering and chattering, but his body is weak. And there is aural delirium. He wakes himself yelling out for Celeste. For Torrance. And his phone still has not turned up. He suspects Andres has taken it. *Stolen his phone*. Karel is singing; his voice, altering without transition, slows to an ooze. Someone else, more than one person, has come into the room where Emil is trying to sleep, and the two infiltrators speak unintelligibly to one another. Somehow, he understands—the iboga—and as he is trying to absorb what they are saying about him, a bright small beam of light jabs into his eye and causes him to raise up.

"Andres?" he says, to muffled laughter. "What is it?"

"Jus' checking you." The voice seems, as Andres does, to come from the doorway. Emil brings up a hand to block off the glare and brushes something, a shirt. Flesh. "Go back to sleep." The light shines in one eye, then moves to the other, taunting. Emil comes off the bed, snarling, hunched, and his open hand claps what feels like an ear. The blow makes a staggeringly loud report, followed by the sound of throttled laughter. Drool. Violence brings Emil back to himself, but he is not done. He swings at Drool again and fails to connect. The mood of absurdity breaks, a shift audible in the sound of sharply intaken breath. Drool understands he has been slapped, struck hard. Amused astonishment turns to rage as Emil's animal strength leaves him.

"Relax, Drool." Andres's voice is very close. "Cuz is messed up on something. He not well."

Emil is shivering again, commingled sickness and rage. His cousin has put himself in Drool's way, and from the sounds of it is shouldering him out of the bedroom. "Sleep, E," Andres hisses at him. "You're sick."

Emil complies simply to avert fainting. Downstairs, Andres is hollering. It is his first night at 9 Noel all over again.

What time is it? He sits waiting on the edge of the bed until he has enough strength to dress himself in a clean shirt and rumpled trousers. His phone is beneath the bed, where it has been all along.

The gratitude he feels toward Andres is disproportionate, but he is not safe in Celeste's house in his current condition. When his vision is partly restored, he gets moving. Andres is in the downstairs sitting room—perhaps Drool is with him—playing a video game. In his haste to be away, he's putting himself in fresh danger. He is in no fit state to drive and yet he does, weeping sweat from forehead and chest with the effort of staying upright behind the wheel, navigating by memory to a house in the hills above the city bowl. He had brought her here after the night in Kampsbaai.

He parks in the road and hopefully rings the gate bell. "I need your bathroom," he tells Tamsin, who has come out to see who it is, and she turns unspeaking and leads the way into the detached clapboard house. In the ground floor galley bathroom, Emil throws open both taps to mask the noise of his retching. Long tendrils of clear bile jerk out of him; at last his heaves slacken, and he drinks from the tap lying bent over so his weight rests on the cool porcelain. Even when the water runs tepid, he goes on drinking.

"Can I come in?" Tamsin enters without awaiting an answer

and squats over him, where he lies on the floor, to nudge the back of her hand against his hot throat. "Definitely running a fever." Flinching at the contact, he lets her pull him up to a standing position and lug him into a bedroom where, with a judo maneuver, she gets him onto the high bed. With the covers tugged back, she wrestles his sodden shirt up over his head.

She is sitting near the foot of the bed saying nothing, nor looking at Emil. Waiting for him to sleep, perhaps. The room is cozy, square with tall ceilings; it offers a view onto the cropped yard and the back fence. He is unperturbed by Tamsin's silence; even the possibility that his sudden appearance at the house has disturbed her work does not trouble him. She quits the room when he begins dozing and returns with lukewarm soup. Attempts at feeding him do not come to much: he manages four spoonfuls and then must clamp back an impulse to gag. Tamsin drops two brown pills into his dry palm and waits while he pushes them into his mouth. Aspirin, she murmurs, as if begrudging him an explanation.

The rushing noise that brings him awake is persistent, familiar. It is not rain but the television playing in the next room, the faint wittering of facile voices. The sheets are very smooth against his fever-dry skin, the hot stiffness of his prick. Piqued, he goes and stands partway in the living room doorway to spy. Tamsin, in boy shorts and a flesh-colored singlet, sits reading in an armchair with her knees up. Every so often she darts furtive glances over her book at the gameshow on the television. This furtiveness is both curious and endearing;

Tamsin is unaware of being observed. He steps forward from the doorway, making a sort of cough as he does so.

"Your phone's been ringing," Tamsin tells him. "Your lover, I'd guess."

He makes a noise in his throat to signal a slight amusement. "I have to get something from the car." He dresses and goes out front, leaving the gate ajar behind him. He reenters the house with the black notebook beneath his shirt. The remark about his lover: a reference to Bolling? He had not for an instant considered going to the German's house rather than here. Why?

"There's a southeaster on the way," Tamsin says as he scans his text messages. "You took a while to stop shivering. How do you feel?" The book, resting face down on her belly, is *The Thief* by Jean Genet.

Bolling *has* telephoned. Three times. His mother has too, also Andres. "I'm hungry. Can we go out for something?"

"The Southeaster. It'll be here in a few hours." Tamsin's reluctance to go out seems to lie elsewhere.

He looks around the house, nakedly assessing. A comfortable house, if far more modest than Bolling's. There are prints of Caravaggio's work—two of them—on the walls. There are a handful of artists whom he recognizes easily by their style, and the Italian is one of them. Quarrelsome men and women, a kind of brawling tension. "This your place?"

"I didn't buy it, if that's what you're asking. My mother got a huge advance on the first book, which she used for the down payment. I rent from her. You oughtn't to overdo it, you know, going out. There's grapes and hard cheese in the fridge. Some sliced ham from Woolies. I know you didn't love the soup. First though you could wash."

Tamsin comes into the bathroom when he's beneath the shower. He cannot see what she is doing through the steam, and she leaves almost at once. Clothes have been left on the lid of the toilet. Gray trousers belonging to Adam, he guesses; the fit is a little wider at the ankle than he likes.

"Where is Adam?" he asks Tamsin.

"He rents a place close to Varsity. He and his girlfriend live together."

"Dipha?"

"Yes. Would it have been clearer if I'd said his Black girlfriend?"

"Maybe."

The restaurant has two levels. It is so popular there is a forty-five-minute wait for a table. Unless, that is, they will accept seats in the smoking section? It is all the same to Tamsin, and Emil accepts.

His phone is ringing and he steps out to take the call; Bolling is on the line. "I can hardly hear you," he barks. "Where are you? You might want to come round. I've got Braeem and a few others over."

At the table, Emil says nothing of Bolling's invitation; he had been noncommittal with Bolling. Tamsin watches him eat as if ravening, finishing his meat before consuming his spinach. Tamsin has ordered a bowl of raw fish and vinegared rice. There is something disinhibiting in the silent way she attends what he is doing. Earlier, she had waited with the same patience for him to fall asleep.

When they are inside a taxi, Emil confesses where they are bound. Tamsin casts an eye over his attire and her own; neither is dressed for a soiree, but she does not protest. "What's at Bolling's?" she says.

"He has company he thinks might be interesting."

Braeem Shaka himself opens the door. He nods a greeting but does not give his name. Tamsin shows no sign of recognizing him, but for Emil, the height and stilted manner are unmistakable. Bolling's house too retains its familiar atmosphere, at once cozy and airy. The German is seated cross-legged on the floor of his salon, talking to a white-bearded Creole man wearing a suit jacket. A third man perches nearby on the settee but he seems inattentive. He carries himself like a bodyguard.

"Ah, Tamsin." Bolling's greeting is ambiguous. Emil observes that Tamsin is the only woman present, that he himself merits no welcome. "Koos, a moment," Bolling interrupts the one with a white beard, stands, and goes to the kitchen, returning with tumblers of what must be whiskey for Emil and Tamsin. He gestures for them to find places to sit. "Should Braeem accept Kob's offer of talks without conditions?"

The question is general but everyone, including the well-built young man, is looking to Emil to answer. Lightly, he says, "Refuse."

Shaka asks, "Do you know what it is Kob wants to discuss?"

"That hardly matters." It is Tamsin who answers. "Unless it's to do with holding the referendum you're calling for."

"Why refuse?" Bolling wants to know. "What's your reasoning?"

Emil looks at Braeem. "You're trying to build a movement; why not keep building."

"The message is popular but I'm hearing people ask, is this the right messenger?" the one with a white beard, Koos, asks. Why, Emil wonders, has Bolling, as host, not presented everyone by name? "Is this guy really someone of our community? Some of that talk about you being an astroturf is propaganda coming from around the governor, of course. Not all though."

"Astroturf? Why? Because he went to Stanford Law School?" Tamsin says.

"Folks where I live would see gaining admission to Stanford as a plus. The American dream is still alive, in this country at least," answers Koos.

Shaka gestures with a shrug toward Bolling. "I'm not sure Lukas sees the American dream as a selling point."

"What's the problem?" Tamsin presses. "America or the American dream?"

"Both."

"Everyone loves America, or at least no one I know actively hates it."

"A hot mess that hangs together because of anthropocentrism, religious and secular," Emil says, and wishes the words back instantly; a regurgitation of Bolling's own view back to him in a tone salted with irony. It is the wrong moment for the German to learn that one of his notebooks has been stolen.

The others are watching him with a little wariness. He has seen the expression on Tamsin's face before; it is the same unreadable look she directed at him on the drive back from Dead Woman's Beach.

Shaka is first to guess the source of Emil's remark and he gives Bolling a pointed look, musing, "An acolyte, eh?"

"Quite." Bolling sounds abruptly very English, although he might be agreeing not with Braeem but with Emil. Very like the German to miss one of his notebooks but to say nothing of it, to fold the theft into the ongoing game he is playing with Emil. Smiling to himself, Bolling adds, "My views of America are beside the point. Is it helpful for Braeem and his movement to be associated with the US?"

"Your views are what, exactly? Standard anti-imperial stuff?" Whitebeard, who is almost certainly an academic, says.

"Not really." Bolling shrugs but is clearly keen to go on despite not wanting to divert the conversation. "Even its artists default to 'aw shucks' responses to critiques of their country. We're fuckups, we get it. Iraq, financial crisis. All of it. But we're influential and good-hearted and everyone wants to be us . . . so . . . That's the subtext of big American novels over the last, let's say forty years."

Silence. Their eyes are on Tamsin, who takes a slug of her whiskey but is silent. While her arrival had discomfited the others at first, Bolling alone seems hostile to her presence now.

"There *are* rumors you don't speak argot, or not very well," the professor points out to Braeem.

"And you spoke English at your rally. Why?" Tamsin.

"That's the direction the Creole community is moving in. Breaking free of its colonial language. We didn't need to focus-group the language thing . . ."

"Before this devolves into a free-for-all," the white-bearded man is saying, "what's the real story about the deportation from the States? It might be helpful to know."

"Campus politics," Bolling answers smoothly.

"It was because of BDS." Braeem takes in everyone. "Let's get into it, actually. It's no secret."

"BDS."

"Ja. Boycott, divest, sanctions. It's to do with Israel. I didn't know a thing about it for most of my first year of law school, and then in March, right around the time of the spring frenzy over summer internships, an American Jewish woman, someone I didn't know very well, invited me to a BDS meeting." Shaka, pausing, gives Bolling an unreadable look. "Not sure why I went. As I say, Molly and I didn't know each other well. Perhaps I needed a distraction from the internship madness. I was halfheartedly trying to set something up back here, a legal clinic paid for by a law firm in San Francisco, but I was also tempted by the Silicon Valley law firms, one of which I'd done a sort of pre-interview with. There was lots going on in my head and maybe some of my jumping into BDS was to postpone dealing with the huge decision in front of me. Anyway, I attended a demonstration which the university determined got out of hand, and this led to eight people, myself included, being arrested. I didn't spend a night in prison, although I was ready for that. The police took us to the station, simply booked us and let us go. I didn't ever think I might have violated the terms of my scholarship by getting arrested. I should have—after all, if aspiring lawyers don't read the fine print, what good are they? Someone else took the trouble to look into the terms of my scholarship and bring it to the attention of my dean."

"Who?" Tamsin wants to know.

"There are interest groups," Bolling says.

"Yes, let's just say someone connected with one of the groups that opposes BDS."

"So what happened?"

"The law dean called me into his office, and he told me to bring along someone I trusted so I came with Marty, a Trini friend of mine, Black and Indian—a dogla, he said was the term for it back home. Brilliant guy, incandescently smart but also savvy. Holden, that's the dean, was alone in his office. This surprised us both, even though we had no idea what was up. He didn't waste time with niceties, Holden. He said, 'You were arrested recently by campus police. This means you've violated the terms of your scholarship.' Marty didn't blink, which was good, cause I sat there unable to react, to think. 'Which terms?' Marty asked, and he took a piece of paper from Holden's hand. I could see the dean had circled a section on the page. Marty scanned through the document and looked Holden in his eye. 'It wasn't someone in your office that noticed this,' he said, and Holden shook his head no. I thought to myself, he's recording this conversation. It sort of jolted me. I kept thinking we should be recording it too.

"I was still obsessing when Marty said, 'What do you plan to do?' And Holden said the university would have to rule whether I was in violation or not and then take action, and that there wasn't much wiggle room as to that ruling. Marty said, 'There's an appeals process.' Again, he wasn't asking.

"'Yes,' Holden answered. 'If you appeal, it will go before an arbitration panel.' He was warning us. Arbitration is how businesses and universities stack the deck against you. It's not your peers on the panel. It's donors and senior administrators of the university. In this case, the priority would not be justice, or even leniency, but managing reputational risk. Holden knew this and wanted to be sure we knew it too. I was surprised when he admitted, 'Whoever alerted us about this wasn't acting out of any sense of rectitude.'

"That was when I understood how toxic the fights around BDS had become, and not only at Stanford. I was like cannon fodder blundering onto a battlefield and getting mowed down in the first volleys. 'If the Law department tries to sit on this,' Holden said, 'there'll be a stink.' Another warning. After the meeting, though, I felt a bit of sympathy for Holden, having this thing dumped in his lap. He was trying to be fair about it. Marty said, 'He's not going to take a bullet for you,' meaning Holden. 'Nor is Stanford Law.'"

"Did you appeal?" Tamsin asks.

"I didn't. I left Holden's office with Marty and we went off campus and got blind stinking drunk. Marty didn't try to influence my decision. He went to high school in Miami; he knew how America worked. Only when we were shitfaced did he give me advice. He said, 'This is the Bay Area, some high-powered ACLU lawyer will take your case and blow it up into a big free-speech brouhaha in the courts.' I didn't though."

A silence. Bolling turns to Emil once more. "Is Kob keeping Myambire in the loop? Has Errol said anything?"

"You want him to pump his own father for information?" Tamsin demands.

Is this Bolling's interest in him, Emil wonders? The Errol angle is one he had not considered but which now seems so obvious.

Playing peacemaker, Braeem asks Tamsin, "What about your own family: any government connections there?"

"My mother writes crime novels." Tamsin laughs. "My dad is a farmer."

"What's her name?"

"Is that germane here? What are you asking from Kob? Besides the referendum."

"A moratorium on foreigners—all foreigners—buying property in Cabo for five years while the government gets some affordable housing built. Locking in priority hiring of locals in certain sectors, that sort of thing."

"The Movement folks will definitely go for those." She raises an eyebrow. "What if Kob offers you an official-sounding job?"

"No jobs. I'm a community organizer. Or I'm Governor."

"He's not going to let you stand outside and piss into his tent."

"That's what I told him," Koos puts in, nodding at Tamsin.

"We'll see." Shaka is uncomfortable.

"I need to rest," Emil tells Tamsin in a whisper. "The fever." Strength is leaving him, and he can hardly remain upright.

Tamsin stands. Koos shoots Emil a look of exasperation.

"Please," Bolling says with cool formality. "Feel free to go lie down upstairs if you're not well."

"I should get him home." Tamsin is equally detached. Does anyone else besides Emil perceive her eagerness to leave?

Bolling walks the two of them out through the garage, one level below; Emil had not known the exit existed. "Take the car if you like, rather than wait for a taxi," Bolling offers in the same distant tone. If he notices how closely Tamsin holds Emil about the waist, he gives no sign. "The key is in the ignition."

"I have a notebook of yours." Emil had not planned to make a confession, but here it is.

"Eines meiner Schwarzen Hefte? Hold onto it. I don't read those. Nor does Braeem, as it happens." Bolling laughs as a meaningful look passes between him and Tamsin.

The storm has turned in its course. Either this or it is already dying, to judge from the faintly humid air blowing in through the taxi window. There is some tension in Tamsin which she cannot conceal: she glowers straight ahead, one leg cross-tucked under the other.

"Apologies for dragging you away." *What am I to this woman?* There had been a surprising strength in her grip on him. *What is she to me?* The men in Bolling's house have likely wondered the same.

Tamsin shrugs. "They weren't interested in my two cents. Except Bolling, who hates women but is too shrewd to pass up good advice. What black notebook were you talking about?"

"I took a notebook from Bolling's house when I was there."

"Ah. Was he drowsing post-coitus? You know Heidegger called his notebooks Die Schwarze Hefte?"

Emil giggles with a silly sort of relief. "Heidegger."

"Martin Heidegger, yes."

Fever returns during that short night, and with it comes a nausea, a belly sickness as from food poisoning. Tamsin wakes—perhaps it is the sound of air gusts flapping at the latched window. The storm has come down on them after all, although the wildest bits are far away, probably on the flats, which get the worst of everything in Cabo. Intermittent rain moves crosswise over the city. It might be six o'clock when Tamsin is wakened by Emil stumbling about, probably to fetch a glass of water from the kitchen.

Storm and fever might well be linked. In the afternoon, when Tamsin enters her spare room and sets her long hand against Emil's throat, she muses that he might be dead if not for a hectic flush in the cheeks. He does not stir when her weight settles on the bed, offering license to frankly stare. The eyelashes, long and upcurling, part slightly so the sclera show, as if rolled back in his head. Even in illness, Emil's form retains its neatness. He sleeps with arms at his sides and the toes primly pointing.

Only fever, Tamsin reminds herself as she climbs into the bed, shunting Emil a little roughly to one side to eke out space; his weight is inert. With her own body, she warms him, pushing out the fever. Steady heartbeat. After a few moments of this, she gets up and goes to find a washcloth. She likes him like this, as fever has made him. Pliant, unguarded. She folds down the coverlet. It is easier than she's anticipated to undress him, so easy that as she levers his shorts over the angle of his feet she hesitates, suspicious that Emil is feigning. His penis has another color than his belly or the inside of his thigh, darker: a Black man's penis. He has a sprinter's form, calves that are hammy and strong, fine ankles, and wide, high-arched feet. When they'd swum at Silvermine, she had failed to notice his feet; the nails, cut down, are crescent-shaped and opaque as mother of pearl. A standout winger at King Edward's school is how her brother described Emil, whom he called Silva. He is too compact, lying here, to be a rugby player, in spite of the muscular thighs.

Emil is shuddering in his sleep, lips muttering. Tamsin bundles him once more under the duvet.

She has begun to read to him from Cioran—the aphorisms are brief—and then when the Romanian is too bleak for her, she reads random snatches of *Studies of Hysteria*.

I get along quite well with someone only when he is at his lowest point and has neither the desire nor the strength to restore his habitual illusions.

Reading aloud, she is surprised at how often she perceives alien, even opposing meanings in the words.

A spell when Emil is strong enough to stand and walk. In the sitting room, he props himself in front of the television, although he does not seem to watch. "Bolling's very rich, is he." Tamsin lays her book face down next to her armchair. "Why is he here?"

"His family has business interests, I think."

"What's your involvement with him?" Tamsin says it so casually, he is alerted.

"As you see it. He's an acquaintance." His voice is a little wheezy.

"You're not infatuated with him? I wondered if he might be sleeping with Braeem."

"I don't get the feeling Shaka inclines that way."

"*You* must be quite rich," Tamsin muses. "Errol Silva, eh. What's the old saying? 'There are no poor Creoles in eGeld.'"

"And no rich ones in Muttie," he finishes. "I drank ibogaine tea in Bolling's house," he says after a little time has passed. He is full of confessions these days. "He gave me a glass without telling me what it was. I experienced lucid dreams and in one of them, my mother took me for tests to determine if I might be autistic. I was about four years old. That rang true. She never said anything when I was growing up but I always felt . . . observed. It was a kind of trauma for her, I think, waiting for someone else to see what she saw in me. My father sometimes hinted that I was odd, only because I was cut off from my cultural roots. Nothing more. Of course, my mother began doubting her own perception."

"I can see that. Sort of like being universally gaslighted," Tamsin says. "Does Bolling see what your mother sees, do you think? In you."

"I don't know what Bolling sees." He has tired himself out with talking.

"You have a . . . an affect which I suspect draws Bolling. A sort of innocence of other people. Why did he give you the iboga?"

"I didn't ask him. You've done it?"

"No. I very nearly went to an ayahuasca retreat once in Kleinmond, but it wasn't for me. Ayahuasca has gotten very trendy. In Holland, I think, they have ayahuasca churches. People dressed up in white lying about in their puke and shit." Tamsin comes over to join him on the couch. He is slow in averting his eyes; her breasts swing easily beneath the singlet.

"You're afraid you'd play mind games with your patients, I think? Your subjects." Is he seeking an opening?

"I'm a historian, remember. But I had the opposite concern, actually. That I would fall for my patients, the hysterics and the narcissists. Get off on neuroses."

"Is Bolling a narcissist, do you think?"

"Bolling? No. Shaka is the narcissist. It's latent, but it's there. He's rather ecstatic about his experience in the US. He's working toward martyrdom but with an off-ramp, so there'll never be a need to sacrifice himself fully. No need to die. Bolling is a romantic, a reactionary. He's drawn to fascism's hatred of modernity but he loathes the fascists' fetish for competition, I suspect. The fixation with biological fitness. 'Man is alone in the world, in tremendous eternal isolation. He has no subject outside himself; lives for nothing else.'"

Emil gives her a sharp look; he has read the passage, or one very like it, in the notebook.

Tamsin is amused. "Know who wrote that? Otto Weininger. Someone who would have found the Nazis irresistibly alluring had he lived long enough. I bet your friend Bolling knows a lot about Weininger, who influenced the Nazis' preoccupation with mysticism. Like Wagner and Nietzsche. Unlike those two, Weininger was Jewish. And Viennese. Like Freud. So, Bolling and I both have our Austrian patron saints. There's an Austrian for everyone really. Popper, Kraus, Hayek, Zweig, Wittgenstein. If you were to begin idolizing von Eiselsberg, say, we could be a proper trio."

Now he is being mocked—he and Bolling both. *Von Eiselberg?* "I would think you and Bolling would get along then," he says. His arousal remains, but it is the right moment to return to bed. *Don't push your luck.*

"Doubtful," is Tamsin's only answer.

Biographical information on Von Eiselberg is sparse, and most of what he finds is in German. But Emil notes that Billroth, a mentor of Von Eiselberg, expressed racist sentiments concerning an influx of Jewish students into Vienna Medical School.

In the notebook, he reads:

> *Hobbes' claims about the viciousness of hunter-gatherers are a clear red herring: early humans engaged in mostly ritualised conflicts that rarely led to mass casualties or deaths. Modern humans in fact unknowingly charge foraging peoples with another, more serious crime, in our eyes: a refusal to fall in with the dictates of civilisation.*

As Emil sleeps, Tamsin slips the black notebook out from under his pillow, sits on the floor of the spare bedroom, and resumes perusing it.

> *Contemporary humans disdain hunter-gatherers as a pesky holdover from an era when we were the rivals of wild beasts. The silent law of modernity—one of many—is that man may attack or subjugate what is natural, is frequently called on to do so, but he must contend only with those of his own species.*

Her intuitions about his sickness are being borne out. He barely stirs and, growing cold, Tamsin returns to her own room with the notebook. In the morning he is restive once more, like the pre-vampire who experiences two sorts of sleep. Several times that day, Tamsin laves him with the washcloth, on each occasion observing that he is immaculate rather than beautiful in any common meaning of the word. Her recitations from Cioran and other texts have accrued momentum, and it is unclear whether they are for Emil's benefit or her own. Not that it much matters. It is, Tamsin decides, on these unseen moments of selfishness that caregivers survive.

The next morning is different. A strange elation grips him, and he showers and goes out to find breakfast in a café. He returns with croissants and orange juice to find Tamsin agitated. "Esme's coming. My mother. She's flying in this afternoon and she's going to stay here."

"I should head back to my aunt's anyway." He's not sure what the fuss is about and sets to putting the things out for breakfast. Is this Tamsin's way of turfing him out?

"Come with me to Scarbs. To Scarbrough. I already told Esme I won't be here."

"Why?"

"The dynamics in my family are . . . complicated. Adam gets clingy and competitive when we're all together, and Esme tires of Adam's neediness and tries to put me in the middle as a buffer, and it just becomes a shitshow."

"Why should I come with you, I mean?"

"Well, you'll just end up at Bolling's if you don't."

He had not considered this eventuality, but she has mentioned it now, giving it the ring of truth. "So, you're my defense against him? Do I need guarding then? From Bolling, I mean." He might be flirting with Tamsin—he is uncertain—but in any case she is unwilling to flirt back.

"How successful a writer is your mother?" Emil asks, when they are driving.

"Oh, she's had four or five bestselling novels. Her trilogy about Bululani and Duiker, Black and White detectives in eGeld, rode a multiculti wave of fame. I've read two of them. I think Esme went about it pretty shrewdly. The setup for the books, I mean. Japhet Bululani is the senior partner, the older cop who is cynical about life. His partner Duiker is White, new White and guilt-free so it doesn't sound defensive when he describes his compatriots as flawed. Duiker is married to a Creole woman and plays football—I mean soccer—with his Black buddies on the force. It was a winning formula."

New Whites. Small Whites. Emil wonders, but doesn't ask, whether Tamsin considers herself a new White.

They are south of Kampsbaai, where he and Tamsin had first met. This flank of the peninsula is less densely settled than the other; the only settlement he can name is Llandudno, and he scans the road signs coming into view with interest. Nordhoek. Kommetjie. At the end of Kommetjie, beyond its lighthouse, an old yellow-skinned man with long narrowed eyes and outturned nostrils sits on a broken chair next to the road. In him, the Boesvolk blood is strong. He offers a two-handed wave in response to Emil's nod.

"They ought not to swim there." Tamsin shakes her head. A knot of yellow children are up to their necks in the ocean playing some game that involves a great deal of bobbing and ducking. None is likely a good swimmer, but perhaps they understand how far out they can venture and which places to avoid. Here and there, barely submerged rocks cause the water to dimple and roil. Tamsin points with her chin at a splintering sign planted in the sand. *No swimming: Waste runoff*. The heedlessness of the children has touched her mood. Emil in turn becomes a little withdrawn.

To cheer them, Tamsin drives first to a place for swimming above the village of Scarbrough. A bit like Silvermine, she says, save that swimming is not allowed. It is a reservoir that provides the city with drinking water. "Bloody hot." Tamsin flaps her hand to fan herself. "Rangers patrol up here, but most afternoons they retire to their shed for a kip." She has parked the car in the lee of a tor, though there is scarcely any shade. "We're going to earn our swim," she says, gesturing toward the foot track they will follow. She seems to relish the prospect of trekking two kilometers uphill.

They come under immediate assault from sandflies. Emil is beating them off his neck and shins the whole way, but it pleases him how well he manages the exertion. He has recovered from the fever.

At the edge of the reservoir is a perimeter where the grasses and scrub have been cut back. The shallow water is the same tawny color as at Silvermine, but the reservoir floor is concrete-lined. "Scarbs is down there." Tamsin is pointing toward the opposite shore; in the haze, it appears farther away than it is. "We could walk to the house, but we'd have to leave the car."

His head aches. The sun casts a flat white glaze off the

reservoir surface, which is reflected by the low sky. The place has an atmosphere of apprehension that he acknowledges is his own mood. They are trespassing in a place without cover of tree or bush. But there is more: a little way back from the water, knuckle-like boulders of sandstone or some other friable rock sharpen the ambience of a consecrated space. He hunts for signs of how the Boesvolk might have used this place a thousand years ago, supposing of course there had been water here then. Braeem Shaka's anecdote about Dead Woman's Beach has loosened something within him: a sense that he too can claim these stories as his own history. A feeling of roots even if not quite as Errol means it.

Tamsin slips free of her dress and slippers, leaves them where they fall on the scrubby ground, and levers herself into the water. Sandfly bites mark her upper back and arms, the skin hectic and already wealing. With his thumb, Emil peels a mandarin from his pocket and eats it in two bites. A dark bundle hits his shin as he is teasing open a second mandarin: her swimming costume, bra, and shorts. Perhaps an invitation, although Tamsin is not even looking toward him.

At last, he enters, dragging his feet over mossy, smooth concrete. There has been no letup from the sandflies and he dives and resurfaces, pulling in an unwieldy breaststroke in Tamsin's general direction. She's the better swimmer, but his greater strength would ensure that he would overpower her. Idle musing: a reaction to the illness he has experienced and the persisting weakness, but which he cannot now easily shake off.

The way he's looking at Tamsin seems to convey something of this dark thought. Just an idle musing, he tells himself again. Paddling her arms in a kind of half freestyle, she circles around him and exits the water. Trying for nonchalance, Emil treads water. Best not to be overly solicitous with Tamsin. When he looks up, she has vanished, and curiosity pricks him to follow.

She's squatted on her heels within a tight copse of five or six stones leaning like dolmens, chin on chest as if an engrossing thing lies between her feet. Pissing, he guesses from the posture; attempting to retreat, he treads on a thorn and feels a stabbing pain in his heel that causes him to freeze before starting again to duck out of view. *Peeping Tom*. Tamsin is aware of him. Her eyes meet his and then they shut in a long blink; bowing her neck once more, she defecates in a hot rush. Her left hand is scrabbling over the surface of the thin soil, grasping at dead leaves, something to wipe herself. An automaton, he backs out of that place with its animal stink and slinks back into the reservoir.

The pattern that has set in between them over recent days has in an instant shattered and, for Emil, without volition. When Tamsin reenters the water like a soiled naiad, her hair piled on the crown of her head, he reacts to her unfamiliar air of vulnerability by lunging at her. Id and ego.

He's lifted Tamsin clear of the water but his feet scrabble over the reservoir floor, and they fall backward into water of a depth somewhere between waist and knee. He pushes inside Tamsin, whose response is a kind of acquiescence; at one moment she tightens her clasp on his buttock, a gesture he perceives as encouragement, or pleasure, although she is perhaps simply shifting her grip to avoid drowning.

It may be that he has ejaculated, but his erection has yet to subside. Tamsin, matter-of-fact, pulls on her dress and retrieves her swimsuit. The dampness of their skin draws a burring frenzy of sandflies and they are driven from the reservoir's edge, Tamsin swatting her sunhat in wide arcs to fend them off. She is breathlessly laughing all the while at the fury of the attacks, the impossibility of defending against them, and now Emil is laughing too, and they lurch down the track, and neither is sure how momentous what has happened ought to be.

Scarbrough is less than a village, more of a hamlet of twelve, perhaps fifteen houses. In the last bungalow (keys inside a flowerpot, the left one near the front door), Tamsin's first act is to kneel at the driftwood dining table and tap out three lines of white powder for each of them. After the second line, all sensation leaches from Emil's gums. His teeth feel like wood chips and his erection persists even now. Tamsin snorts what remains. The drifts of powder, scattered by her haste, gather in the runnels of the tabletop.

Cocaine makes her ugly, limning her eyes red. For reasons that are not entirely clear, he has removed his shorts and lies shoulder to shoulder with her on the floor of timber slats, which are rotted from the effect of damp ocean air. Nothing comes out of him; it is as if he is stopped up. The veins in his glans protrude. "Cocaine can cause priapism," Tamsin says in a dissociative sort of tone, and she draws in her feet so her legs are folded into a hill, as if lying on the wood floor is giving her backache.

He wakes wanting again to go inside her. The cocaine has worn off somewhat but his vision remains sharp-etched, and he perceives the gooseflesh on Tamsin's arms, her belly, as obscene. Her thighs hold him, and at the same time her hand is guiding. "Not there. I'm not using birth control." He ejaculates: the fluid leaking from his prick is clean as ichor. Tamsin has rolled onto her flank, but it is not clear whether this is meant to dissuade him or invite him.

A gray light comes in from outside the windows. What wakes him is the sound of Tamsin's hunger pangs, her belly creaking like an oar. A gruff booming bark comes from down the hill, something in it so wild he might be dreaming again, but then he recognizes the sound of olive baboons, perhaps more than one.

He gathers Tamsin up and carries her through to the nearer of the house's two bedrooms and falls asleep next to her but not touching on the bare, stained mattress. His prick is a small and insensate thing.

The vacation house has sat vacant over the long winter months, the windows latched tight against cobras and the clever fingers of baboons. The close interior harbors mold and mildew in the cupboards and single bathroom. Emil feels it tickling his nose and throat. In the old-fashioned murmuring fridge is a hard cheese, marmalade, and olives. Tamsin has removed bricks of unsliced bread from the freezer and set them to thaw on the counter. In the pantry is a stovetop kettle and ground coffee wrapped in foil paper.

He washes his clothes in the bathroom sink with carbolic soap. Out on the stoep, Tamsin is finishing a cigarette. Her fingers worry at the sandfly bites on his belly and neck, as if she is making a tally. Wound about her from knees to torso is a striped cloth. The exposed bits of her—throat, ankles, behind her knees—are even more welted than his own flesh. Off somewhere, bull baboons are raising their woofing grunts again.

He draws out his penis and, rearing a little to avert backsplash, pisses off the stoep into the dying grass. The front lawn falls steeply away from the house and on down to the fence, a garden overgrown with reddening watsonias. She squints and jerks her head in the direction of the next house. "Mrs. Marcus is watching you." The windows are darkened and the place, as rundown as their own, is too large to be a summer cottage. "Adam loved his foreskin as a boy," she adds, conversational. "We were constantly telling him to stop yanking on it."

A causeway runs below Esme's house, at the bottom of Scarbrough, between the village and the retreating ocean. The waves break farther and farther off the strand. In back, the house has a porch with woven rainproof furniture. The land, unfenced, abuts a bald blackened hillside that must be public land. The gorse is reestablishing itself after the blaze that cut it back a few seasons ago.

While he reads from the notebook, indolent flies, small enough as to be scarcely visible, rove across his arms and torso, eking moisture from the skin.

What might an ethics of contingency look like? To most modern peoples the idea would represent a secular analogue to quietism, fatalistic and Luddite. The view is not wrong, but the question is moot. Adoption of such an ethical system is no more plausible than eradicating belief.

They are slumming, voluptuous in their filth. His tongue and teeth are furred, and there is a rind of dirt he cannot get at beneath his fingernails. Tamsin stands next to his chair, wearing her bandeau, and near enough for him to smell the same mildew odor he detects on himself. Sawdust and carbolic soap.

"There's a cobra living in the garden. Nomvuyo says she's watched it come onto the stoep to sun itself." Tamsin takes in his naked chest, his belly. It is not vanity, this going about without a shirt, but too few clothes. Nomvuyo is the cleaner; she lives just on the other side of this hill. "I need to call her." Emil thinks to slip his hand under Tamsin's wrap, but it will have no effect on his penis, so he reopens the crime novel he has been attempting to read for a day and then closes it.

"I'm not sure I met Bolling by accident."

"What do you mean?"

"We met in a bar in Muttie seemingly at random but he knew things about me, knew I was in med school, that I had moved from eGeld."

"He was reading you, probably. Trying to pick you up. He invited you back to his place?"

"Yes. It was that night I drank the iboga. We went to Bolling's to look for a friend of his. I think he said it was Shaka."

"That night in Kampsbaai . . . he seemed to know what you were thinking."

And exactly where to find me, Emil thinks, but he says, "And then, the other night, Bolling brought up my father and I wondered if it was ever about me."

"I'm sure your vanity didn't take too big a hit. Anyway, I don't think Bolling was really looking for information as much as signaling."

"Does Shaka have a chance, do you think, of creating a real movement?"

"I don't know. He'd rather still be at Stanford, wouldn't he? On that beach, he came across as a little ambivalent. There's some rage in there, certainly, but I'm not sure that it's the condition of the brown man that riles him up. My guess is, that's Bolling's calculation too."

"What do you mean?"

"Bolling's curious to see how far the whole thing can go, but he's not politically motivated. He's not dreaming of Creole power."

Vivian telephones as Emil walks into the small car park of the Scarbrough general store. "We're arriving next Saturday," she says. He has forgotten the Christmas season, which is now here. "The twenty-second. A quick visit. We've had to shift our plans back so your father can take off to Lusaka on Christmas Day." Such a brief visit that he will see his parents only once.

"By the way," his mother tells him, "your aunt would love to hear from you." An oblique note on which to end the conversation, not least because his mother seems to little care why he has had no contact with Celeste.

Returning to the cottage laden with bread and coffee and meat, he meets a team of brown men, Creoles, dressed in ill-made but carefully pressed khaki uniforms. Beaters. Drivers of baboons. With every stride, the leader breathes into the whistle clenched between his lips, producing a noise like the courting sigh of some prairie bird. His fellows punctuate this with a smart rap of their knobkerries on the lids of rubbish bins. All five eye him as he passes, but none returns his nod. He assumes Scarbrough residents employ the men: an odd livelihood, guarding the vacant second homes of wealthy folk against half-tame primates.

He's set down the provisions and is unlatching the gate when a blue Mini rolls up and halts alongside him. "Hi," the woman driving calls through the window in a good-natured if overfamiliar tone and gets down from the car. Her style is close to his mother's. There are chocolate-colored shoes, almost moccasins, on her feet of precisely the sort Vivian wears to go to the shops. In the same assured voice, she tells Emil, "You're not delivering groceries, are you."

He is on the point of answering but merely smiles. The woman comes nearer. Her eyes are gray, the face carefully made up. *Too young to relinquish sexual vanity entirely.* A reflexive thought, with something—too much—of Bolling's voice in it.

"Friend of Tamsin's?" she decides. "I'm Esme." He notes, sourly, that she is ever so slightly taller than he.

"Esme?" Tamsin calls, coming out to them. Her feet are bare, the toenails a little muddied. On the tilted path, just inside the gate, Tamsin kisses her mother's cheek very close to the lips. A provocation.

"Gone native, Tams? Thought you'd be in town."

"I needed space to write. You've met Emil? I thought *you* were in town."

"So I am. I came to find you, give you lunch. Both of you. I have the feeling you could help with something I'm working on," she tells Emil.

"You two go on." Emil is walking into the house to put away provisions. "I'll stay here."

"Oh, I really hope you'll join," Esme calls after him.

"Leave him alone, Esme."

He is still hiding out in the kitchen drinking warmed-over coffee when he hears Esme saying, from very near, "I'm just using the little girls' room." There are footfalls on the front stoep. "Where did Emil vanish to? I'm serious, Tams, about picking his brain."

She insists on peering into all the rooms—it is her house. Tamsin waits in the kitchen with Emil, smiling; the tour concluded, Esme enters the kitchen. With a glance at Emil, she asks Tamsin, "You've not had Nomvi in?"

She insists they all ride in her car to lunch. She navigates the high, switching roads with a two-fisted grip on the steering wheel, her concentration one level below mania. They are descending to sea level on the opposite coast of the isthmus and Esme relaxes enough to ask, "What will we have?"

Tamsin ignores her mother. "Where's Adam?"

"At his place, I'd imagine. I invited him to join, but he insinuated that we'd subject his girlfriend to excessive scrutiny."

"Dipha? Dipha from eGeld?"

"I think that's who he is seeing. I haven't met the girl. Like father, like son, I suppose. What will we have?"

"Oh, I'm sure you've picked already."

"It can't be Olympia's. There's a red tide in."

But it is after three p.m., and only one place remains open, a pleasant enough Mediterranean restaurant overlooking the dock in Simeonstown, nondescript enough to be plausibly Greek or Turkish.

Esme orders a bottle of rosé. "Where are you from, Emil?"

"Kayalami, outside eGeld."

I went to KES, he nearly adds, just as Tamsin puts in, "Emil is a KES old boy."

"How did you find King Edwards? Adam hated it at first. I would send him to a coed school now, of course. Going to school exclusively with other males ramps up testosterone levels."

"Adam hated it all the way through." Tamsin is definitive.

"What are you doing now?"

"Medicine. Fourth year."

"I thought you might not be from here. I know it's politically incorrect, but Muttie folks have gotten so chippy. I don't like the mood down here."

The remark is directed to Emil but Tamsin responds a little spikily. "What mood?"

"Anger. It feels angry. I'd say it's an us-against-the-world sort of vibe."

"In town? Where have you encountered this mood?"

"In town, yes. But I stopped to fill up at a petrol station I frequent when I'm down here. It was the same there."

"Do you mean uppity?"

"I mean sullen. They act as if I've screwed them out of something."

"Are you here researching the next book?" Emil asks. He is trying to head off tension, but other motives might be in play. He likes Esme. Or is it that, as the junior partner in whatever the thing with Tamsin is, it pleases him to see a new facet of her. "And do you prefer to be called Marva or Esme?"

"I have become Esme Astor. Honestly, I *have* thought about making the name change official. Marva's a very olde-worlde, Slavic sort of name. Glamorous but also a little bit gray and Soviet-bloc-y, isn't it. In some ways it tethers me still to the housewife I used to be. Anyway, I'm here in Muttie to launch a new book."

Tamsin says, "Where does the wealthy White woman get herself murdered this time?"

"An Englishwoman, yes. I sent you the manuscript."

"I'm sure I never received it." Tamsin takes another large swallow from her wineglass. "Can I guess the plot, do you think?"

"Go on then."

"Alright. Slow down, Emil. You have to drive two boozy old cows back to Scarbs. Here goes: A woman has been strangled on the orders of some medicine man, you call him an umlimo. Some sort of sacrifice, but it's not clear for what. A Black police captain is assigned to the case, youngish guy, name of Simphiwe or Andile. Andi, as he calls himself, is ambitious, wants to prove himself, also prove the country has moved past racial justice, is meritocratic. By the end of the book, Captain Blue, as Andi Bululani is affectionately known, isn't so sure he can ignore racial justice. He solves the case, earning plaudits, but he's not sure the right guy has gone to prison. Everyone else is happy, but he feels like the victim of a conspiracy."

In oblique response to Tamsin, Esme says, "You probably don't read crime novels, but if you follow a template too closely, you lose your audience. Tamsin makes it sound much simpler than it really is. You have to innovate."

He eyes Tamsin. Vaguely drunk, she sounds sardonic, but not bitter. Nor does he flatter himself that she is acting out for his attention. Esme too has drunk quite a lot but shows few effects of the wine. As they walk from the restaurant to the car, Tamsin tells her mother, "Let Emil drive, Ma. So you can sober up some for the ride into the city."

Esme has put on the car radio, and a news item holds their attention. An orderly noon demonstration in the administrative district of the City Bowl turned violent without warning, forcing police to cordon off streets where looters and vandals remain. Although the bulletin made no mention of Braeem Shaka, Esme announces, "I've been hearing rumors this Braeem Shaka is fronting for drug lords."

"I don't think he is." Tamsin's voice is flat with suppressed feeling. "He's many things, but . . ."

"He's the reason people in Muttie are getting so chippy. Part of it. It's mad to talk about being owed reparations by Black people. Isn't it. It's just absurd. As if it was the Movement that created Partition and separated everyone. I'm going to sound non-PC again, but Black people suffered worst under Partition. It's not ambiguous. It's not a victim Olympics. And the idea that Creoles had zero complicity in the system, that's revisionism."

Tamsin laughs so hard her face turns redder. Catching her breath, she says, "It's made you rich, Muttie."

"Oh, it's my livelihood for sure. Not denying that. Can't bloody live here though."

"Anyway, I'd heard there were talks going on between Kob and Shaka."

"What talks? What's to talk about when you're inciting looting and vandalism."

Esme leaves Tamsin and Emil before the front gate of the cottage. "Tams, you're bringing Emil to the book launch, you hear?" Esme kisses her daughter on the nose and receives a clumsy embrace in return. Watching the car move out of sight down the hill, Tamsin mutters, "I owe Dad a visit."

News of rioting in the city casts a pall over the Scarbrough house, but neither of them is inclined to discuss what it might mean for Shaka. In the cottage, there is no radio or television, and Tamsin goes out to sit in Emil's car two or three times to hear if there have been any developments before giving it up.

Over the next days, the last in Scarbrough before they return to the city, Errol attempts to ring several times, without success. Emil is thankful the mobile network is so poor.

"Tell me of a time when you felt normal," Tamsin asks as they sit in the garden absorbing the sun. "As a child, or in your teens even."

Roused from a light sleep, Emil has no ready answer. He lets a little time pass before venturing a response that does not feel inadequate. "Playing rugby. On the rugby field I felt normal."

"The elation of running the ball, scoring a try, that sort of thing?"

"No. Or not only that. Also in the changing room, or training. Being with the other members of the team. Camaraderie."

"I wasn't friends with the other players," he confesses to her, later still. "I wasn't the most popular member of the team, but I was part of it, you know."

Are he and Tamsin much alike? Will she redeem him, be both the alibi and trigger of his humanity? His worth to her is no clearer now than before. He expected Tamsin to disavow him before her mother, put distance between them. *Emil is my assistant. I'm mentoring him.* He finds that he quite likes the amorphousness of the relationship.

The cottage retains its utopian squalor. They are squatters, lying about, scarcely stirring from the house. The fugitive mood breaks when the cocaine runs out and Tamsin must wait a day for Ekow to make his delivery.

From the porch, Emil watches as the familiar silver-blue car pulls to a stop in the road. Ekow gets out, unlatches the gate, and mounts the stairs with a bouncing step. His hands are empty but then he is wearing a coat. Emil cannot tell whether the dealer has seen him. His eyes are concealed behind sunglasses. *Of course he has.* The silence, the mutual refusal to acknowledge the other man, feels foolish. He wants but cannot bring himself to call out to Ekow and dispel the animal feeling. And what is there to say?

He reads: *What is the backlash against 'cancellation' and political correctness but master morality—a sly co-optation of Nietzschean slave morality that adds manufactured victimhood to the long list of tools the wealthy and influential wield against the powerless.*

Tamsin has done a line or two, but she is being oddly self-denying with her package of cocaine in spite of the privations of recent days. She sits now on the edge of the bed absorbing Emil's scrutiny. Unmoving but for the butterfly-slow blink of eyelashes. The quality of his erections, their persistence, changed when the cocaine ran out and the only thing left to him was zoll. He pulls down his shorts to let her see that he wears her underwear, a lime-green pair that he lifted from her tote bag a day earlier, the feel of them in his hand enough to stiffen him. There had also been a tube of lip balm, a stick of mints, and a dog-eared paperback novel by Gabriel Matzneff. The book confused him. *She reads French and German?*

His prick, his runner's thighs have stretched the underwear beyond salvage (the slipperiness of the silk keeps his penis in a state of more or less permanent hardness). Seeing him in her briefs draws no reaction. Her fingers are on him, tracing the nearly healed sandfly weals, but the excitation is all on his side. Very likely, she finds his shallow cross-dressing banal, predictable, although for this too there is no evidence.

If he loves Tamsin, it is for this reason. He has absorbed enough from her—also from Bolling—to recognize the banality of his love, and he has ceased to think of himself as emotionally deficient.

She delves one hand into the waistband, pulling at the elastic. He reclines on the soiled mattress, obedient to her hand. More banality: here is what he has sought—power that does not need to coerce. At last, he's ready. Now, each time is like this, complaisant, Emil pretending to be only half awake.

Afterward, overstimulated, he wills Tamsin to go to the other room—it is smaller but no less filthy—and sleep. She is being deliberately obtuse; her hip is glued against his. "It's a common response, postcoital revulsion," she told him a few nights before, reading his mind as he'd once suspected Bolling did. It was no admonishment. Anyway, she prefers talk to cuddling. Although the back of her hand presses along his throat. Still feeling for fever.

"Esme didn't want custody of Adam?"

"I think she did, but there were other things going on. Her second book was about to come out, my father was getting into his cows and sheep, and she was having serious doubts about getting up every morning at five to crack ice off paving stones and milk the cows. My father had suddenly become immensely bohemian, and a little reclusive." This is how the conversations often go, the answers tangential to the question but perhaps more illuminating.

In the morning, they climb the hill to the red dam for a last swim. The heat has been holding steady but the weather is on the point of giving way to squalls.

Perfunctory farewell in the car (in their interaction there is little space for lingering embraces). Tamsin will go out of town for a few days to visit her father. And Emil is back at 9 Noel, the weightless atmosphere of the flats, which he might as well never have left; it is more or less the same, in part because he's blanking from memory the circumstances of his leaving. The front door is unlocked. Halting in the hallway frowsy with cooking smells and low light, he calls out to Andres, testing his own theory.

"Where you been, Cuz?" Andres replies. "Your parents are arriving any day now." He does not emerge from the sitting room.

"I know."

There is no further response from Andres. Is it that Emil may as well not have been absent from his aunt's house or that he ought not to have returned? He has become a prodigal son: clearly unsettled by life at 9 Noel, trying to escape it but seeming to be incapable of doing so. He is a second Torrance; his cousin surely long dreamed of moving out of his mother's house before doing so at last.

And yet Emil could return to eGeld. Andres will be fine, whatever comes, or not. Something else has been keeping him in the south. Muttie is a dream, meaningless but also preordained. The same applies of course to eGeld, but eGelders are better collaborators in the fictions of contemporary life: aspiration and opportunity. What Emil has not yet worked out is whether Stadmutter too revolves around a shared delusion, one in opposition to eGeld's own utopia, or instead around a refusal, perhaps an inability to rally its people around abstractions. In some sense, this is the question Shaka seeks to answer.

In the glassed-off arrivals hall of the regional airport, Tamsin goes directly to her father, her small case jerking and clacking over the tiles. "Pa" is what she had begun to call him as a mischievous nine-year-old. "Robin," she says now to draw his attention, and then in the child's voice she had once used to pierce whatever was distracting him, "Pa Robin."

"Tams." Her father bends to greet her, all sinew and smelling of iron tools and wood. *I will call him Robin.*

Squeezed, Tamsin holds back a grunt. "Farm life agrees with you."

Robin ignores the pull handle of her luggage, hoists it to his shoulder with one arm, and walks off. She sees why. The provincial airport at New Dublin is not designed for pull suitcases. "I hope you brought sweaters?"

There had been rain in the afternoon when she was aloft, and the atmosphere has a loaminess akin to breathing in fertile soil. A windless cool prickles her bare arms. So unlike Stadmutter, which is about six hours due west and south by car. The hinterland has dry, mild winters that are an extension of autumn. Still, she has had to steel herself for the abiding cold in her father's stone house.

"I have sweaters." This is their rapport: answers gestated, oftentimes offered days later, a slightly distracted pensiveness, gentle ribbing, blank stares. They are in Robin's pickup truck, which he calls his everyday car because of its small flatbed and which looks too small for him. He sneers at modern monster trucks with their rear cabs and chrome cylinders. "We're magpies, Tams," he will tell her at least once during her visit, meaning humans.

"Nice of you to come visit your dear old dad."

"I couldn't bear the idea of you alone, crying into your Christmas lamb." *Your father lives in his own head*, Esme had told her once without rancor. *It's you who should be farming, and Robin writing books*, she had thought at the time. Would her parents be married still, if it had fallen out so?

Here they are: twenty acres of flatland, mostly pasture, with some land given over for maize and tubers. Part of an inheritance, the land allowed Pa Robin to give up being an ad copywriter and become a gentleman farmer; in spite of a guilt that seems not to have ceased, he'd accepted.

In the half a year since her previous visit, the farm compound—the main house, a converted granary, a cow barn—has undergone changes, many too fine-grained to be evident to Tamsin. An unfamiliar car is in the scrubby yard near the front door, an inexpensive foreign two-door that looks a little like a toy. "Not the sort of car I pictured Brenda driving," she says, and then frets that she is being snide.

"I'm going to leave the farm to that woman, Tamsin. We all break our backs, but she makes it work. For anyone else, a bequest like that would be a curse, but not Brenda."

Does Brenda share Robin's bed? Her father's monkishness has long seemed eccentric, perhaps even a cover. If it ever came out that Robin was romantically involved with an employee, Esme would claim to have foreseen it in some form or other; the tale of the White farmer and his Black wench would find its way into Esme's writing.

In a taxi on his way to Bolling's, Emil reads the piece of paper in his hand, and not for the first time, although he is not precisely trying to memorize the words.

> *The Teutonic world—Berlin and Wiens—birthed the most exalted cohort of intellectuals the world has yet known: German Jews. I need name merely a few: Wittgenstein, Marx, Einstein, Benjamin, Mahler. Germany's role in this*

> *is only tacitly credited, if ever, and this blinds us from noting a dialectic that should be plain: the intellectual intensity of the German hothouse contained within it the seeds of shattering glass.*

He has gnawed over that last sentence: there is something perilous in the image of shattering glass, something that needs explanation. Also, this particular note carries a dark echo of Tamsin's joke that the three of them—herself, Bolling, Emil—could each have their "own Austrian."

Bolling seems to intuit Emil's mood the instant he opens the door to him. Near-imperceptibly, the German withdraws, as if he cannot help himself. But then, Bolling's modus operandi is to present little to nothing of himself while extracting everything from you.

"Where are you off to?" A roller suitcase, ordinary, sleek, stands in one corner of the salon.

"Just back actually. Hamburg."

Business? "What's happened with Shaka? Has he been arrested?"

"Braeem? I don't think they got him, no. I would have heard from him and I haven't." Bolling sits in what must be his favorite chair; Emil though is agitated.

"But why did he go ahead with the march so soon? The talks with the governor were going badly?"

"They seemed to be getting pretty serious. Substantive, you know, but I wasn't involved day-to-day."

"You're not worried? Fifty people arrested?"

"Do you want to sit? I wish he'd talked to me before going ahead. His timing wasn't great. I also suspect Kob set him up."

"The governor? How?"

"Nearly a hundred looters? There are always opportunists, spoilers around public demonstrations, but so many is no accident. I think Kob used his contacts, prison gangs, to sabotage the demonstration."

"Sounds very . . . conspiratorial."

"I agree. It does sound like a conspiracy theory. But it's what I'm hearing."

"They've never once mentioned Shaka in the news reports since the march. That seems deliberate. Deprive him of publicity. Actually, I've been meaning to ask how much of Shaka's politics come from you."

"Depends what you mean by *my politics*."

"The . . . fascism-adjacent antimodernism. That stuff."

"If you're asking did I stoke Braeem's nationalist instincts, I didn't. My politics are very personal. A Haitian-German thing, you could say. Braeem used to talk about a third way, social democracy with free-ish markets. But there's not much traction around the world right now for the idea of pursuing a universal good. It's all zero-sum. He understood that. I simply convinced him that ending Partition speeded up identity fission rather than reversing it."

"Identity *what*?"

"Widely shared experiences are vanishing. We're breaking down into ever smaller groups, intersecting and overlapping, maybe, but with nothing—not music, not sports, definitely not news—that cuts across all groups. After Partition, Creoles began looking for new ways to separate themselves from other non-Whites. From Whites too, but not so fiercely. They were already an idiosyncratic people, mixed heritage, European-based language, animist beliefs, and then they've marginalized themselves to the point where having a semiautonomous enclave is probably the best way forward."

"What does your father think?"

"I'm guessing you know his politics. He's hopeful but he's not optimistic about integration." Emil's answer comes after a slight hesitation. "When he was about eighteen, he met a Black man in his town, which was very unusual during Partition. This man made a lasting impression: he spoke argot perfectly, coming into a Creole town and moving about fearlessly. He was an agent of the Movement during the struggle years, and he brought my father into the Movement. And he continued to do it long after my father moved to eGeld, but very few Creoles were receptive to outreach from the Movement."

"Braeem—you gave him . . . iboga?"

"He's very careful about what he accepts from me. And he's allergic to . . . mysticism. There's quite a bit of the technocrat in our Braeem."

"How does it end, with you and Shaka?"

"I don't know. With us drifting out of one another's orbit, much as we drifted together."

Much later in the night, Emil remembers the most pressing reason he came to see Bolling. Careless of whether he's waking the German, he intones, "*Germany made the greatest cadre of intellectuals the world has known.*"

"Ja?"

"That last sentence."

Bolling, lying uncovered near but not next to him in bed, has moved his arm; the crook of his elbow no longer covers his face and muffles his voice. "What is it? The intellectual heat of Germany contained the seeds of breaking glass, something like that? A speculation about the inevitability of what happened in Germany, which was not Britain, not France. Working through the central reason the immensely productive intellectual and commercial flowering of the Jewish minority ended so very fucking badly. In dialectical reasoning, thesis A—that the German-speaking world in the early twentieth century was a great place to be a Jewish intellectual—generates antithesis B: the German-speaking world was incubating not only Jewish genius but the ferocious if not universal backlash to it. To put it more prosaically, a Faustian pact was made. In the case though of Germany and its Jewish intellectuals, which is Faust and which is Mephistopheles?"

"Meaning that German Jews could be seen as the devil, as the side with the most to gain from the bargain?"

"I think there were Jews that perceived great benefit in assimilation, rightly or wrongly. And the German political class also saw great benefit. From an economic standpoint, killing off a class of highly productive people makes no sense. The logic of antiutilitarianism is deeply unsettling for Anglos, particularly Americans. So they continue to fixate on the

Nazis. Every few months a new book comes out in New York or London about the Holocaust. The Americans, of course, were only too willing to siphon up German-Jewish scientists who managed to escape."

Later still, it may be near dawn but the room's heavy blinds admit no outside light, Emil says, in what sounds to him a form of intimacy, "What's a Haitian-German identity anyway?"

"Oh, it's a sort of in-joke, although the synthesis of that particular dialectic is a deep aversion to the States and France. The problem is I have no interest in going back to Berlin, so it's a blessing I stumbled across Muttie. The Romantic in me was sucked in at once. Germans *love* this place. There's something here for all Germans. Really. The ones fleeing gray *imbiss* lives. The surfer tech bros from Munich, the township martyrs. Subconsciously, I knew this, and that's probably why I avoided visiting."

There's roast beef and sweet potato pottage keeping warm on the Aga stove. Robin comes downstairs from making the fire in Tamsin's room and pours out wine from a bottle in the cabinet. "An off-label claret." She cannot tell, as often, if he is being self-mocking using words like *claret*. *Both of us have a submerged Anglophilia*. In her childhood there had been many Whites like her father, similar in manner and taste.

After his first mouthful, he snaps his chair back. "I have something for you." Tamsin hears the door of his study open and then Robin returns carrying a slim leather volume, old but immaculate.

"Lautréamont?" She flicks it open and is leafing through. A prose poem. "This is what you read out here, is it?" Robin gets up to water his wine from the tap. Seated, his gangling, long legs knock the farm table's low trestle. "Pa, would you try ayahuasca?"

"That's what Castaneda was into." He swirls his wine. "Not likely. I like hilltops and rock pools and Ted Hughes, and I like these things in an unmediated state. You're considering it?"

"Considering it. It's easy to get nowadays."

"Wasn't Freud against mystical states?"

She shrugs. "My worry is experiencing false memories. That's a very real possibility, apparently."

"Why do you anticipate false memories?" His curiosity is sincere, gentle. In his place, Tamsin would have taken an ironic tone.

"Freud packaged his mysticism better than most." A side-stepping remark that puts Tamsin in mind of Bolling.

Her attention is wavering. Robin, noticing, sips from his wine, and when his glass is empty, he extracts his legs from beneath the table to stand. "I think I'll go up for a little reading, Tams. I've to be up at five but I'll leave you to lie in until six thirty." *Haha*. He kisses her forehead. "Take the wine up with Monsieur Maldoror if you like."

Her father loves unobtrusively, without demand, she thinks as she leans against the porcelain kitchen sink and waits for the tap water to run warm.

Upstairs, she cleans her teeth and then remembers the full glass of wine on the bedside table in her room. *Perhaps one more log on the fire?* She is tipsy and heavy-limbed more than sleepy, a languor from the meat and wine. Under duvet and sheet there is a hot-water bottle, which she sets on her belly. Ordinarily, she dislikes being held as she sleeps, but a warm body would be useful during the nights here.

The book of poems lies face up beside her on the narrow bed, but she does not read from it. Her thoughts stray toward Emil. The skin of his back, his wrists—smoother than her own—which she envies him. He is otherwise imprecise in memory; she can recall little he's told her. Unformed, she thinks. Him? Or rather her impressions.

It is developing into a habit, leaving Bolling's house with something on his person that he has filched. Bolling is still asleep, but Emil is jumpy until the electric gate has shut behind him; and then with a look down the road in both directions, he sets off walking toward the city bowl. He needs to walk off the tension of attempting a theft and getting away with it.

Hunting for a landmark that eludes him, not looking where he's walking, he almost stumbles into a stranger before pulling up short. A woman. Tall and well formed, quite a bit taller than himself, waiting motionless at an intersection but without the particular vigilance of looking out for a taxi or bus. Emil begins to apologize, but she refuses to acknowledge him. There is the inquiring honk of a car horn as a taxi passes in the road, slows, and then speeds up again as the driver senses no interest.

Emil is rooted; some aspect of her appearance commands his attention. She is beautiful but ill-used, a woman that has squandered the adoration of men but still also escaped full ruin somehow. It is midafternoon, but she wears a cocktail dress that is expensively cut, setting off the fineness of her legs and sheer enough to disclose her flesh-toned underwear. The flat shoes on her feet add a demure touch but might serve a more pragmatic purpose: in heels she would overtop most men.

Emil has taken her for a Creole woman but now intuits that she is most likely White and passing, a *dirty White*, in the crude phrase. There are poorhouses full of Whites like this, even if he has never seen them. "How much?" he asks, strangely excited by her contradictions, although it is doubtful he could muster one more erection.

At last she notices him, and something passes between them in a look, longer than a glance. On his part it is pity: in a city such as Muttie, she incites hatred in all who recognize her. White whore passing as Creole to attract White and Creole clients. In the woman's eye he sees an expression both grudging and proud; she has been recognized. The next instant it has vanished and she tells him, "Swart, voetsek." *Fuck off, Black.* He smiles as he walks on, one whore taking leave of another.

The etching he has taken from Bolling is a Kentride. In the upstairs bedroom at 9 Noel, he scrolls through web pages on his phone, viewing image thumbnails until he has eye strain. He has identified the work as one named Harmattan.

Zinc, oil paint, and hydrochloric acid, it dates to 1981, when Kentride went off to exile in France to evade the final tumultuous years of Partition, to Marseille rather than Paris. He used the Mediterranean city as a base for travels to South America and the West African Sahel.

It was not too difficult to confirm that the etching had been done by Kentride. Bolling himself had, in a roundabout way, presented Emil with the clue. "What about you?" he asked, a disembodied voice, at one moment in that long night.

"What about me?"

"When will you return to medicine? *Are* you going to be a surgeon? I am the only one who will ask straight out."

A little time passed before Emil answered, although he said only, "I don't know."

"You can do your specialist training down here just as well," Bolling pointed out. "You could live here, in this house. I'd only request that you keep an eye on the place, my Mntambos and Kentrides particularly, which I plan to keep here. I'll be away more than not, I think."

The six forms depicted are of a dubious humanity, syncretized androids, their faces concealed beneath space masks that resemble Tuareg headdresses, with elongated torsos and willowy arms. On initial viewing, he had taken all six figures to be women, but at least one, the second from the left, displays ambiguous male genitalia.

What will he do with this thing, which he can neither display nor sell? Bolling will of course miss it sooner or later, although it would be very like him to notice its disappearance and say nothing. The etching already haunts him: no matter how he dresses it up, he has acquired a memento of what has passed between himself and the German. Whore. A subliminal realization that had drawn him to the woman in the road.

He wants to have done with Bolling, but severing the relationship will not be simple. First, though, that same night, he telephones to test how alert he is.

"That woman, the one in the attic, what happened to her? I forgot to ask."

"Hospice." Bolling is pleased he's rung, he can tell. "Still hanging on. I visited her last week. She gets more radiant by the day, that woman. An extreme form of terminal lucidity, maybe. She asked me to bring her back here. I suspect whatever drugs they have her on there probably don't give her such great dreams."

Over the four days of Tamsin's visit, she has only one encounter with Brenda. On Christmas Eve. She is roused with what feels like needless urgency by Robin kneading her shoulders. Six a.m. Damp chill pours in through the open window. "There's hot coffee downstairs," Robin says, with a sternness that brings her awake.

"What, is one of the ewes lambing or something?" Tamsin says, but he has already hurried from the room. The coffee, oily, black, makes her gag. Unsalvageable even with heaps of sugar, but she forces several mouthfuls standing next to the kitchen window and then burrows through the hall cupboard for rubber boots.

Brenda and Robin are winding up the milking and there's nothing much to do. "What the fuck is the urgency?" Tamsin asks, and Brenda half turns in response to this greeting, lips tight-smiling. She has a steeliness that owes to her brisk manner rather than any angularity.

Tamsin stands back, awed by the enormous slab-sided cows and by Brenda's brusque handling of their teats. She feels like a schoolgirl in the farm manager's presence.

A second Black woman wearing jeans and a poncho, younger, with sharp aboriginal features, now follows the sheep dog Merrie into the cowshed. The dog is known to the cows, which do not trouble as it sniffs at foreleg and withers. Noticing Tamsin, the woman removes her hood. She seems too shy to speak. *Scenting what?* The subtext of farm life is more impenetrable than Lacan.

Without turning from what he's doing, Robin says, "Xoliswa, this is my daughter, Tamsin. Take her with you to the pigs, will you?" And he whistles Merrie to remain close. Xoliswa glances at Tamsin. Xoliswa has the air of a younger person even if they are of the same age, not precisely diffident but seeming to anticipate that she will not be taken seriously.

And yet all the while they muck out the pigs and attend to myriad tasks that fill the entire morning—hunting firewood, checking the apiary, inspecting goats—Tamsin has no doubt: here is a Brenda in the making. Xoliswa is patient in giving direction, she is deft and alert, and is disinclined to idle talk, a reticence that arouses Tamsin's interest.

Her accent is traceless. At St. Catherine's, Tamsin's high school, Black girls had made up most of her class; whether from eGeld or Port Elizabeth, they talked in accents like Xoliswa's—that is, over the phone they were indistinguishable from the White girls, as if the end of racial Partition set in motion a locution shift.

Xoliswa sits with Tamsin and Robin for a lunch of hot maize porridge and cold leavings from the fridge: broiled chicken, pumpkin greens. "Where's Brenda?" Tamsin asks, as if the kitchen is not too cramped for the three of them. The swell of pride at having been of use to Xoliswa has not faded.

"It's Christmas Eve," Robin answers. "Her family is in Warrenton." Half listening to farm talk and irritated by the ticking Aga stove, Tamsin overeats, particularly the mealies. She is grateful when Robin pours out small cups of more oily thermos coffee and offers to wash up. "Tams, go with Xoliswa."

Xoliswa and Brenda are as impenetrable as anyone Tamsin has met: real cowgirls, she thinks. Men's women. Ready to muck in where needed, yet unmistakably women. Part of her fixation with Xoliswa is a response to the lack, or deep veiling, of any curiosity about her. Do they think she is overly fussy? Clumsy, frail?

And yet there is a crack in Xoliswa's mask, not quite a warming (it seems unfair and unkind to label her frosty) but something. As they walk to count the goats, Merrie trotting between them, Tamsin intercepts the woman's glance in her direction. Xoliswa holds her eye, and Tamsin is ready to interpret the look as a signal.

Maldoror is rough going and slow, but on Christmas morning, Tamsin persists in reading while the farm is blanketed in sleep. The sun is beginning to show as a wan, watery eye when she sets the book down.

She lies very still, unwilling to leave the warmth of the bed. She is really waiting, as in childhood, for her father's approach. Daddy's girl. When she had been the only child of Esme and Robin, he would tiptoe in alone on Christmas morning and tickle her awake. The image is too maudlin to be other than a false memory. Her brother has more of their father's temperament: obstinacy, and shadings of guilt over every decision. Still, she and Esme are better equipped for the country as it now is, and which increasingly belongs to capitalists. She slips from the narrow bed, pulls on a pair of socks, and delves her hand into her suitcase.

Of the gifts Robin receives, he is most pleased with the book by the Martinican writer. He rubs his fingers on a tea towel in between bites of egg and toast, reading to her from the flyleaf. Tamsin is not sure about the study of hysteria she has received, unknown to her and from a quick glance revisionist in slant, but the second book is piquing, poetry by a Czech or Romanian woman whose name rings vaguely familiar.

The landline telephone rings; Robin gets up to answer it. "It'll be your mother," he tells Tamsin. "I thought it was you," he says down the receiver. After several minutes, Tamsin accepts the phone from him.

Esme turns waspish when Tamsin asks after Adam. "Gosh, Tams. You could call your brother directly, you know. Shall I put him on?"

The asperity is not entirely unexpected; when Adam and Esme quarrel, Alice invariably takes the side of her grandson. Tamsin is solicitous. "Are you feeling a little outnumbered?"

"Will you come? Otherwise, Alice won't see you."

"Not till March. I didn't want Robin to be alone over the hols." Robin has stepped outside a moment, but she drops her voice. "Don't begrudge him."

Esme's laugh is curt. "Your father's never been lonely a day in his life."

They use up the day reading, napping, and taking Merrie out to walk across the fields. In the afternoon it is Tamsin's job to peel and chop the ground provisions for Christmas dinner. She is antsy, preoccupied by the conversation with Esme, and with Xoliswa, who has edged ahead of Brenda as the ideal match for her father.

By five p.m., when they sit for the soup, the kitchen and sitting room are feverishly hot with baking and broiling, and because Tamsin has emptied a bottle of Gryskloof by herself, despite it being a mediocre-to-good vintage. Mercifully, there are no cocaine cravings, but it is less clear, now she is entirely drunk, whether she wants Xoliswa for Robin or for herself.

Hinting, she tells him, "We'll never eat all of this food by ourselves." *Let's invite Xoliswa over.* She cannot say it, not least because it is the tritest of fantasies. That, and alcohol has an uncomfortable tendency of making her wheedle.

"A bit of music, yes?" Robin says, getting up.

"Will you turn a profit this year?"

"Strictly break even." He laughs perhaps because he has no need to be profitable, nor of the government subsidy he receives each quarter. "The squashes will do well. The price of mutton is up but beef has gone down. Once I pay wages, there's not much left." Despising money, he'd once said, is the way to know its true value.

Her mouth and tongue are coated with tannin, altering the savor of the soup. Still, she eats to avoid passing out. Sitting upright is an effort and there is a burning sensation in her chest beneath her breasts. "You said something once about going organic. The feed, fertilizer."

"I'm still considering it. We've discussed it, Brenda and I. It would mean a great deal of change, more labor-intensive work, more hires. I'm always nervous hiring new workers, foreseeing in my head a moment when I'll have to let them go. I actually hadn't planned to take Xoliswa on. Brenda convinced me that we could use the help of another full-time person, and she was right."

"Can't you find other Brendas and Xoliswas?"

"Not so many women want to go into farming anymore, Tams. And young men, well *they* bring a whole host of problems with them."

"No complications with Xoliswa and Brenda?"

"Like what?" Robin is amused. "Are you asking what I think you're asking?" He laughs and laughs and does not stop. Abruptly, she is laughing too, and also crying, and she moves her emptied soup bowl to one side, distressed by the rawness of her emotion. *He doesn't need to be rescued any more than I do.*

She gathers herself while Robin returns the roast to the oven and fetches the rum pudding. Reseated, he fills both their wineglasses from a fresh bottle. "To us. And my hareem."

As if she needs to get any more drunk. "To your hareem!" But this wine, definitely not a Gryskloof, is smooth; on her tongue its voluptuousness matches with the sweet potatoes swollen with animal fats. So medieval, an arbitrary holiday featuring eating and drinking into a mindless satiety.

"I've thought about it," Robin admits. If he's feeling the wine's influence it does not show. "It would get complicated and you know I haven't much patience for complication. But yes, I've thought about it. Spending so much time doing mindlessly fatiguing work with someone, you might be surprised how easy . . . I think I've also magnified Xoliswa's inscrutability into more than it is. Frankly, I've conjured her into a divine shepherdess who crafts couplets in the bush."

"I see that," Tamsin says, encouraging him. "Her aura of mystery, I mean."

"What's kept me from . . . seeing where it might go is Brenda, actually. I didn't see a way to ask her permission, and as I see it, I'd need Brenda's permission."

"Brenda's married?"

"Divorced. She married some ne'er do well, oddly. A carpenter. Well, perhaps not so odd. Women that have their own lives together do that startlingly often. It's probably the only time Brenda has set a foot wrong."

"So what about her, then. Brenda?"

"I thought about that also!" Robin's laugh is merry. "Still think about it. Look, Brenda must marry me, not I her. You see the distinction? The farm is mine now, but it is going to be hers. And not because of guilt. She's the better farmer between us. There are two ways to resolve the situation. Either she marries me or I work for her."

Tamsin is failing to understand. But the questions do not seem so urgent, here over Christmas dinner, with the man she loves best.

The taxi that brings Emil to the city's most extravagant hotel, the Mount Nelson, is immaculate. The driver, an ex-soldier, is mute for much of the ride and then abruptly chatty just as they pull up to the grand, walled entrance.

"Come up," Errol tells him when he calls from the hotel lobby. "Your mother's just getting finished."

A fib, perhaps; it is Vivian who opens the door of the suite. Their embrace is fonder than the one they shared in the house at eGeld, but then he is not the person he was then. Can his mother sense the shift that has occurred? Errol has come out of the bathroom and he gives Emil the simultaneous shoulder clasp and handshake that Creole men do. He smells of talcum powder.

"Muttie agrees with you." Vivian sidles up to the wall mirror to slip earrings into her ears. "You've lost a few pounds, you're closer to your rugby weight. Where are you taking us for a drink?"

"Not far. Ten minutes down the hill, walking."

Vivian is pulling on flats. "I don't walk places at night, Emil."

"Perhaps you will in Vienna? Or Bern?" Errol gives Emil a meaningful look that he does not understand. "Anyway, a car is out front waiting for us."

"Muttie is changing," Errol notes, drumming his fingers on the table of the place in Breestraat. Emil had made a reservation, although there is time for not more than one drink before dinner elsewhere with the Wilsons. Errol's remark is framed in general terms, but it is actually an observation about the tall, thin, Black hostess, and more obliquely about race in Muttie. The woman's accent is suggestive of the DRC or another francophone country.

"So . . . Celeste and Andres. What should we expect?" Errol quizzes Emil.

"Everyone's well."

Vivian does not let him sidestep so easily. "You've been busy."

"This girl's an immigrant." Errol's scrutiny tracks the hostess.

"Which girl?" Vivian asks, turning around to take in people at other tables.

Errol is grinning openly. "What does Andres say about Shaka? He supporting him?"

Errol knows nothing of Emil's direct interactions with Shaka, about which he does not forget. "He thinks Shaka is American and doesn't trust him," he responds, careful, neutral. "Are there plans to arrest him?"

"Arrest who?"

"Braeem . . . Shaka."

"Stay tuned."

"Your father has been . . . in contact with the governor. Acting as sort of an unofficial liaison."

"Race business," Errol adds, but he does not seem displeased to have been given the role.

"I'm sure there's a lot of pressure on Kob?" Emil says, as drinks are delivered to their table: a beer for himself, a martini for his mother, and for Errol, a whiskey.

"It's out of his hands now." Errol is fairly gloating. "It might not surprise you to learn he's relieved to not have that responsibility. As I say, stay tuned."

"We hear so little about Torrance." Vivian touches Emil's hand.

"Me as well," he jokes darkly. "He's doing night school. Getting his diploma in sound engineering."

"Is he bright?" Vivian sounds doubtful.

"Yes. Ambitious as well."

In the hired car once more, Errol says, "If Torrance is bright and ambitious, he needs to be in finance or law . . . we need more of our folk in hard science."

Emil feels a sense of dread about the dinner that he cannot account for. The responsibility for it going well is not really his. As patriarch of the extended family, as the one who will get the bill, Errol had selected the place: a glass-walled restaurant atop a rock cliff that overlooks Tafelbay. Inside are many holidaymakers from eGeld; a sartorial fussiness gives them away.

Celeste and Andres have arrived before the Silvas and taken seats facing one another near one end of the table. And here is Torrance, moving a little furtively, just as the first wave of greetings is complete. Is the casual greeting that passes between Torrance and his mother and brother something to which the three have agreed ahead of time? It presents an odd contrast: Emil has shaken Andres's hand and kissed his aunt's cheek before taking the seat next to hers. Vivian is beside Andres; Errol and Torrance occupy the table's head and foot.

A predictable and inevitable lull following the moment of reunion. Emil drops his voice to ask, "How are things with Rinus? I've not seen him in some time."

"How could you?" Celeste gives him a mock-severe look. "We've not seen *you* in weeks."

"I've been helping a friend prepare for medical boards. I didn't mean to vanish."

"You were badly sick with some sort of flu, though, last I saw you. Andres was very protective."

"Yes, I remember. He and his friend Drool took care of me." An irony is missed by Celeste.

"Your governor is up for reelection next year," Errol says,

addressing the Wilsons, after the main courses are served. "All you think he will win?"

Andres looks up from his phone, which he holds between his knees. Celeste looks diffidently toward her younger son.

"Middle-class people and the wealthy think he's a safe pair of hands," Torrance begins cautiously enough. "I don't know about that, but he's a good politician. Goes out and talks to people, takes credit for things that are going well."

"Why not a safe pair of hands?"

"Kob? He's a bit too pro-business. Quietly, of course. As I say, he's a shrewd politician. Taking care of big business with tax breaks. Small companies, not so much. Policies, you could say, that have created an opening to the governor's left."

"In other words, if this Shaka guy could run for governor, Kob would have to break sweat to beat him."

"If?" Vivian prompts.

"That oke has already left the country," Andres tells the table. "That's what I'm hearing. Left in a hurry after the riots, the looting, and so on in town. Gone back to the States, I'd bet. Shaka is a gang boss, he's been a gang boss all along. That's all I keep hearing."

"Meaning it was deliberate?" Vivian sounds skeptical. "He sent people out to smash up the city."

"The *Star* is saying it," Torrance puts in. "Of course, it's the governor's mouthpiece. One of them."

"So the new narrative around Shaka is he's not a nationalist, just a thug?" Errol says, trying to catch the attention of a waiter, any waiter.

Celeste says, "What do you mean by nationalist, Errol?"

"I mean all that talk about Cabo for Creoles, Celeste. Demanding reparations from the national government. Maybe you missed that?" Errol ignores the look his wife shoots at him. Addressing Torrance, he says, "What about if the Movement puts up a candidate against Kob. Is he beatable, do you think?"

"Depends who," Andres answers quickest. "Anyone remotely like that last one, then no chance."

"And if the Movement stood a White candidate against Kob rather than a Black one, what then?"

"Same result," Torrance affirms. Andres nods.

Vivian says, "So is it a racial thing?"

Celeste is laughing. "It's a Movement thing. The Movement stands for eGeld, in my view. It's for people in eGeld. Not here."

"Unpack that for me, Celeste."

Torrance prompts his mother. "You mean it's a party of extreme capitalism?"

"Let your mother answer for herself."

"No, that's it. What Torrance is saying. It seems cruel, this free market. People always worried about being downsized, or your rent being raised."

"For workers like me," Andres says, "free markets mean bosses hiring people they don't have to pay a living wage. Folks from out east, know what I mean?"

"You can say Black people, Andres." Errol is earnest rather than mocking. "We all know who you mean. You'd vote for this Braeem Shaka, I take it?"

"Nah. He's foreign. American, Angolan, something."

"American?" Vivian sounds genuinely puzzled.

"And he's a false prophet. Him and the Movement folks are as bad as each other."

"So you're basically for the status quo. Let things go on as they are. What has Kob done though? Point to one substantive achievement." Errol twists his lip. "And don't mention basketball leagues. Kob didn't start those."

"I can live with Kob. I didn't say I love him. Ma's the one likes him." It is not clear whether Andres is teasing his mother or taunting his uncle.

"I'm no fan of Kob," Torrance says. "I'll probably stay home next year."

"I do like Governor September," Celeste admits. "I think he does quite a lot for his people."

"Tell me. Like what?"

"Community-building. Swimming pools, parks. Mediating between the gangs. He ended that gang war in Tygerburg, didn't he? Crime has gone down in Paarl as well."

"You don't think that might be because Kob is in deep with the gangs? From when he was police chief? Leave that to one side, though. What about job creation? What's the unemployment here?" This is not Errol in his lawyerly guise, but in agitated, hectoring mood. Vivian is warning him off with her eyes.

"Not so much in the way of jobs, that's true," Torrance concedes.

"What about training and higher education? Technical training, vocational, that sort of thing."

"It's expensive. I'm in night school, I know."

"And yet lots of people are out of work. You know what unemployment in eGeld is? Seven percent. Know what it means? Wages have gone up even for menial jobs." To Andres, Errol says, it's because of Kob that there's downward pressure on your wages from cheaper workers. What Kob needs to do is get you in some training program so you can earn more, keep moving up."

"But what if I don't want that. I mean, I'm getting ready to shift into driving a forklift truck, and you're right, there's less competition for that work, but getting constantly retrained? Constantly shifting jobs? I don't want that."

"You want to stay a forklift driver? Okay. You'd only be putting off the inevitable, Andres. Sooner or later, there'll be the same competition for forklift drivers as there is for, for . . ."

"Bricklayers. Or concrete busters. Ja, maybe."

"You've just confirmed for us, Uncle Errol, exactly why the eGeld model turns off most people in Cabo," Torrance says, jumping in. "Relentless striving for bigger jobs, bigger paychecks—it isn't for me."

"But racism is?"

"I'm an antiracist," Torrance says. He means it, Emil thinks, but he has not used the word accidentally; he is aware of being audited by the Silvas.

Errol throws significant looks at Celeste and Andres; neither takes the bait. "An antiracist surrounded by racists."

"Maybe. There's racism in our community, sure. You hear casual slurs against Black people. Some people vote solely based on race. But it's complicated, Uncle Errol. Young folks here kinda worship African American culture. They do. And there are racists in eGeld. Of all colors. And let's face it: all the top, top people in the Movement, they're Black, aren't they? There's Simpson, who's White but he's like eighty-five years old. And that woman who claims to be both White and Creole, the party secretary. Anyway . . . the heads of the big banks are all both Movement and Black, aren't they? Cliquishness is not so different from racism."

"He makes a point, Errol. Quite a few points, actually."

"We're not perfect." Errol makes a rueful face; Vivian's interjection has, as intended, opened space for her husband to soften, to conciliate. "God knows we need more Creoles in the Movement, bright folks, Torrance. Bright folk."

"Creoles in the Movement appear as tokens, Uncle. Faces in the crowd, keeping up a multiracial image. It seems there's more room for Whites than Creoles." Torrance has been emboldened. Celeste's mouth twitches with suppressed feeling of some sort.

Errol's face is still. "Am I a token? Is that what I seem?"

It is Andres who replies. "I don't know. You've done pretty good, Uncle Errol, far as I can see, but you're not president."

"Who said I wanted to be president? And is that what it would take for Creoles to feel part of this country? A Creole president? Would you vote for a Creole president if he were in the Movement, Andres?"

"I don't know."

"You know September was in the Movement for a few years? Governor K, as he likes to be called." Errol is suddenly weary. "I didn't recruit him. But he expected to get some ministry. I think it was Sports he wanted, and it didn't happen, so he quit the party. Anyway, let me stop. I'm not winning any converts here, I can see that. Dessert, anyone?"

"You didn't talk much over dinner," Vivian Silva tells Emil as the three of them ride back to the Mount Nelson. Errol is nodding from the whiskey. An appraising remark rather than judgmental. He has the impression she is crediting him for something, and it is true that the two families navigated a quite difficult evening fairly smoothly. Although Emil's feeling, as the Silvas took leave of the Wilsons in the restaurant foyer, is that it had not turned out as Celeste wished. She had embraced her nephew as if uncertain when she would see him next.

"Now you can answer your own questions. You've seen Torrance at close quarters."

"Yes. He seems wise. I think he knows his worth." *Worth to whom? Errol? The Movement?*

It is after midnight when he enters the house at 9 Noel, and he longs to examine the Kentride etching before he sleeps, craving it as he had once longed to pore through the black notebook. Andres and Celeste are at the kitchen table having a nightcap and, he suspects, waiting up to see if he will come. He finds an odd comfort in joining them, although he takes a beer rather than rum. His arrival, and willingness to sit up with them, cheers his aunt as a sort of endorsement; after all, he could easily have taken a room at his parents' hotel. He smiles to himself. He is here because Tamsin is away and because he cannot go back to the Bolling house, the scene of his great crime.

"You're not in the Movement, are you, E?" They have been talking aimlessly; Andres's question seems to have been prompted by Emil yawning.

"I'm not. Isn't that what they say about our generation, that we're not political enough?"

"You don't think, do you, that if we all joined the Movement, there'd be no more race issues in this country?"

"Let's not talk any more politics." Celeste is checking her phone. "We can leave that stuff for the fancy dinners. Let's agree to disagree."

"I have another question." Emil makes his face serious. "Why did Torrance move out?"

The question catches Celeste by surprise. "Torrance? He wanted to live with Anne. They've been together three years."

"He never comes to visit, I notice."

"He's busy. He's got night school. Work. We talk all the time, nearly every day. Why? What do you think is going on, Emil?"

"Nothing. I'm asking because we saw him tonight. It made me wonder."

"We're good. All of us." Andres is firm.

"I'm off," Celeste announces. "Rinus called me a taxi. It should be pulling up just now."

"Goodnight," Emil says, and he follows his aunt from the kitchen. "I need to sleep."

What lies beneath? We are palimpsests, Bolling has written in his notebook. As Emil is looking up the meaning of the lascivious-sounding word, a telephone call comes from Vivian. "We have to leave early. No, don't bother rushing over." His parents are already at the airport. "A few things before I forget. Your father wants to do something to help Torrance. We're sure you can be helpful with that."

"Yes."

Also, and more importantly, that gap year you wanted to take. Traveling and taking time out. Now's the moment, I think."

"It's not too late," he agrees. "But I like it here."

"Always the contrarian."

"Celeste knows you're leaving early? She was keen for you to meet Rinus."

"Your father is going to phone from the airport. We'll see you when we see you, I have a feeling."

"I'll keep you apprised. Oh, and thank you." *For what?*

"Always, Emil."

Emil is late for Esme's book reading, which is taking place in Stadmutter's largest bookshop, in a seafront shopping center. Cardboard cutouts of two figures flank the bookstore entrance: the novel's White and Black detectives, presumably. Just inside, hardback copies of *A Garroting in Margate* have been stacked high. Late, but he takes time to leaf through a copy. On the inlay cover is a photograph of a younger Esme with pale streaks in her hair. *Esme Astor is the real deal*, the blurb reads. Below this is praise for an earlier novel, *The Muti Defense*, which he guesses concerns some sort of sacrificial killing.

He has seen Tamsin, seen the empty place beside her, but she has not noticed him. The reading has begun and he remains where he is, behind arced rows of seats that are entirely filled. Esme is a fluent reader of her own prose: breathless and with an instinctive rhythm. The tale is a familiar one, a mid-level detective who refuses to be fooled by evidence that has gulled his superiors. The culprit, influential, attractive, is White.

It is the turn of the other woman on the stage to speak, and she tells Esme, "I wanted to emulate you, let's put it that way. I've been rereading *Stone's Throw*, your very first book, which influenced my latest novel, *Abalone Wolves*, quite a bit." Raising her voice to tamp down the hand-clapping, she continues, "Tell us about Captain Blue, Esme. Japhet Bululani. Is he based on a real-life officer?"

"Not at all." Esme looks into the faces of her public with what seems myopic focus. "Bululani—he's a contrast with the detective of my first novel, a woman of mixed heritage with her own quite idiosyncratic demons. He's a more arresting character, I find. For starters, he's older, about fifty. He's a man. He's also got a black-white view of the world that is constantly being tested by the cases he's handling. I'm confident I'll be writing more about him."

During the Q and A, there are no surprises until a young White man accepts the microphone and standing up, announces, "Your books seem a little disconnected from life in this country. Do you have a responsibility to remind your readers it's a bit of fantasy?"

A small murmur, pitying perhaps, runs through the audience. Heretic. *Why come to hear a writer you don't like?*

"It's as you say. It *is* a bit of fantasy. I thought you might accuse me of cultural appropriation, you know, writing from the point of view of a middle-aged Black African man. In response to that unasked question, there are truths in my books that are never captured in news stories. And at the end of the day, if all I've done is encouraged some woman, somewhere, to write, and write from a different perspective than her own, then I'm content."

The reading is breaking up; there is a scramble as audience members join a lengthening line to get their copies of the novel signed. Tamsin has seen him. He watches her approach—what has it been, a week since they parted? She holds him, a finger behind one ear, to kiss his cheek.

"How is your father?"

"Robin is well. You'll come back to the house for dinner with us? Esme's editor. Nellike too." That must be the woman that shared the stage with Esme.

"Let me get a signed copy," he tells Tamsin. I'll come look for you."

Esme, when his turn in line comes, is businesslike. "Lovely you came, Emil." The distant sincerity of fame.

Just as briskly, he asks, "Would you write it out to Vivian?"

Afterward, he rides to Esme's house with Tamsin for supper, which is being put on by Esme's publisher, Martin Tallow. The country's biggest publishing company, Tamsin says. The house has been reordered in some way since he last visited, some of the furniture has been stowed perhaps. Four brown men in white aprons and black clothing wait in the kitchen for delivery of food.

Here is Adam with Dipha, and then several guests are swarming into the living room. Tamsin points out people. Martin stands next to the editor of *Garroting*, as she calls it. Esme's friend, the poet Simone Burgess, is also here. Simone lives in an isolated hamlet down the peninsula.

"Literary Stadmutter," Tamsin says with what sounds like unironic pleasure. She picks sweetmeats from the tray of a waiter going by. "The writing ecosystem here is tiny and so it breeds lots of feuds. Feuds on feuds. 'He stole my agent,' she mocks. 'She plagiarized parts of my prose poem.' In fact, Jacob Mason from the university's writing department would be here ordinarily, but he's got some beef with Simone."

The poet is strapping. She is in conversation with a striking woman. "Adam, there's your fave author." Tamsin gestures with her chin. "Children's book writer," she tells Emil, holding his arm.

"Voetsek, Tams." Adam, too, is enjoying himself. He tells Dipha something that makes her giggle.

People-watching quickly palls for Emil. "So, the visit with your father was fine?" Emil says. Tamsin waves the question away. Her attention is repeatedly drawn to Jillian Lord, and as if to cover her interest in the editor, she tells Emil, "Simone hates big events. She does small readings for six or seven in the living rooms of friends."

Nellike has found time to change clothes and she's not the only one: when Esme enters the room, the publisher Tallow starts to clap, and the other guests—they are now ten—take up the applause. Esme wears a long close-fitting dress that sets off her figure. Here, she is more than a celebrated novelist fresh from releasing new work to her audience. Woman, mother, perhaps even lover. And yet, even surrounded by those that are, presumably, her closest intimates, there is some hesitancy in coming to stand in their midst as the handclaps slowly die; doubt or reticence flickers in her eyes before the alter ego restores itself. That self-scrutiny even in a moment of clear triumph strikes Emil as a trait seldom seen in men. Esme deflects the attention with a brisk "Let's eat." Tallow takes her hand and, kissing it, leads her in to sit.

There is chilled soup for supper. Springbok loin. The dining room is too small for so many bodies. Martin is like a handsome satyr near the head of the table, surrounded by women—Jillian is there, Nellike, who seems to be drinking too fast, Esme herself at the head. It is his triumph as well as the writer's, it seems. From the kitchen comes the sound of the chef issuing curt instructions to the servers of food and drink.

The poet Simone is on Emil's right. He and she have exchanged a perfunctory greeting and left it there. The waiters never let the glasses stand empty but are careful to avoid hovering, or to be overeager in recharging a glass. Simone is prudent in her drinking, and so too, he observes, is Esme, but the other women are giddied already. Jillian conceals it well by sitting quite still; the telltale is her eyes, which are heavy and slow-blinking.

He himself is in a fey mood, which he attributes to several factors, including his decision—made prior to the conversation with his mother—to leave Stadmutter. He has hoped for a moment to speak with Tamsin about this, but that moment does not come, and tonight is not the night for it anyway. It is right that she celebrate her mother. And so Emil drinks with a kind of caution, sticking with white wine. The din in the room absolves him of the need to make conversation, and in fact seems to be having a similar effect on others. Perhaps the asymmetry of women and men is similarly influential. Emil and Adam are only boys to Jillian and Simone. Whatever its source, the atmosphere provides tinder for a quarrel, some silliness that flares as the diners are being served an overrich, tiny dessert of tiramisu.

Someone farther down the table, Martin probably, has made a throwaway remark about the Movement.

"You used to be National Party once, isn't it, Martin?" Adam had been talking closely with Dipha but evidently eavesdropping. He leans away from her abruptly. A question that seems calculated to ambush the publisher, embarrass him. The National Party, now disbanded, had been the architect of racial Partition.

"Weren't we all, Adam," Martin answers, with a straight face, and then, exchanging quick glances with Jillian, lets his lips quirk in slight amusement. He next turns and murmurs something to Nellike on his other side, and she collapses in giggles.

Esme has a curious reaction to this exchange. Her eyes are downcast, and her face and neck color faintly, but whether in response to her son's remark or her publisher's is not obvious.

Adam falls into sullen silence, as if drunk, which he is not; his coloring would give him away. He seems cowed by the glib way his mother's publisher has drawn the sting from his comment.

Emil feels a sudden—a misplaced—pity, not for Adam but for the woman next to him; misplaced because Dipha is not overawed or excited at being in the room. She is not here on sufferance, a token, to use Torrance's term from the other night: Dipha comes from eGeld, where such a monochrome scene would be unimaginable, and she comes from a family at least as wealthy as Emil's own. This crowd is indifferent to her youth and her Black skin, indifferent more than hostile, although the view of many Whites, Tamsin included, is that the country belongs more and more to Dipha rather than themselves. The meaning of Emil's own presence here is fuzzier: he is brown, but he is also from eGeld; were he from

Stadmutter, a real Creole, he might feel he were at supper on sufferance himself.

He is curious what Dipha makes of the racial crusade her boyfriend has taken on. She must tire of Adam sooner or later; he has more growing to do than she. To Dipha and himself, Emil adds Esme as one standing in some way apart from the others at dinner, although he cannot say why.

Tamsin cups her wineglass in both hands and directs a meaningful look toward her mother. Whatever appeal is in that glance, Esme has no desire to answer it. Some game is going on with poor, hysterical Nellike. Esme is in some way part of it, a not entirely passive foil to Martin, whose provocations are mounting. Nellike is struggling to remain upright. Jillian, also tight, is trying to coax Simone into something. The poet holds her eyes tight shut; her entire frame quivers as if with panic. With every new interaction, Emil slips further away: the old dissociative tendency, somehow renewed by what he has experienced in recent weeks.

"I need some fresh air," he announces to no one in particular, and leaves the supper room, which breaks the glamour of dinner. The kitchen is empty; the waiters, dismissed, have let themselves out of the house.

Tamsin has followed him outside, and then here too comes Adam, trailing them in a curious echo of that night in Kampsbaai. He disapproves of their interaction, although Emil guesses Adam himself does not understand why. Adam jabs a finger at Tamsin. "Do *you* know any Black people, Tams? Not even Black friends. Acquaintances. Colleagues?"

"Not really. As far back as high school, whenever I started getting close to anyone Black, I'd start second-guessing my motives. Do I actually like them, or is it guilt? There was one girl in my year at St. Therese's. Lindi, who I got on with, I can't remember what drew us together. We got along very well, actually. But bit by bit, I pulled back. It was the fact that she felt different from me that made me racist, do you know what I mean? Maybe she understood what was going on because she gave up trying to maintain the friendship. In a sense, I think I'd decided I *was* racist and couldn't help it, our history and all."

"I remember Lindi," Adam admits. "But that makes no sense, Tams. That's why you lost touch with her? I had a crush on Lindi, I think she came home with you one school holiday."

Emil's phone is ringing; Errol's name flashes on the screen. He moves a little apart from Tamsin and Adam to accept the call.

"Emil, listen. Stadmutter is going to see some heavy police action in the next day or so. Federal police conducting rolling sweeps to pick up quote unquote subversives, meaning Braeem Shaka. I don't entirely approve. It'll only martyr the man, but Kob doesn't have a bloody clue what he's doing."

Emil resists sharing this intelligence with Tamsin; there will be a moment for that later. The party is breaking up, although several guests wait in the kitchen for coffee to finish brewing. He looks in but does not enter: Tamsin is there talking to Jillian. He approaches Esme to wish her goodnight, and she gestures for him to sit. "I hope you enjoyed supper." She gets straight to the point. "Look, I wonder if I could ask for your help with the book I'm working on. I'm going to need some guidance getting the argot dialogue right. Do you know anyone here in Muttie I could consult with? A student at uni would be great, but anyone who speaks fluently. I'm looking for someone for about a month. The dialogue could be worked out over the phone after an initial face-to-face meeting."

"You're setting the new book in Stadmutter?"

"Yes, Muizies specifically. The book will center on a surfer criminal gang, and Muizies is perfect, charming but a little down on its luck. You know Agatha Christie surfed there?"

Emil thinks a moment. "I'll ask my cousin. If he's willing, I can pass you his number."

He is pushing back his chair to stand up, ending the conversation. But Esme is not done. "The detectives trying to smash the crime ring will be Creole." She glances at Martin. The publisher is staring into his phone. "Fentanyl, abalone, you know." Andres *could* be useful, Emil thinks wryly, but he has not his older cousin in mind but the younger.

Tamsin comes to stand between Esme and Emil's chair. It is Martin she is looking at. "You might want to check on Nellike."

"Kitchen," he says, deflecting the pointed remark. "Simone is making coffee."

Tamsin turns to Emil. "Quick word?" She jerks her head and he follows her outside, catching sight of Nellike in the kitchen. Her eyes are closed, and the counters seem to be steadying her.

"Let's go back to Scarbs. Tonight."

"I need to go to my aunt's house. I was just leaving, actually."

"Why?"

"Your mother, she asked me to connect her with an argot speaker for the new book. I thought Andres, my cousin, might know someone." A partial lie.

"I'll come with you. This dinner party is going to drag on. Nellike may well sober up and have a few more glasses of wine. And then tomorrow is Carnival. It will be chaos."

"Sure." He resists the urge to compound the earlier lie. "Grab your things."

He is in Celeste's bed. Tamsin is with him, the two of them alone in his aunt's house. That no one else is there had raised Tamsin's suspicions, and so he had given her a brief tour of the place, leaving out Andres's room. In Torrance's old room, she made no comment, and they passed quickly to the master bedroom, where she looked over Celeste's perfumes and creams. More than once during her exploration, she said, "Are they avoiding you?" But then she had fallen asleep at once in Celeste's too-soft bed and he had removed her shoes and skirt before lying down next to her and picking up the notebook.

Germany achieves by accident what America, with its soaring intentions and 'manifest destiny', can only aspire to: civilisation, in all its opulent cruelty. Perhaps because Germany is better able to grasp the duality of the word.

And then an unexpected text, unlike any he has read thus far:

I sat and watched swifts for an hour and more, enthralled by the beatless acceleration of movement, their arrowing flight. For me these birds are more arresting than any machine man has made, any algorithmic calculation. The swift is born to what it is. So too the jaguar or the killer whale or the mole, all having an essence man lacks, and this turns on its head Sartre's arguments that existence comes before essence. My marvelling at swifts is meaningless. I would watch the death of a swift with the same detached wonder. Beauty and vivacity accrue no right to go on living. So it must also be where humans are concerned.

An argument both more and less impenetrable than many of the others. Lying beside Tamsin, reading under a low light, he grasps that understanding Bolling's writings is not entirely a matter of having read the right philosophers. And he has complied partway with Bolling's invitation to throw out his assumptions. Present dislocations have equipped him with a keener intellectual, even emotional vocabulary, but he concedes frankly that it is these shifts that make it so difficult to countenance returning to eGeld, to his old life.

The Kentride etching is a new source of anxiety. He cannot continue to trust it will remain safe at 9 Noel. There is no lock on the door, nothing to bar Andres or even Drool from snooping through his belongings. After caching it somewhere it will be safe, he can leave this city: his preference is to leave the country, taking cues from Bolling's notebook, from the German himself. And Tamsin.

He is reminded of his father's brief warning over the phone only when he and Tamsin are on the way to Scarbrough. The police—there are very many of them, some in camouflage carrying machine guns—have set up a roadblock on the outskirts of Ottery, a Creole township. One of them, big-bellied and in the blue and khaki uniform, straightens up and chops his hand with exaggerated slowness. Tamsin winds down the window so they can hear him out.

"Where are you going, Meinherr?" His tongue is working at something in his teeth.

"Scarbrough."

"This one's going to Scarbrough," the policeman calls, consulting his sergeant. Another man responds with a shake of the head.

"Do you live there? That's your permanent home in Scarbrough? You'll have to turn back unless you have proof of residence."

"Is it an accident?"

"I can't say. Do you have proof of residence?"

Tamsin says, "Give us five minutes please. We're checking." She winds the window back up and pulls out her phone.

A call comes in on Emil's phone as Tamsin tries presumably to reach her mother. "Can you come to the house?" Bolling, but an unfamiliar number. "I need you to do something for me. I've texted you the new security codes." He's gone.

"So?" Emil asks Tamsin. The policeman approaches again and raps on the window glass.

"We have proof of residence back in town, officer," Tamsin says, shading her eyes with one hand. "I don't suppose you'd accept a photo? On my mobile?"

"No, mevrou. You'll need to go and physically get it."

Tamsin nods and waves at the officer, then rolls up the window.

"The road on the other coast is open, apparently. Let's just go around."

"I need to go to Bolling's. He asked me to stop by, no idea why. It won't take long, I hope." He is peeved at himself for agreeing, or at least not refusing. But he is curious too to learn if this is about the Kentride etching. Bolling has had ample time now to discover its absence.

"Drop me back at Esme's. I'll wait there."

Bolling is not at home. The house feels shut up, unoccupied. On the high kitchen table is a cheap mobile and a note. *Only call me on this phone*. He leaves the phone and note and passes upstairs. The door to the main bedroom has been locked, but the second room has an air of recent occupancy. The bed is roughly made.

He opens both wardrobe doors. Sitting there on the spacious floor is Braeem Shaka, long legs drawn up against his chest. "Where's Bolling?" Emil demands without thought.

"Good to see you too." Shaka pushes out of the wardrobe and, sidestepping, goes into the bathroom and closes the door.

He seems shaken. Emil gives him a moment. Downstairs, he takes up the burner phone; it has one number, foreign, in the contact list, which he dials.

"Ja."

"I'm in the house with Braeem. What's going on? He was hiding in a wardrobe."

"Keep him there. They have an arrest warrant for him. Insurrection, drug trafficking. They've already been to his mother's house. Don't let him leave and don't give him his phone."

"Where are you?"

"Let's just say out of town."

The phone at his ear, Emil examines the contents of Bolling's fridge. "What do you want me to do? Other than tell Braeem to stay here."

"Stay there with him, will you? I have his lawyer figuring out a strategy. Lay low a few days and I'll come back to you with instructions." The line hums; Bolling has ended the call.

It would be nothing at all for Emil to walk out of the house and go on to Scarbrough. It would be the sensible move. The house is well stocked; Shaka is not apt to starve. Emil cases the downstairs rooms, weighing his options. The small office off the kitchen from which he took the black notebook is locked. Indecisive, and then sliding into inertia, he sits on the couch, gathering himself, checking the news. What does he owe Bolling? Braeem?

It might be possible for Shaka to wait for an opening to sneak away from the country. If the sweep fails to unearth him, will eGeld pull back swiftly and risk losing face? All is speculation, and nothing of it is Emil's problem. His primary concern is to not get caught up in a mess he cares little about. Also to avoid selling Shaka out, accidentally or no.

Here Braeem comes now, barefoot and dressed in loose, soiled-looking exercise pants. As if they are simply mates, hanging out, he flops on the couch next to Emil. "So, what's going on out there?"

"I'm sure Bolling has filled you in." Shaka's choices are, of course, harder than Emil's own. To remain in hiding is to fall into a sapping kind of martyrdom. In fact, all of his choices lead to martyrdom from here, including giving himself up and facing the charges laid against him. His lawyers could turn it into an international affair, a development the government would oppose, not wanting to draw the world's attention to the country over a fresh set of racial injustices.

There is no television in Bolling's salon, but the sound system has a radio, and the news contains a few details that seem culled from a press release. Police action . . . Ottery, Tygerberg, North Wynberg. A few suspects have been arrested and taken away in a helicopter.

Shaka dozes off. Emil gets a good look at him. He is a disjointed figure, especially in sleep, his parts disparate, ill-fitting in some way that cannot be tied solely to the lankiness of his arms and legs.

The news reporter: "One eyewitness here in North Wynberg said the operation recalled the country's earlier troubled history, a reference to the widespread raids carried out during the era of racial Partition."

Emil walks through to the kitchen, withdraws Bolling's burner phone, and thumbs out a text. The reply comes almost at once, and he goes to a kitchen drawer and fetches some keys. Before leaving to pick up food, he changes the security codes.

Most of that day, Shaka sleeps on the couch. In response to Emil's suggestion that it would be more comfortable upstairs, he merely closed his eyes and turned on his side. Emil has unlocked the door to the main bedroom and gone to lie in Bolling's bed, his belly filled with oversweet Thai food. The house for once fails to work its soporific effect on him.

Bolling's room is as austere as might be expected, and contains nothing to explain why he keeps it locked. In the dark wood armoire are formal shirts he has never seen the German wear, and another Kentride on the wall, from a different period, less ethereal, less arresting than Emil's own.

From Bolling's window is a view of scree plateau, a sensation of high altitude: Godsetafel off to the West and Louwenkop—the lion's head—straight ahead at a range of about a mile. In between is public land, with no development nor any paths Emil can see. Almost surely there are bergies out there, the granite formations providing ample shelter for indigents to live out of view, perhaps even with access to sources of fresh water.

He has missed three calls from Tamsin. He will need help, her counsel, but better for the moment to be reticent. *Something family-related came up. Sorry. See you tomorrow.*

He wakes at midnight to piss and sleeps again. His own phone and the burner lie next to the bed but he does not look at them.

Seven a.m. Bolling has sent a flurry of messages. *I have a farmhouse just the other side of Constantia, right beneath the Sauerboom. Very small. Tight window of about three hours to move today. Eight o'clock is a great time to be on the road. Commuters.*

There is no protest from Shaka when Emil tells him to gather his things so they can move from the house. Shaka drives. It is Emil's idea. Shaka's height and his nearly emaciated frame are distinctive, but a complete disguise would invite more attention, so Shaka wears nothing more than a baseball cap and two days of beard. Emil pushes the driver's seat up close to the steering wheel to conceal those long legs.

"Bolling says, keep your head down while he works something out with your lawyer," Emil tells Braeem, and receives a nod. He is a little less surly this morning, a benefit perhaps of not being alone. And he seems relieved to be on the move.

"Do you have a mobile?"

"Got rid of it weeks ago. I have a tablet in my pack."

"There's no one you need to get word to? Family?" Emil has taken cash from a drawer next to the bed in Bolling's room and spread it about his person. Another ten thousand rand are in his backpack. He holds the phone and the money; essentially he is Braeem's minder, but this seems less risky than the alternative. *Take no one else with you*, Bolling had said, meaning specifically Tamsin. *Don't take any elaborate routes to get to the farmhouse. Trust in the appearance of normality.*

Tamsin's advice was good: the road on the peninsula's other coast is unwatched, which baffles Emil. The roundabout drive to the farmhouse takes more than two hours.

They are in among the great wine latifundios which produce less desirable, more acidic wine than hinterland vineyards. It is well situated, the house Bolling has directed them to, in a copse right up against the mountain. There is cloud cover above that does not stir, trapped by the mountain and air currents, and creating a pocket of terrain more humid and overgrown than its surroundings.

Emil watches as a stream of coaches peels off the highway onto the approach roads for Groot Constantia and Ou Kerkshalle, the best known of the tourist wine farms. The back road Bolling told him to watch for is here, tarmac giving way to a gently inclined dirt track nearly overgrown with veldkruide. He is nervous about damaging the low undercarriage of his car but Shaka, humming, seems to enjoy driving off-road.

No one will stumble on this place by chance, which makes Emil wonder at Bolling's purpose in acquiring it. Shaka steers the car through a stone arch that serves as a front gate and parks in the front yard. A farmhouse with no farm to speak of. There is a small plot that could support chickens, desiccated old pear trees in the orchard that will need coaxing to bear fruit. The pig run is mostly intact. Stands of bamboo have been allowed to grow in profusion, to cover over the house and most of the shed that might have once housed chicken feed and shovels.

Emil scrabbles his fingers in a flowerpot in the yard for the door key: a glint of brass in several inches of water and silt. He opens the door and steps back. Shaka stoops to enter. Somewhere within the house, a dead thing gives off a smell sweetish and faint. Most of the downstairs is taken up by the kitchen and dining room, which has ceilings of a reasonable height. The meal table is an immense spavined thing with rough-hewn edges. Presumably inherited furniture.

The upstairs rooms are as dingy as he feared, but there are mattresses on the beds. Sleeping rough in Scarbs has prepared him for this. Bolling is paying the bills; the toilet gurgles into action when he presses the flush.

He cannot make a phone call—there is no signal on either of the phones Emil is carrying. Out front in the pebble yard it is the same. Braeem does not care. He has no phone. He is out back on the small porch sitting in a wicker chair, reading from his tablet. *Reading what?*

"I'm going to the nearest town to get some things," Emil tells him. "Make some phone calls. What do you need?"

"Beer."

Parked in the car lot of a Pick n Pay supermarket, he sends Tamsin his location. *I need you to meet me here.* Scarbrough is twenty-five minutes away by the back roads. He switches phones to place a call to Bolling.

"We're here. At the old farm. I'm getting supplies in a place called Oudekraal. The fridge is working, right? I forgot to check."

"Ja. How is he?"

"He's not saying much. It must be a lot to take in."

"I'm certain." Bolling sounds noncommittal.

"Someone is going to relieve me in a day or so, I hope?"

"Someone like who?"

"I don't know. One of his supporters. Someone who was in your house that night. There must be someone. I'm not going to stay indefinitely."

"There is no one."

"And you're out of the country."

"I'm out of the country, yes." Bolling laughs but does not seem abashed. "Do *I* owe you something?" More laughter. "You're the only person I can trust with this. Anyway, if anything changes, I'll let you know."

"Anything like what?"

"The government deciding to cut a deal."

"Is that what you're working on?" Emil asks, but Bolling has rung off.

He hadn't liked that *Do I owe you something?* with its particular emphasis. Bolling knows about the etching. He knows and is using it as leverage. Taking it had seemed a fair exchange for sex, but a different trade entirely has taken place.

He is at the checkout counter paying for groceries—with cash—when Tamsin phones him. She is outside.

He experiences a rush of gratitude when she asks, "What have you gotten yourself into now? You don't look so good." And when she has learned what has happened, "I'm glad you didn't bring him to Scarbs. What's the plan?"

"I'll give Braeem three days, Bolling rather, to sort something out. After that, I'll stock up on supplies and leave Braeem the cash and the secure phone."

"He's not suicidal or anything?"

"Better judge for yourself."

"Fuck. We go in your car. I'll leave mine here."

Tamsin has understood the German. "Bolling absolutely wouldn't want me in on this. You know that, right?" A few moments pass before she asks, "What's Bolling's endgame? Why did he decide Braeem wasn't safe in the city? Seems needlessly risky driving down here."

At the farmhouse she advises, "Pull the car in a little closer," pointing to the house itself. And as they enter the front door, "Don't think you're not going to tell me your motives for getting pulled into this as well."

Braeem looks up without much interest from where he sits on the porch. Emil wonders what medications he might be on, something for anxiety. He has installed himself here perhaps because the interior of the house is dank and claustrophobic, never mind in need of a good scrubbing.

But then he does something unexpected. "One moment," he says, standing, and almost tiptoes across the creaking deck slats to retrieve a third chair from indoors. A host attending to his duty.

Emil presents Tamsin as if she is a stranger, and there is an awkward moment, which she breaks by nodding and turning to look off into the terrain.

Braeem, nodding to himself, slips away again and returns with three bottles of the beer Emil has just bought clasped in his long fingers. Tamsin, who has not yet spoken, accepts one. Emil goes to put groceries in the fridge and pantry.

"I couldn't get the radio going," Braeem announces on Emil's return. The porch is an island of relative cool, the surrounding trees, avocado it looks like, tempering some of the summer heat. Tamsin has positioned her chair opposite Braeem's, and it seems entirely natural to sit out here, sweating and drinking beers.

Braeem has been trying to tune the radio on an old-fashioned phone, which is lying beneath his chair. "Calm down," he tells Emil, with a trace of amusement, almost a smirk. "There's no SIM card." The phone emits a static AM drone, which Emil had heard earlier but not identified.

"There's nothing new," Tamsin tells him. "No developments."

"A helicopter went past but I couldn't see it, couldn't tell where it was going."

Emil says, "It might be one of the fire service ones. I've hidden the car under some bamboo."

Shaka tilts his chair back, rocking a little and drinking his beer. He is suddenly agitated. "Who's this . . . White woman?"

he asks as if waked from sudden sleep to find a stranger next to him in the bed.

Tamsin smiles. "We're friends of Bolling."

Redundantly, Emil echoes, "We both are."

"You don't trust me," Tamsin observes, giving Emil a silencing look. She stands up. "You don't mind if I have a look around the place?" She takes her beer with her.

"It's peak fire season," Emil says, filling the silence. "That helicopter was probably on its way to Kirstenbosch. A routine patrol." If, as seems certain, Braeem is taking some medication for his state of mind, he cannot be left alone in such a secluded place. The sudden shift in his manner, the wooden responses.

Tamsin does not return to Scarbrough that first night nor the nights afterward. Emil had known she would stay, but does not flatter himself. She has taken a psychiatric interest in Shaka but refuses to discuss with Emil any of her thoughts or amateur diagnoses.

Later, Tamsin fucks him in the smaller of the mildewed bedrooms, and he frets that Shaka, lying in his own filthy bed not two meters away, is hearing every intake of breath. Afterward, she shushes him when he seeks her reassurance about Braeem's mental state. The same thought about Shaka listening has occurred to her as well.

There is nowhere to go in the bed, which might be cozy under the right circumstances, but Emil has the feeling of attempting to sleep in a cooling oven. The old-fashioned windows open barely more than a handspan.

By morning, he is calm. *Don't overthink.* In Stadmutter, shifts and turns of this sort are frequent. The city has a low threshold of normality. And so he is up and about at seven a.m., getting better acquainted with the farmhouse and its environs. He estimates that the main house is more than a hundred years old, stone and brick, with wooden beams visible in places in the ceiling. With work, some charm might be restored, but for the moment crumbling mouse turds litter the dining room and kitchen. A dead mouse somewhere explains the sweetish foul smell, but he cannot locate it. Standing in the kitchen with one hand on the great iron stove, feeling its sighs, he cannot bring himself to shift it and see what lies behind.

Out back, the pear trees have endured the withering heat better than the apple trees, but then they produce small slow-ripening fruit good only to make brandy. Or they would if they were not barren, but he is thankful they are tall and leafy enough to obscure much of what is here from passing helicopters.

"I'm going for supplies. We need mouse traps, sheets," he announces. Tamsin is confining herself to the bedroom. Emil suspects she is (unnecessarily) giving Shaka the opportunity to acclimate to her presence. Braeem had gotten up shortly after Emil; even now the vibrating thwack as he rocks his chair on the deck slats carries through the house. "How's Shaka's mental health, do you think?"

"Garden-variety anxiety. The rocking, the foggy moods, probably the effects of Xanax. Taking it impairs clarity of thought and so Braeem stops every so often. Or forgets."

Scant reassurance, he thinks, driving out past Oudekraal to buy the sheets, a rehearsal for the escape he may be compelled to make later. Beyond the Creole townships is a village with familiar shops: Woolworths. Clicks.

He curses himself for forgetting to bring the burner phone with him. On his return to the farmhouse, he bypasses the mart with the Pick n Pay and sees Tamsin's car is as she had left it.

Back at Bolling's farm, he curses himself again for neglecting to buy a board game or two. There are no books, nor a television. What is there to do to avoid driving one another mad? With Tamsin in their bedroom and Braeem on the patio, Emil is at loose ends unless he wishes to while away the hours in the dank dining room. Going out to walk the land somehow seems riskier than driving. So he sits on the porch not quite facing Shaka and contemplates whether to press Braeem to open up or leave him in a state of distraction.

Tamsin is no help. She too sometimes comes to the porch—the dust and grime in the bedroom seem to aggravate her allergies. She is mirroring Braeem. Neglecting to wash or change clothes, although she has not brought much with her. Rocking back onto the rear legs of the porch chair and maintaining that posture as if daring gravity to topple her. What had Tamsin told him next to the black lake of Silvermine? Something about helplessly falling for her patients?

Braeem seems to be building a tolerance for her presence, but he does not talk to her, although it might be truer to say he does not speak.

Emil too feels himself being pulled into new depths of inertia, a torpor that causes him to hanker for the relative comfort and serenity of 9 Noel. The elements here are unease, listlessness, swells of wanton feeling, cruelty that lacks the will to action.

And he is triangulating once more, even with Bolling gone, replaced by someone for whom Emil is beginning to feel active disgust. Bolling's ideas seem now to be mostly philosophical idling, a highbrow trolling. Braeem on the other hand seems to have been merely cosplaying at being a revolutionary.

And so he limits the amount of time the three of them pass together. He lacks the appetite to nag and coax Tamsin and Braeem to cook, tidy up, or wash themselves. It is because of him that Tamsin is here in this rotted uncomfortable house. He goes to the shops and buys beer and expends some energy to ensure the household does not sink into deeper squalor. Each of them takes it in turn to patrol the property to its limits at dawn, noon, and dusk, and it is the one task carried out without fail despite its blatantly being make work.

In the Schwarze Hefte, he reads:

The ultimate modern transgression today is not to be a fascist. Fascism is familiar at some level; we all understand its realpolitik—the red pill over the blue. But who is willing to own up to the thoughtcrime of nihilism? Is this not the reason humans hate the Earth, hate nature, for its utter disinterest in our projects?

Shifting preoccupations keep Emil from making much headway with Bolling's writings. He is overthinking the timing of trips to the shops. The risk of Tamsin's car parked in the supermarket lot for a few days. There are grotesque symmetries between Shaka and Tamsin that lead Emil to vacillate between trying to put a stop to it and plotting his own departure from the farm.

And then quite by chance, on the fourth day (the fifth?), he lances the wound of Braeem's moroseness to gain access to the man.

It is an effort to dredge up the words, but he says, "How well do you know Bolling?" He has been thinking about the German—who has left off communicating via the burner phone—and the mounting evidence that he has washed his hands of Shaka.

"Depends what you mean by 'know.' If you're talking about his views of the world, politics, then quite well. How well do you know him?" Braeem pauses, oddly grim-faced. "Don't bother. We both know him equally well, I'd guess." Braeem has been, it seems, wanting to talk. "Did you know he's only been in the country a year? Or are you curious as to what he's doing when he's not filling notebooks or drinking his cocoa tea?"

"Is he much involved in the family business?" Emil is trying to piece together where Bolling might be.

"Not really. I think when he's exploring one of his spots, Casamance, Oran, he might do a little bit of very preliminary bizdev, although I think BD is probably exaggerating a bit.

You know what cosplaying is, right? He cosplays as an investor looking for returns."

"Do you miss America?" Tamsin has managed to step out onto the porch without making any floors creak.

Shaka slows his rocking. He is laughing and he laughs harder than seems warranted, as if Tamsin has made some daft joke. "I feel the way I would about someone that had jilted me. I remember the good things though when Bolling is on one of his tirades. Yeah, getting a scholarship to Stanford Law felt like being anointed. Maybe Oxford would have been just as much a headfuck for a kid from Tygerberg, what do I know? I had minor anxiety attacks pretty much every day before I traveled."

"What was Stanford like?"

"It was probably a good thing I ended up there and not at Columbia, say, or Harvard. Folks left me alone after they realized I wasn't going to play the race card. I was foreign and brown but not Latino, and not Black, which took a while to sink in. Stanford's not as leftwing as people might think. It's very libertarian, blockchain and start-ups and all that, but also live and let live. I pushed back on libertarianism at first. I said it could work in Sweden or the Netherlands, homogenous countries that don't have entrenched inequality, but not in America. The other students knew almost nothing about where I came from, only about racial Partition. I represented a view they hadn't heard before."

"Were there aspects of Stanford you didn't like?" Emil asks.

"Oh, of course. America too. Even though we're set up to love it, aren't we? But Stanford, it was too big an opportunity, too big a vote of confidence for me not to love it. Bolling got that, without me needing to tell him, that I didn't have the liberty of disliking Stanford Law, or turning it down. Not when it was offering me so much."

"He was sympathetic? Bolling?"

"Nah. Just acute in his observations. I've been able to talk about it, America and Stanford, with him in a way I haven't really with anyone else. He's never visited but he knows all that singularity, life extension, libertarian craziness inside out. I stopped telling him, 'You ought not to have an opinion about the place,' because he knows it better, far better than I.

"Anyway, long story short, what I loved is exactly what he hated about the US. That American-type certainty and conviction was what I wanted for myself. And I wanted to be able to say things like, I am doing well and doing good."

"Someone, one of your classmates actually used that expression?" Tamsin pressed.

"No. It was the ethos of the place, though, so of course I began to feel that this was what I wanted in my life too, to do well by doing good."

Shaka allows his eyes to meet Emil's from time to time and seems more congenial than in the previous days. In a small group, his self-deprecating frankness, the way he's slipped into a slightly American diction, is endearing. The contrast with how he had come across on the beach when he seemed actively anticharismatic is startling.

It would go differently if Bolling were present, of course.

During the gathering at the German's house several weeks ago, Braeem had been withdrawn, not sullen really so much as inhibited. It might be that Braeem begrudges Bolling his affluence and perhaps his easy freedom from ambition. For Shaka, the German is inextricably tied to America, and he seems to have begun to re-engage with the place since he met Bolling. At any rate, Shaka has exhausted himself, used up several days' worth of words; he stands and goes indoors.

"We should get your car, bring it here," Emil tells Tamsin, with more roughness than he means. "There's a spot where we can hide it."

"I don't think anyone's worrying about my car, Emil." Their interaction has grown stilted, terse. Something to do with the heat, with Tamsin copying Shaka, with disavowing one other, or perhaps it is their relationship when in Shaka's presence. Perhaps the rutting for hours in the bedroom is also a consequence of tension. In some curious way they both prefer that Shaka overhears them fucking rather than talking. Emil is aware of distancing himself from Tamsin, but feels helpless to stop it, or at any rate unwilling to do so. A necessary step before his own departure.

He lets the matter of her car lie. And he concedes that Tamsin's mirroring of Shaka may not be wholly conscious, though he has pointed out to her that she is doing it. He cannot understand her resistance to accompanying him to the supermarket: there is no opportunity at the farm for the two of them to talk frankly, but she is insistent about not leaving Shaka alone, an echo of his own fear that irritates him.

And then one morning, she proposes that they go out to buy beer and a few other things. "We won't be long," she tells Shaka, who is in his habitual place. She insists on driving, and she pulls on a vape pen, not offering it to Emil. "God, that's good. I haven't dared light up and risk setting Braeem off."

"Setting him off?"

"By refusing to let him partake if he asked. THC's interaction with prescription meds, particularly psych meds, is unpredictable. And what if he's stopped taking his meds and the zoll triggers an episode?"

He cannot resist. "You're not a clinician."

"I *have* studied biology." Tamsin is at once enervated and set loose. "If he has an episode, we'd have to take him to a hospital or somewhere."

"Bolling probably knows a doctor that could take care of it quietly." He holds his hand out for the vape pen, testing Tamsin.

"Where is Bolling?"

"Abroad somewhere." Inhaling zoll, he is reminded of his ambivalence toward its effects on him.

"Pulling our strings from outside the country. Wow."

"I'm not going to babysit Braeem forever."

"Why are you even involved at all? Braeem's relationship with Bolling is weirder even than yours. I don't get the sense of any strong affection between them. I'm guessing Braeem wasn't getting sucked off, what do you think?"

"He better not have been," Emil says in mock possessiveness, and the two of them laugh like manics. *See, there's a lot we need to talk about*. When his face is serious once more, he says, "Shaka is more useful to Bolling than I."

"Is he, though? I'm not convinced by Braeem the revolutionary."

"You mirroring him: is that a psychoanalytic technique?"

"Don't be bitchy, Emil."

"I'm not. You've been rocking your chair just like he does."

"I didn't notice."

Inside the Pick n Pay, he tells Tamsin, "I told Bolling the last time we spoke: one more week. We'll see how useful Braeem is to him. I will pile food in the house and leave Shaka by himself."

Tamsin is too shrewd to make anything of what he has said, which leaves her out. She doesn't respond at once.

Outside in the parking lot, just at the edge of hearing, there is the buzz of helicopter rotors as Emil finishes loading the car's trunk. Both of them make a show of not looking up.

"When next you speak to Bolling, if you're still in contact with him, tell him I'm minding Braeem. He won't like it, but he will understand." Tamsin says.

"Give me your car keys."

Tamsin switches the vape pen from one hand to the other and rummages in her shorts. "I don't have them. Shit."

He tenses in anger. Tamsin goes to sit in the passenger seat. The ire passes. He takes his place behind the wheel, fiddling with the car radio before turning the ignition key. "We'll come back after the groceries are in the fridge."

"It doesn't matter." Tamsin's voice is resigned.

It doesn't, he realizes.

"What's the point?" Tamsin gestures toward the radio. "It doesn't really matter what the news says. Does it?"

"Let's go to Scarbs. Just go," he says, wanting to say more but doubting the moment. Nothing stops them from leaving.

"What's stressing you?" Tamsin asks. "Braeem himself, or getting caught?"

"What's keeping you here?"

"Adventure. Excitement. Curiosity."

"And Braeem? He doesn't come into it?"

"Tangentially. I'm here for you, Emil. Braeem didn't ask me to come. You did. Answer *my* question."

"What's stressing me? Extricating myself. From this . . . from the farm, Braeem. From Muttie." It sounds so self-absorbed, he hurries to add, lamely: "Extricating us from the farm."

"But I don't want to extricate."

"You're ready for the consequences if we get caught?"

"You know, I'm not sure how hard they're looking for Braeem."

An answer that silences Emil; he too has nursed the thought that they are involved in a game, their strings being pulled by . . . whom?

The exchange with Tamsin has torn something loose inside Emil. The three of them are on the porch having a third beer, and then a fourth, instead of lunch. Emil joins in.

"And the BDS thing?" Tamsin asks. "How did you get sucked in? Details, details," she presses in a teasing voice.

Somewhere high overhead, another helicopter. It feels like too much effort to look up.

Braeem says, "I was invited to attend a meeting, where they treated me as some sort of authority in deference to my personal experience of racial Partition, I think. The fellow student who invited me, Seema, had told the people at the meeting about me and well, long story short, I got in deep very quickly. I was pulled in by the atmosphere. I didn't know that much about Israel. It's a bigger deal in eGeld than here."

"Yes," Tamsin puts in. "It's ironic Palestine is one of the few leftie causes the Movement held onto after the end of Partition."

"It's true. As I say, I wasn't equipped to answer the question I heard a lot, which was whether Israeli policies reached the level of a racial partition. I read more and more so that when I went to meetings, I could satisfy the expectations of the group's other members that I be an expert on segregation. To be honest, I wasn't convinced that the parallels were exact, or that tying the Palestinian situation to Partition was the right move, but that's an issue of strategy. I sympathized with the Palestine cause, but I realized it was for different reasons than the Movement. For them it's purely racial, settler colonialism and all that, but for me it was the beginning of a fixation with representation and power dynamics."

"What do you mean?" Emil asks.

"Well, the BDS movement was . . . is a symptom of how the world has failed to rally around Palestinians as it did Black Africans suffering under Partition. All the scenarios I gamed out in my head pointed to the Palestinians remaining relatively powerless, and without a state. Somehow they weren't sympathetic enough to win that support. Whereas here, we held free elections, and we became a poster child rainbow nation. But Creole emancipation didn't take place following one man, one vote, and with time many of us here in Cabo perceived that we were being set back."

"But that's just Creoles losing their guaranteed place in the middle of the hierarchy," Emil says. "I don't see the connection." It is exactly the response Errol would make, Emil thinks, but it is right.

"Yes." Tamsin gives Shaka a critical look. "Much of that sentiment is false consciousness stuff. Zero-sum thinking. Say what you like about the Movement, but they've worked hard at being multiracial, reaching out to Whites that were amenable. The greatest resistance to the rainbow nation came not from Whites but from folks down here."

"Listen, no pushback. I'm only saying Creoles' sense of injustice, of being colonized, continued—in fact it increased after the end of Partition. It's real and needs to be acknowledged."

"Exploited even." Emil has not intended to say this, not so acidly.

Braeem shrugs. "As I say, it's real. It's an issue that needs to be defused. The problem is that Creoles don't view themselves as part of this country, and it's not clear they ever will. But it's also true that most of us aren't political enough to want to formally secede from the rest of the country. There's sort of a sense that Cabo is Cabo, that while it's attached to the country geographically, it's separate enough to do its thing. To be sort of autonomous in the minds of the local people."

"You don't agree with that," Tamsin says.

"No. There's a bias in favor of states, and Creoles need to recognize that. You see it in the common argument made against Palestinians. The people were there, they had their olive groves and their houses and their herds of goats and sheep, but there was no formal state. States offer protection and that's why most of us belong to them. In my view, Creoles need to shit or get off the pot. Get onboard with the whole rainbow nation thing or break away completely, or push for a deal like Catalonia."

"And it occurred to me there's another way the Palestinians parallel Creoles more than Black people in this country. Another argument used to beat the Palestinians is that they barely scratched the surface in terms of exploiting the land they were living on. Judea and Samaria." Shaka says the names wryly. "The economic rationale: Israelis made the desert bloom and that sort of thing. It's the same argument the Movement always beat us with. Cabo is too beautiful and valuable to be allowed to languish. 'Traditional beliefs cannot be allowed to stand in the way of opportunity.' I read that in an op-ed. Cabo would be so prosperous, so much richer if we opened up the economy fully, liberalized labor markets. All these technocratic fixes that would completely alter our way of life. I definitely agree with Bolling on this: the great modern sin is resisting progress, particularly the technological sort. There's not much sympathy for peoples that aren't voraciously exploitative of the resources in their vicinity."

Braeem finishes one bottle of beer and gets up to retrieve another one from the fridge. In the interim, Emil is struck by how persuasive, how cogent he has been even under the influence of alcohol. Far more so than on Dead Woman's Beach in front of a crowd.

"All of which is a long-winded way of saying that a Palestinian state, if it ever comes into being, would be under immense pressure to match Israel's start-up-nation trajectory. Here's your state, show us you deserve it."

"What's wrong with joining the rainbow nation?" Tamsin threads a stray lock of hair behind her ear. "There's room for a semiautonomous, animist province in the union."

"It's theoretically feasible, but reversion to a smaller ethnic-based state seems more attractive, more viable. If only slightly. Everywhere, big multiracial states are unraveling."

"You sound like Bolling," Emil observes.

"On some things. I don't fantasize about going back to hunting and gathering, so we disagree there."

Tamsin says, "Because hunter-gatherers represent the greatest threat to the state?"

"To state values, too. The mass of citizens pulling together toward deeply abstract goals. Modernity. Progress. Innovation. God." Braeem stands up. "I need to have a siesta." There is an edge of anger in his abruptness, but it may be that he simply needs to eat something. A pause before he lurches indoors, and the hard look he gives Emil is not entirely accidental. "I've read far more of Bolling's writing than he knows."

"Do you trust everything Shaka says about Bolling?" Tamsin asks in the bed later, her voice not especially hushed. She wants, unwontedly, to talk not fuck.

"Not everything, no, but he describes his ideology accurately." Letting a little time pass, Emil adds, "You read Bolling's notebook. It's in there."

"I skimmed it."

"You're worried Shaka might be misreading Bolling?"

"Not really, and yet in Braeem's shoes I would be suspicious of him, his motives, if not resent him outright. I'd resent you too, because of how Bolling treats you."

"I'm not sure Bolling has thought through ulterior motives. After all, Shaka isn't running for office, and if he was, Bolling wouldn't have anything to do with him." He is straining to remember something Bolling had once said or written about natural revolution. "Will you see what you can find?"

Tamsin's breath is sweet and foul. "What do you want me to look for?" And then, "Yes."

Sudden laughter convulses her, and it goes on until Emil is squeezing her to still the spasms, and then he gets up to fetch a glass of water from downstairs, moving on tiptoe in the darkness, mindful of the skittering of mice.

Shaka agrees to go out the next morning with Emil to find a spot on the property that has a mobile signal. They step off the porch and move away from the house, staying close to the mountain's roots. Shaka is grunting, slapping at the insects pricking his forearms.

"There's cell service here," Emil says, halting. "I'm ringing Bolling."

"What for?"

"Updates."

"I know what he's going to say, if he even answers: 'Lay low. I'm working to get this thing fixed.'"

"You don't think he can?"

"Not really. Lots of folks have money to throw around. Plus I'm one of many Bolling projects, you know that." Braeem is moving again, limping slightly. A stark view of Bolling, jet-set provocateur with money and amoral instincts, sowing political tension in his wake. In one country, a left-leaning malcontent might win his favor, in another it might be the neofascists. A conspiratorial vision, and so not easily dismissed.

"Let's cut around," Emil says, gesturing in the vague direction of the main road. The network is tenuous; the call has not gone through. "I want to check if there's a fence over on this side."

There is no path, and the way is overgrown with creeping briar. Emil is winded after fighting through it for a few minutes. Braeem, stepping high, meets less resistance. Where are the wild things? Other than birds, there is no sign of anything moving. Not so much as a dormouse rustles in the undergrowth.

The road, a dual carriageway, is perhaps three hundred meters ahead. One moment there is the generalized noise of traffic, and the next it is the susurration of rubber hurtling over asphalt. Emil keeps walking. "At Stanford, why didn't you appeal the decision to cancel your scholarship?"

Emil is on the point of repeating the question when Braeem tells him, "I don't know. Even today. I really don't. Bolling says I didn't want to lose my innocence. For once, I suspect he's picked the easiest answer. Should we head back?" Something in the way he says it communicates to Emil a sudden anxiety.

And then, back on the farmhouse patio, with a few gulps of beer down him, he goes on as if he has been gestating a response.

"I thought I could get another scholarship. And of course it seemed romantic to be a martyr for a cause, even one that I was conflicted about." He glances up; Tamsin has come to join them. "I sort of buried myself in a delusion. I also went down a rabbit hole. Seema, the woman who invited me to the meeting—she too was arrested—called me once or twice. It had gotten out that I was losing my scholarship. That my visa was to be canceled. She was sympathetic and I think quite guilt-ridden. But the only person I really saw at that time was Marty."

"What rabbit hole did you go down?" Tamsin asks.

"The legal grounds on which a Jewish state was carved out. The provisions are so rickety, it seems fair to say it was political—and humanitarian—sentiment that clinched it. But I was also wondering if anyone ever tried to make a similar argument on behalf of the First Nations people or the Roma. Suffering is such a slippery thing to quantify, still less to compare."

"You were curious if a similar case might work here?"

"Yeah. It wouldn't. I got that pretty quickly, but I went on procrastinating when I should have been preparing to appeal. I was stewing in grievance on behalf of aboriginal people all over the world, keeping my own self-pity at arm's length. I was also thinking of the ways I was implicated in what our friend Bolling calls 'instinctive pro-modernity.' I had never taken pride in my ancestry, though I wasn't ashamed of it exactly. In the US, I realized that many of the nicknames and taunts we used for each other when I was growing up were slurs. I had one friend we called Hotnot because of how he looked. And there was an older boy who everyone, even adults, called the Griq, G-R-I-Q, short for Griqua. The sort of casual and stupid racism that goes on all over the world."

"EGeld is a lot more PC about these things," Tamsin says through pursed lips.

"I mean," Shaka continues, "there was African blood in all of us, but we never talked about that, never even joked about that. We didn't mind talking up our Asian roots though. *He's Malay, that one*, someone might say. Or we'd call Tamil guys Chuti. *Sup, Chuti*, or *Sup Benchhod*. We were very good, all of us, at spotting people's roots and ranking them, and somehow it was better to look like a boesman than to look African, even if that implied one's ancestors were savages. Anyway, long story short, I was melting down in an immense identity crisis when I should have been fighting to stay at Stanford."

Tamsin preempts Emil's next question. "Did they arrest you?"

"Nope. I hid out in a friend's spare bedroom for a couple of weeks, and then I came to my senses and turned myself in. Customs and border patrol got me on a plane within three days. San Francisco, Amsterdam, eGeld.

"By then I was consoling myself that Coetzee had also been kicked out of America. Not that I'd ever given a shit about his writing before, but the parallel gave me something else to fixate on. I read two of his books on the flight. That feeling of dissident kinship dissipated the moment I landed. I had been kicked out of America—I had squandered my opportunity, something that almost no one in my community ever got, and I had wasted it on something utterly futile."

"Didn't you try to pass yourself off as an American?" Tamsin asks.

Shaka is laughing. "For about two days, yes. Lucky I didn't get killed. How do you know?"

"There are some parallels. Coetzee got the same reception from his family, from other people he had known. You blew it, that sort of thing."

This cultural slippage in her speech, Emil has noticed it before—*you blew it*—even if he does not fully understand what triggers it.

"Ja. The dean at the uni here was noncommittal about letting me complete my degree. He wanted to know if I would be willing to sit the third-year exams. And here's me on my high horse, thinking, I've just done two years at Stanford, studying with future Supreme Court judges. I had come down in the world through an unforeseeable sort of bad luck. I still wasn't really coming to terms with it. I was living in my mother's house again, and the fact that she was entirely sympathetic and the only person not blaming me only made it worse."

"So you were ripe for someone like Bolling to take advantage of."

"You might say he's invested in me, rather than taken advantage," Shaka says, a coyness creeping into his tone. "I'm sort of like a start-up. He saw potential, he invested."

"And what's the expected return?" Tamsin says, playing along. Shaka shifts his buttocks in the chair. The subject seems to excite him.

"That's what I've been trying to puzzle out."

"Did someone introduce you to him?"

"No. We met in eGeld. I was up there looking for work. Maybe five months into my return. I had to force myself to go. As you know, I don't like eGeld, I never have, but it was time to 'shake body,' as they say, and easier to do that there than down here. My mother, who was worried about me becoming depressed, didn't want me to go. But I thought it ought to be a breeze. I've lived in Northern California, and San Francisco is a much bigger ecosystem than eGeld."

Tamsin asks, "By the way, you presented as Black at Stanford or biracial?"

"Neither. It was assumed I was biracial and I didn't address it. What's that got to do with what I'm telling you?"

Tamsin inclines her head, a gesture that might mean *Go on*, or *wait and see*.

"So, I met a couple partners from a London law firm, and they invited me to join them for a late drink at their hotel. I think they wanted to loosen me up a bit, see how I could handle the networking side of things. The rainmaking, as they call it. I was more nervous than I ever would have been in Cupertino or San Jose, and so I had one or two beforehand, which relaxed me nicely. I swear they were gearing up to make me a verbal offer when their phones rang, something had come up, some client emergency, and off they went back to the office, apologizing and promising to call first thing in the morning. I was dealing with the anticlimax when Bolling came and sat at the bar, and right from the start he had strange energy. Reclusive. I had been in a hole for months, and the conversation with the law partners had awakened my social instincts. So I didn't tell him to piss off when he asked to show me a video. It was the one of him sleeping rough on the streets of Berlin, which he'd turned into an art installation. I didn't know what I was looking at, but that was beside the point—he wanted to seize my attention. Before I could make out what was going on, he slipped the tablet into a satchel and asked, 'Interview, right?' He had an accent, which I thought was Dutch. 'Something like that,' I said, and immediately wondered if the lawyers would plant someone in the bar to approach me. Surely not, right? But Bolling, he always hides in plain sight, doesn't he, he never pretends. He said enough to make me curious about who he was, and then he was gone. 'Let's meet next time I'm down in Stadmutter.'"

Emil returns to the patio from taking a piss out front of the house just as Tamsin passes the vape pen to Braeem. He finishes his sentence before drawing on it. "I stood in that bar and admitted to myself for the first time that I hated the chumminess between Black folk and White folk you see at fancy bars in eGeld. It seemed a kind of coziness that excluded brown people.

"That was all I thought about after Bolling left—Bolling, the only other person in the bar who looked in the least like me. Later, he told me, 'The Creole is a new man, eternally so, always on the point of learning himself,' which at first confused me and then nudged me."

"Weininger," Tamsin says, and she looks to Emil to see if he remembers.

"Whatever," Braeem says. "My understanding was, Creoles need space to develop in our own way. To understand properly who we are."

"Recreolization?"

"Something like that. Creoles being Creoles—a people reclaiming their essence so they can go back to being more than just not-Black and not-White. That night I decided I wasn't much of a believer in meritocracy. The eGeld model. Roll up your sleeves, work hard, and it will come together. Not sure why I went on believing in it even after it became clear that White people didn't believe it, when they started leaving the country talking about quotas."

"And you?" Emil says, turning to Tamsin. "Will you leave too?"

"Oh, I'll emigrate at some point." Tamsin is skilled at deflecting his hostility, his aggression when it surfaces, which is not frequent. "Before the transformation happens. My German is not bad, if a bit higgledy-piggledy, seeing as I learned analytic terms before I learned *Ich bin*."

"Bolling showed me just enough inner fascist to let me know where he wished to lead me," Shaka says. "'Go ahead and invoke blood and soil. You can do it here, at this foot of darkness.' That's what he calls Cabo. He refused to talk Conrad though. He wanted to talk about animism. 'Creoles have ten thousand years of history here in these mountains: invoke it.'"

"Bolling is not really a fascist," Tamsin hedges. "I'm not saying that in an appeasing sort of way. I sort of sense he's too ambivalent about power for that."

For Emil, listening to Shaka and Tamsin is like relearning his own innocence. He has misjudged Tamsin, undervalued the difference in their experience. Though she shows no sign of reading his thoughts, Tamsin has a percipience, revealed in flashes, which makes him wonder how much she might be veiling. Is she any less acute, any less perilous than Bolling?

Also this: as Shaka has unspooled more and more of his

biography, the less Emil is able to know and perceive Tamsin. She is, in some sense, passing out of view behind Braeem, a planetary movement that cannot be accidental. If they are caught by the police, how will he respond, not least if presented an opportunity to save his own skin? Would he sell out Braeem and Tamsin by playing the youthful naïf influenced by an idealistic but manipulative couple? In his thoughts, they are as good as lovers already; and he suspects Tamsin would resist turning on Braeem.

"I don't know it either. He's not a populist. He's along for the ride because he's deeply skeptical of modernity."

Emil says cautiously, "Romantic nihilism."

"Hmm," Tamsin murmurs, noncommittal.

But Emil is not done. Against his better judgment, he says, "*To be anti-modern is to fellow-travel at least part of the way with fascists*, according to Bolling." The words earn him a pitying glance from Shaka. Why had he not guessed it before: Tamsin and Shaka have good reason to view him as Bolling's creature, his agent within the farmhouse.

In that heavy, humiliated lull, Emil gets up as if needing to piss again (the beer!), slips out the front door, and makes for the trees of the dying orchard. After a minute he stumbles onto one of the tiny pockets of signal to be found across the compound and dials a number in his contact list.

"Emil! I never answer this thing, you know. Things still hot down there?"

"That's why I'm calling, actually. Is there still a need to be . . . careful?"

Audibly, Errol relaxes, assuaged by the coded speech. "I've not heard anything in some days. I think this thing has turned into an embarrassment for us at least. Something that we might have to let die a natural death. It doesn't help that Kob is playing his own game. He's been cooperative only up to a point, you know what I mean. Why you asking?"

"I'm worried Celeste's boy could be caught up in this thing. Deeply. But I'm handling it. It's under control."

"I hope so. I don't think his mother could handle a blow like that."

"But why would the governor obstruct?"

"He's triangulating. You know folks down there don't like the least whiff of Movement involvement. The federal police have been withdrawn. If Kob's boys are still looking for our guy, they're not looking very hard."

The line has begun wavering, and it seems a good moment to end the call. Emil tells his father, "The network here is poor. Thanks for this. I'll take care of the cousin thing."

"Yes. Yes." Errol's impatience is directed at himself, something in his vicinity is distracting him. Emil hangs up and checks the burner phone. He is breathing hard, startled at how easy it was. Rather than head straight back, he walks out toward the road, not troubling to conceal himself from passing cars. The conversation has buoyed him, mostly assuaged some of the resentment he feels for Tamsin.

He will leave the farmhouse tomorrow, to avoid witnessing Tamsin's transfer from his bed to Braeem Shaka's. He had anticipated it, carried the knowledge within him that it would happen at some point once the three of them were in the house together. Tamsin herself had warned him about her susceptibility to narcissistic or hysteric patients. And she had characterized Braeem as exactly this: a narcissist.

Aware now of acting solely for himself, Emil tells Tamsin, "They've called off the search for Shaka." The calm he felt after speaking to Errol has dissipated.

Tamsin is stoic. "You spoke to Bolling?"

"I spoke to my father."

"You'll tell Braeem? It's up to him to decide what to do."

"You tell him."

Tamsin sighs, put upon. "You're leaving." It is not a question.

In the morning, the long-delayed question. "Where will you go?" She touches his arm in a meaningless way, as if to ignore the tension.

"Back to eGeld, eventually."

"Breaking free of the vortex? I spoke to Bolling, you know," she adds. "I called him from the burner. He wasn't surprised to hear from me. You told him I was here."

"I didn't. He didn't want you here."

"Do you want to know what we talked about? I asked what his plans are for Braeem."

"He has no plans for Braeem. He's not coming back."

"Ja. I suspect Braeem's relieved about that. You're leaving to go find Bolling, I think. That's my feeling." She says it not with any jealousy, which would move Emil, but only a kind of certainty.

Emil catches the laugh, contains it. "I don't know where Bolling is. I don't have any secret knowledge."

"I said *find* him. You have an idea of his haunts. And he seems to know where you are. Perhaps it works both ways."

"I can help you bring Shaka to Scarbrough if that's what you want. You can hide just as well there."

"He won't move from here, and I've grown used to it. It'll be hard to emerge into normal life. Maybe I've found my level, walking around barefoot in a filthy T-shirt and living on zoll and beer. Are you in love with Bolling, do you think?"

"You've asked me that before. Are you in love with Braeem?"

"He wants something from you, Bolling. Do you know what it is?"

"I'm sure you'll tell me."

"Oh, I don't know either. Listen, this advice is going to sound utterly banal, but don't sweat medical school."

"Thanks. Thanks, Tamsin." He does not know what else to say.

At the last, separation is swift, blank, and without recrimination or rancor. In the kitchen, he corners Shaka as he is grabbing a beer out of the fridge. He is sparing in the information he passes along. Let Shaka wonder whether it has come from Bolling. "I'm about to leave." Braeem's response is to nod tightly, to accept the burner phone from Emil's hand.

There is little to carry away with him: the notebook, now somewhat in disrepute, two shirts. Phone and wallet. He spends a half hour wandering from the bedroom to the porch out back, as if he might be forgetting something. In the bedroom, Tamsin touches his arm again, his wrist, as if he is the one chosen to break out from among a group of prisoners. He is excited to leave but already anticipates the riptide that will come in the next days—jealousy, resentment, self-pity. "You can telephone if you need anything," he tells her. He cannot read her expression.

A persistent itch he must first scratch sends him directly into the city, to the house on the ridge overseeing the ocean. The security code for Bolling's front gate has been changed, as he has anticipated. And then, as if taking part in a treasure hunt, he rushes to the house at 9 Noel, fixating on the stolen etching lying unguarded in his cousin's old bedroom.

Andres is in the kitchen, a pale blue hard hat and gloves next to him on the table. "I'm back to work, Cuz." His jauntiness catches Emil off guard.

"Where? Where are you working?" Perhaps the disability checks have been discontinued.

"Hotel in the city bowl. Night shift."

Is this all Andres has missed, a sense of purpose? As usual he seems scarcely to register that Emil has been absent, but then this is unfair: has Emil not trained his aunt and cousin to expect nothing from him, least of all his presence?

"Getting time and a half. Hotel needs to open in nine months for some big conference. We got Kob himself coming by the site to inspect and three crews, working around the clock."

"Where's your mother? Any word from Torrance?" Questions for which answers are meaningless, questions that are beside the point. He is both more and less pleased for Andres than he's anticipated, though maybe this is merely a general relief. His aunt's house is an oasis of cleanliness. The old sheets on Torrance's bed are unfathomably smooth; glancing through the window there is the impassable south face of Godsetafel, so close he might as well have relocated to the city bowl.

The Kentride etching retains for him its eldritch, astral quality. All his things—his books and few clothes—are accounted for. After two nights of sleeping through to mid-morning, he perceives how tightly wound he had been in the farmhouse.

Another day passes before the house at 9 Noel reactivates that extratemporal quality he has experienced nowhere else. He is girding himself. Also testing boundaries. The second night and the third he goes to his aunt's bed and sleeps there naked, frotting against her cotton sheets despite the absence of any desire. To understand, at last, whether any of his actions in Stadmutter carry consequences. Has Celeste slept in her bed since he and Tamsin occupied it not so long ago? He is more alone here than ever in the house. Andres is working the night shift.

He is more protean in Stadmutter, at moments ribald, envious, sluttish, none of which had been true of him before. But is he more interesting? Less bland? Or is it that he has made a futile exchange: one sort of slipperiness for another?

Celeste appears the next evening. He has come downstairs and finds her at the kitchen table drinking a medicinal-looking tea from a clear glass. Celeste has gained a harried look. Rinus has something to do with it. "Have you moved in with Rinus, Aunt Celeste?"

"More or less, love. He lives north of the city and running the car back and forth, here to there, to work, it was getting to be too much. It's an hour and a half each way."

"Why not ask him to move in with you?"

"I did, you know. It's already too many men in the house, he said. He's old-school, isn't he. Territorial. He said he'd move in if I kicked Andres out. We had a fight after that. Big fight. I thought about breaking up with him, to be honest."

"He doesn't like Andres?"

"I don't think that's it. He's just old-fashioned. 'He's too big to be living off you, that one,' he said. That didn't bother me too much, Andres pays his way, you know, and now he's working again he's making up for when he couldn't. But then Rinus says to me, 'Keep an eye on that Andres of yours. Something's funny there.' I knew what he meant but he wouldn't say it straight out so I cussed him off. Turned the air blue. But he was laughing. My language didn't bother him. He just kept saying, 'Something's not right there. Something's not adding up.'"

"What does that mean, 'something's not right'?"

"Come on, Emil. He means Andres is gay. A fairy, as Rinus would put it. After our big fight, I came home and I nearly flat-out asked Andres if he's got a girlfriend and why he doesn't bring her round and all that."

"Would it bother you if he is? I don't think he is," he hastens to add, for Celeste's peace of mind. *He does seem very close to Drool.*

"Oh, it wouldn't bother me at all. He used to be so sensitive and his dad dying didn't help any. He was about fifteen and suddenly he was bullying other kids, flying into a rage. Torrance had to talk to him. It was really hard on Torrance, having to act like a bigger brother. One thing Rinus has taught me—and I'm grateful for it, Emil—is I can't only worry about Andres. I have two sons, and I've behaved like I've only the one."

"Have you spoken to Torrance?"

"Torrance doesn't answer my calls, love. It's my own fault. I let that happen. Salvage it, Rinus tells me, salvage the relationship with your son. He should know, he didn't talk to his daughter for eleven years. It's different with girls, of course. But I listen to him. Just keep calling, just keep trying, he says. And when he answers, because he will one day, arrange a meeting in a neutral spot somewhere, a café or something. Ask him to bring the girlfriend, bring Anne. It's good advice, that. One day, he'll pick up. Have you spoken to him?"

"Not recently."

"It's the one thing I don't mind Rinus getting on at me about." She drains her glass.

Emil waits for Torrance in the parking lot of an industrial complex of warehouses and light manufacturers. Somewhere on the peninsula north of his aunt's house with an unimpeded view of Godsetafel; at the limits of vision, he can make out the cable car station set into the mountain. A cable car sidles down to the base station on an unseen filament, visible only in the moments it reflects in gleams and flashes the westering sun. From this vantage he can see die Teufeldirk in back of Godsetafel: The Devil Knife, a near-perfect stylization of a mountain with its triangular faces. Summer is growing very late: the dusks shortening, the air ever so faintly thickened by humidity. He will be glad to evade Stadmutter's wet sunless winters.

"Cuz," Torrance says, wary as ever, and yet without conviction. He sounds, for the first time, like his elder brother. Emil has missed his approach.

"You're avoiding me. Your mother too. And I'm leaving Muttie and wanted to tell you she wants the two of you to reconcile."

"Good for you. Good for us too." Torrance laughs, keeping his distance. The forgotten man, the striver. The two cousins are no longer near reflections of one another, Emil observes, if they had ever been. Only he had perceived the resemblance, and like so much else that has happened, he doubts it. "You're not an ally, Emil," Torrance tells him. "You only think you are."

"An ally of who?"

"My family. Cabo. It was always going to be about you, your coming down here. It didn't add up, your moving into the house when hiring a flat made more sense."

Rejection causes amusement more than hurt. "What's this about, Torrance? I've come to say bye."

"It's about you, Cuz." A distancing word for both Wilson brothers, *Cuz*.

"What are you saying? There was some ulterior motive for my coming?"

"I never believed you were doing it out of altruism. Family feeling."

"Then what exactly?"

"I suspected your dad put you up to it."

"To do what?"

"Spy, I don't know."

"How do you mean?" *I came to save you*, he does not, cannot tell Torrance. In part because it is a lie. He came to save Andres. But it is false also because he has long since been done with errands. No burden, no mission. "Is that why you moved out? Or was it that Andres and your mother disagreed with you about me?"

"Yes, there was a disagreement. Ma was excited to have you; she'd always adored you. Andres was too caught up in his own work and money drama to care much one way or the other. But he accused me of upsetting Ma with my crazy suspicions about you, and we nearly came to blows. There were already issues festering between us involving my dad, his . . . suicide. Anyway, I went to live with Anne, it seemed like the right moment to move out, and afterward it felt like we'd engineered the whole fracas to make space for you in the house. I say 'we' even though I didn't really want you to come, but it was a dilemma we needed to resolve: I should have been the one to make way for you as the youngest in the house, but I was giving Ma money for her mortgage bond every month and Andres wasn't. She wasn't about to have you kipping indefinitely on the couch, so I chose the lesser of two evils."

"Why did you come the first night?"

"I decided to give you the benefit of the doubt. It was an idiotic move. I thought Ma and Andres would be pleased. Ma was out, Andres and I scuffled. It probably sounded worse than it was. I know how to handle my brother, trust me. After seeing you that first night, I wasn't sure. And then I met your friend at Dharma, and he gave me a weird feeling and all my suspicions about you came back."

"And now?"

"Nothing's changed."

"You should email my father," Emil says. "Tell him your suspicions. He can explain the whole thing to you."

"I emailed him. Never heard back. Not a word."

Emil is startled by this. *When?*

"I have to go to work, Emil."

"I'm leaving Muttie." Why does he sound so portentous, as if the news has some bearing on Torrance?

"Time to return to normal life?"

"I don't know about that. Anyway, I suspect you'll end up there as well. Sooner rather than later." His appeals to his cousin are all used up. Stubbornness has gotten Torrance through, and he seems to be sticking with it.

The year is no longer new; the austral autumn will soon come on. He has the necessary money in his bank account for what comes next. Vivian alone is privy to his plans; there are a few final errands to complete before he departs Muttie though.

And some more score-settling as well. In the very last days, Emil comes downstairs in his aunt's house and finds Drool drinking a beer at the kitchen table. His reaction is pure instinct: he catches Drool's throat and right wrist and bends that arm back between his shoulder blades, forcing him to his feet to frog-march him through the front door. Shoved out of the house, Drool puts up little resistance or protest. Nor does he return and try to kick the door in.

When he thinks of the farmhouse, which is seldom (putting from his mind the fortnight he spent there has been easier than expected), Emil experiences spasms of jealousy but no regret. In some moments, Tamsin is an avatar of himself; they are privileged children with a lexicon born of national inheritance. He feels used too, although the idea is absurd on its face. He has been the primary benefactor of their interaction, he acknowledges; he feels none of the same certainty about relations between himself and Bolling.

Vignettes: night on the Kampsbaai road, a danger perceptible only to himself. And later, Tamsin whispering at his ear as he watched the young girls dance. The enveloping foulness of sweat, cocaine, and mildew of the house in Scarbs, a rehearsal for life in Bolling's farmhouse.

First love? Had he, in the end, hurried away from the farmhouse to preserve his sanity or to avoid ceding her ever more power over him? Why has he given of himself to Bolling, more or less entirely, rather than to Tamsin? Counterfactuals are intricate, but in hindsight, Bolling has been too much a presence in his life, present and absent in every place, claiming ownership over more than is his due.

Scarbrough, in its last summer hurrah, is livelier than he recalls. Kitesurfers are out over the breakers. Driving along the village's upper road, he smells meat char and sees the winking of small wood fires on the beach. Evening had seemed a good time to drive by the house. It seems vacant, the porch light unlit. None of the cars parked out front is Tamsin's, but he circles the village, once more, twice, before returning to the house at 9 Noel.

Days later he spots Tamsin's small red car parked precariously cliffside on the upper road. He has been varying the times of his circuits through Scarbrough should anyone be paying attention. It is early afternoon, and the beach is comparatively quiet. Seeing the car, he slows but does not stop until he is beyond her house. Turning the car about on the narrow road to make another pass, he catches sight in the rearview mirror of a dark slat nearly two meters long, lying in the dust of the road directly outside the gate of the house, where he had first met Esme. Has he driven over the thing? He'd felt nothing beneath the tires. One part, the middle section, is streaked a deep copper. Perhaps just a rusted and road-strewn piece of metal, then. But as he stares, one end of the thing raises from the dust, and then the length of it moves, scarcely perceptibly, across the road away from the cottage. A cobra. The cobra in the garden, about which Nomvuyo had spoken.

The house still appears unused. Tamsin's car might be in Scarbrough, but Tamsin is not here.

It is nearly evening when a taxi comes to fetch him from the house at 9 Noel. He dozes in the back of it on the twenty-minute ride and when he enters the high hall of the airport departure lounge, he is seized by doubts. He is not nervous of being airborne so much as leaving, and he distracts himself by fixating on the inane. When last has he taken a flight? The airport itself disorients him, the army of travelers, perusing news racks, sitting for immense breakfasts, standing about charging their phones.

Other passengers have far too much luggage; some families—emigrating perhaps—are setting out with more than one suitcase for each person. He has with him the case he brought from eGeld, containing more or less the same clothes. He will buy what is needed once he arrives, and the arrangements he has made will see him through the first days. In his backpack is one surgical handbook; the others he has sent back by mail to his apartment in eGeld. Also with him: the Oliver Kentride etching, which, he's decided, he has paid for and so is his entirely; it is anyway safest with him.

From Stadmutter, there are direct flights to Amsterdam in the old country, and Nampula in Mozambique, to Gaborone and Windhoek. He is bound for none of these places, and so he will change planes in eGeld. So too will many of the travelers around him, who are destined for London or Addis Ababa or Kuala Lumpur or New York.

Leaving at dusk, he will arrive at dusk, and those he has left behind—his parents, his aunt, Tamsin—will be no more than midway through their sleep.

Very little, he supposes, will come of the texts he sent from Andres's phone that morning, but perhaps that was the point. The tips hotline of the Stadmutter police service is probably meant for public relations purposes and not actually for finding suspected criminals. As he sees it, therefore, the authorities may or may not go looking for one Quinton Uys a.k.a. Braeem Shaka at a farmhouse on the edge of Constantia, and they may or may not find him there.

His flight is delayed—the aircraft has landed late and must be cleaned and refueled. The delay need not trouble him; he has a four-hour layover in eGeld. He is calm, even welcoming of the detainment. And so it is by chance, strolling through the departure hall when he should be readying to board, that he sees Tamsin, or someone with a striking resemblance to her. She waits in a long snaking line for a flight which has just been called to board. *Not her.* Where is the flight bound? He panics, then takes hold of himself, or tries to, needing to be sure.

It *is* Tamsin. Craning his neck to see the departure information, his heart agitating, he wonders, *Why is she going to Amsterdam?* He scans for sight of Braeem, and, just to be sure, for Bolling. It would dash him, seeing the three of them together here.

He walks toward her, Tamsin or her doppelgänger. Stops. Unobtrusive, he watches from a range of about three meters. He is staggered. She too carries a backpack, one larger than his own. He has never seen her wear jeans and she has dyed her hair anew with the rabbity color he had studied so closely the night in Kampsbaai. The first night. Braeem is not there, not behind Tamsin, nowhere to be seen in that line of passengers. Of course, it would be too dangerous for him.

Once more he starts forward, then pulls up short. A grave betrayal, sending the police to the farmhouse. How does she come to be here? She wouldn't leave Braeem alone; would she? In a few minutes she will disappear through glass doors. If she recognized him now, beckoned him, *come with me*, how could he refuse? How is it they have both come to be here, leaving the country? On the same day. *Betrayal.*

With only one person ahead of her for the document check, Tamsin turns and her gaze washes over him. Not even a hint of recognition. No surprise. It is not her. It is not Tamsin. But it is her. Involuntary steps have brought him near enough to be sure: the height is right, the coloring. He is close enough to see the passport and boarding pass in her hand, even if not to read the name there. It is he who nearly says it. *Come with me.* Her eyes meet his again, and then the passenger line shifts, and she turns and moves through the boarding door.

ACKNOWLEDGMENTS

I wish to thank:

Whit Frazier and Vivek Narayanan for generously reading and sharing incisive feedback about the typescript; my editor Jennifer Alise Drew for being tireless, patient, and thoughtful in guiding me to corral the narrative. Also: my agents Charles Buchan and Kristi Murray for championing the book, and of course my family, Johanna and Emil, Lorna and Eugene, Mojisola and Orlinka for forms of support that are ineffable. My gratitude, long deferred, also goes to Polly and Julian at Cove Park in Scotland, where I first began to put the novel down on paper.

ABOUT THE AUTHOR

OLUFEMI TERRY is a Sierra Leone–born writer, essayist, and journalist. His short fiction has been published in *Guernica*, *The Georgia Review*, *Chimurenga*, and *The Granta Book of the African Short Story*, and translated into French and German. His non-fiction essays have appeared in *The American Scholar*, *Africa is a Country*, and *The Guardian*. He has been the International Writer-in-Residence at Cove Park, Scotland, and a Writer-in-Residence at Georgetown University's Lannan Center for Poetics and Social Practice in Washington, DC. In 2019, he received a grant from the Washington, DC, Commission on the Arts & Humanities. A former juror of the Miles Morland Scholarship and the AKO Caine Prize for African writing, he is the 2010 winner of the Caine Prize for his story "Stickfighting Days." He lives in Germany and Côte d'Ivoire.